The White Jade Fox

The White Jade Fox

ANDRE NORTON

E. P. Dutton & Co., Inc.   New York

Library of Congress Cataloging in Publication Data

Norton, Andre   The white jade fox
I. Title.
PZ3.N8187Wh [PS3527.O625] 813'.5'2   74-23871
ISBN 0-525-42670-1

Published simultaneously in Canada by Clarke, Irwin & Company Limited, Toronto and Vancouver

Designed by Riki Levinson
Printed in the U.S.A.   First Edition
10 9 8 7 6 5 4 3 2 1

Contents

The White Jade Fox

I

Mêng Youthful Inexperience

Saranna faced, not toward the port of Baltimore as the bark drew in, but rather out to the freedom of the sea. All during the voyage from New York she had hardly been able to stand imprisonment in the fusty, cramped cabin. And now that she had good reason to go on deck, she drew in deep breaths of the salt air, as refreshing to her now as the lilac bush her mother had so treasured. She was a sea captain's daughter, and yet she had never before been to sea.

She wondered, not for the first time, why Mother had never sailed so. Many captains took their wives; children were even born at sea, or in strange corners of the world where American clippers lay at anchor.

Mother had had such a hunger for far places. Most of the books she had squeezed out pennies to buy, after Father's whaler had been lost, had been battered, secondhand copies of travelers' accounts. Saranna could see her now, rubbing fingertips over the satin-smooth finish of a lacquer box, telling Saranna of the distant and mysterious China from which it had come. China was a land of pure enchantment for Keturah Stowell's small daughter. Of course, white women were forbidden to go there. The Chinese forced captains' wives to disembark at Macao to wait out the ships' visits to Canton. But Mother's stories had been Saranna's choice over any fairy tales.

"Miss Stowell—"

Saranna was startled out of her memories, memories that ended in sad times which made her both grieve and feel angry at the fate Keturah Stowell had faced so bravely when the news of the loss of the *Spindrift* had come, after many weary months of no news at all. She turned reluctantly away from the rail and the freedom of the sea to face Mr. Sanders, her present traveling guardian—a stiff lawyer with whom she had only an uneasy surface acquaintance. (She sometimes wondered with a small touch of that independent surface levity, unbecoming to a penniless orphan, whether, if Mr. Sanders were ever to smile, his whole countenance might not break brittlely in two.)

But he was not alone this time. The man with him was one Saranna had seen twice at a distance when she had dared, during their voyage, to climb to deck for a breath of air. He was much younger than the lawyer, with harsher features, his skin weathered as dark as a seaman's, though he wore the fine broadcloth of a gentleman.

"May I present Captain Gerrad Fowke?" Mr. Sanders asked abruptly. He might be doing something of which he personally disapproved, but for which he had no choice. "Captain Fowke is a partner of your brother in the new Brazilian venture. He wishes to offer his services in any way—"

Saranna guessed that Mr. Sanders believed such an offer entirely unnecessary. But she inclined her head and the lawyer continued:

"Miss Stowell, Captain Fowke—"

The Captain bowed with a careless grace more in keeping with his clothing than the face above his smoothly tied stock. He moved far more easily with the swing of the ship than did Mr. Sanders.

"I fear I must drop the 'Captain' nowadays, Miss Stowell. Now I am a landsman. May I say that I am deeply sorry your introduction to Baltimore must be for such a sad reason—"

He spoke more awkwardly than he moved, as if he

found the conventional words of condolence hard to voice. Saranna knew sympathy with that, nor did she wish to be continually reminded by well-meaning strangers of her own present troubles. She replied in a voice she schooled to the proper decorous note:

"You are most kind, Captain—Mr. Fowke."

Captain suited him much better than the "Mr." he asked for, she thought. But there was something in the very intent gaze with which he regarded her which made Saranna vaguely uneasy.

Back home she had had little contact with men since her father's last sailing. Her time had been much occupied either with helping her mother in the work of a village seamstress, or in those studies her mother had been determined she was not to drop at their sudden change of fortune.

To her there seemed a boldness in the way Mr. Fowke studied her, and she wondered if she should resent that inspection. If so, what was the proper look or gesture for her to make? Hastily she pulled her veil into place. And from the slight change in Mr. Sanders' expression she gathered that she was doing the right thing. But Saranna also regretted inwardly that it was so necessary to *always* do the right thing.

Mr. Fowke was certainly not handsome, but there was a strength in his features which she recognized. Any man who had commanded a ship carried that air of authority and decision, as much a part of him as his well-tanned skin and those fine lines at the corners of his eyes which came from squinting into the wind.

She also decided, taking advantage of the barrier of her veil to study him, that he might not be as old as she first had reckoned. There had been, and were, many captains in their early twenties walking their own quarterdecks. Boys of seafaring families went to sea as young as ten and battled an early path to command.

Reluctantly, she looked now to the land where she had no wish to set foot. Even to see the port loom out of the distance stirred her resentment. Jethro—the half brother old enough to be her father, the brother she had never set eyes upon in her whole life—what right had he to arrange her future for her without so much as a "by-your-leave"?

She had never learned the reason for the quarrel which had separated Captain Stowell and his only son. But Jethro had broken from the family mold of ship's officer to enter first one of the merchant companies in Canton, and then, eventually, settle in Baltimore, where he was now pioneering in the coffee trade with Brazil. He was an important man in Baltimore, Mr. Sanders had made that plain.

Too important to come all the way to Sussex to collect his orphaned half sister; instead he had sent Mr. Sanders. She wondered now what they would have done if she had not been so bemused with grief and had flatly refused Jethro's order to come to him. Would they have extracted her from Pastor Willis' house bound and gagged like the unlucky heroine of one of those wild romances Mother had always laughed at? Saranna wished now she had spoken her own mind.

Who wanted to go to Baltimore? She had no training in the airs and graces of society. In her secondhand black dress, cut down so hurriedly from her mother's best one, she must make a queer figure. She had already learned that from a careful, if surreptitious, inspection of what she had seen worn by the ladies of fashion in New York.

And Jethro's home, Mr. Sanders had told her, had a lady of that ilk for mistress—her brother's widowed daughter Honora, returned after only two years of married life and the loss of her husband, to again assume rulership in her father's establishment.

The closer the bark approached the wharf the more uneasy Saranna was. And when they were tied up and the gangplank run out that uneasiness increased. There was no one waiting to meet her. She knew Mr. Sanders was eager to be released from his charge of her, to be about pressing affairs of his own. Yet he could not leave her standing here, the shabby sea chest which served as her trunk at her feet.

It was Mr. Fowke who came to their rescue. Behind him drew up a closed carriage of equal elegance to anything Saranna had glimpsed in New York.

"The *Triton*," he nodded to the bark, "is ahead of time. But that is no reason to put a lady to any inconvenience. Ma'am, if you and Mr. Sanders will allow—"

The lawyer welcomed this solution. At his nod Mr. Fowke himself set hand in the rope sling about the sea chest and almost tossed that, bulky as it was, to the coachman to be stowed aloft.

Feeling that she was putting everyone to a great deal of trouble, Saranna perched tensely on the edge of the seat, refusing to take any pleasure in the comfort of a vehicle whose like she had never seen before as they drove through streets she hardly regarded, so eager was she to reach her destination and release her companions from their unwanted responsibility.

The noise and confusion of those streets resembled the roar which had half-frightened her in New York. However, here she caught sight of black faces, new to one from the North. Now they were out of the dock area, coming into streets lined with trees, those trees already well into spring leaf.

Their brougham pulled into a half-circle drive before one of the larger houses and Mr. Sanders went to knock at the door. Saranna, handed out by Mr. Fowke, managed a few words of thanks as he placed the sea chest on the stoop.

When the door opened a black house servant faced Mr. Sanders. Saranna clutched her shawl, lifted her chin a fraction. She was, after all, at her brother's house. Shabby as she was, unwanted though she might really be, no one must guess her inner shrinking from the ordeal awaiting her in this imposing residence—she could not think of it as a "home."

The servant bowed them in. Saranna had only a quick

chance to say good-bye to Mr. Fowke, who did not seem disposed to accompany them, to her relief. The fewer eyes she had to face now the better. Reluctantly, she marched into the wide central hall.

This interior, in spite of all which she had gleaned from Mr. Sanders concerning her brother's wealth and position, was so superior in elegance to the cottage where she and her mother had lived in the village of Sussex, the neat house they had had in happier days in Boston, that she was momentarily bewildered.

There was such a wide spread of polished wood and burnished metal, rich color of rug and curtain, that she could not really distinguish any one object clearly in her first survey. She was not allowed time for a second.

A woman was descending the graceful curve of the staircase, such a woman as instantly centered all attention upon herself.

She had not the slightest hint of any warmth of welcome in her expression. In fact, her delicate features were a little set, as if she were about to engage in some disagreeable duty. Her above-average height, the meticulous arrangement of fair curls beneath a cap which was a confection of black lace and mauve ribbons, the wide, almost majestic swell of her mauve skirt, gave her a daunting air of presence.

As this newcomer reached the polished floor of the hall, Saranna was thoroughly chilled by the level gaze which made mocking measurement of all her own shortcomings and defects of dress and person. Across the frilled collar framing the other's pointed chin the younger girl caught a glimpse of herself in a long wall mirror.

She was as rusty black as a storm-bedraggled crow. Her features were a little too sharp, her cheekbones too clearly marked under the taut pull of her skin on which there was a dusting of freckles, faded only a little under the weaker suns of winter. She still had those shadows under her eyes, painted by weary nights of nursing, the drain of sorrow for a death no courage nor will of hers could hold at bay for long.

Saranna had thrown back her veil when she entered. Still only a little of her smooth hair showed beneath the brim of her old bonnet, but against the pallor of her skin, the dead black of her shabby, dowdy shawl and dress, her hair showed its unfashionable red far too strongly. She had always accepted that she was far from a beauty, but until this moment she had never truly realized just how plain and drab a woman could appear in contrast to one who could claim otherwise.

"Saranna?" The other favored her with another up-and-down stare which catalogued every frayed and rubbed spot, every too-often tied bonnet string, all which was obviously wrong with Saranna. "It should be *Aunt* Saranna, should it not?"

So this was Honora, Jethro's daughter. Yes, by an odd quirk of fate she was aunt to this dazzling mistress of the house, though Honora was her senior by several years.

Honora laughed, a tinkling laugh like two ice crystals, one broken upon the other. "But, of course, that is folly! You are so young, a mere child. We shall call you Saranna. I am Honora—"

She inclined her head regally. It was plain that she was doing her duty, as she believed, graciously, to one far beneath serious consideration.

Within Saranna, resentment warmed into a small coal of hidden anger. But she must never, never let Honora know (*that* she determined fiercely)—never let her know that either tongue or manner could wound.

"You are early, we did not expect you to land before evening," Honora swept on. "Mr. Sanders," for the first time she addressed the lawyer, "how ill you must consider this house is run that a carriage did not meet you. I beg you to forgive me—"

Her small white hand touched his stiff arm, her features melted into a gentle smile. And Saranna (privately irritated at the blindness of men) watched the stiff Mr.

Sanders melt in turn, to wear an almost approachable cast of countenance.

"It is of no consequence, Mrs. Whaley. I believe we had what seamen term a favoring wind to bring us to port. And Captain Fowke was most kind in sharing his carriage—"

"Captain Fowke?"

Saranna was sure she had witnessed a momentary tightening of Honora's lips as she repeated that name. She could believe that her hostess was not too pleased at hearing that. "But—no, I can guess why he did not wait— he must have pressing business with my father—the New York orders. You see, Mr. Sanders—" once more her tinkling laugh sounded, not quite so brittlely this time, "I have quite become a female of business. My father likes to use me as a sounding board for his ideas. La, I can talk like any parrot about coffees, and costs, and the like—not that my poor head gets any meaning from it. Now our thanks to you, dear Mr. Sanders, for your journey to res- cue this poor child—"

Inside Saranna bristled like a threatened cat at the tone of that "poor child." She only wished she dared hiss as emphatically as that same animal.

"Father," Honora was continuing, "asked me to say he would wait upon you tomorrow morning. And, of course, you and dear Mrs. Sanders must dine with me on Satur- day. Mrs. Sanders must have already received my note of invitation—"

Some time later Saranna eyed her reflection in the mirror of a tall wardrobe. Behind her lay a bedroom which would better have housed a princess. But it was given this time, she thought with wry humor, to the real goosegirl, not to one of royal blood in masquerade. Her own black figure blotted out some of the splendor about and behind her.

She had laid aside her shawl and bonnet, refused at once the attentions of the black maid who had been on her knees by the sea chest struggling with its rope when Saranna entered. Now she was alone and able to face facts.

Face facts! An expression she had heard so often on her mother's lips during these past years. Mother might have had golden dreams of far travel, but she had never confused those dreams with reality. Always she had insisted that one must think over any situation carefully and calmly, not rush into things as Saranna was temperamentally inclined to do.

Notwithstanding, Saranna *had* been rushed into this change in her life from the hour Mr. Sanders had appeared without warning two days after her mother's funeral, bearing the totally unexpected letter of command from Jethro—that Jethro they had never heard of or from. She had been overpowered then by the advice of Pastor Willis and his wife, grateful to the Lord they served so firmly and humbly, that Saranna had found a protector and not been left alone at seventeen to make her own way in the world. And, because she had been so dazed with grief as to accept all their arguments then, now she had to adjust to what lay before her.

This room was like Honora looking over her shoulder, saying this is the way we live, and you have no proper place in this house. Above the black of her dress, unrelieved because her chemisette-vestee showing in the vee of her bodice was of the same doleful color. (Mother would hate to see her now, she had disliked her own mourning so much—saying one ought to mourn in the heart and not be a living reminder to all of a private sorrow), her skin had lost all natural coloring. Which made her hair, smoothly braided and coiled at the back of her head, appear too fiery bright.

She had never worn a house cap, but she knew from the study of the few fashion books Mother used in her dressmaking that all ladies, old and young, married or single, were now supposed to do so. Now, regarding the blaze of her hair, she decided there was only one improvement in her appearance she could make in the short time before she had to face the imposing household below.

Quickly Saranna unpacked her sewing box, found a length of rather limp black lace. With energy (to have something to do with her hands soothed her nerves) she began to sew. She was trying on the improvised cap when there came a light tap at the door.

At Saranna's invitation Honora appeared. In the girl's estimate the dress her "niece" had worn at their first meeting had been elaborate enough for a ball. But that paled into insignificance beside the one which clothed her now. Delicate lavender of half-mourning still, but the wide black lace of the skirt flounce filled the doorway, billowed in graceful folds as Honora moved.

Her shoulders were bare under a shawl scarf of the same black lace. And her fair hair, crimped, curled, carefully coaxed into an affectation of loose locks, was only partly covered with a token widow's cap of such fashion as to make Saranna's improvisation equal in dowdiness to the bonnet she had worn earlier.

"Where is Millie? She was to unpack for you—"

"I do not need her—" Saranna began.

"Nonsense, of course you need her. She's a lazy slut. Don't you let her beg off from any task she's set. You must keep an eye on every one of them or they'll shirk their work."

Honora advanced into the room without invitation, seated herself on a chair from which Saranna snatched her bonnet with only seconds to spare. Now the older girl came directly to the point:

"You are in full mourning, so I know you do not wish to meet any company. Unfortunately I must entertain for my father tonight—some of his business acquaintances. Therefore Millie will bring you a tray here where you will not be disturbed."

Or disturb you, Saranna added to herself. Honora was in half mourning, but it appeared she did not believe in seclusion for herself. Though Saranna had no intention of quarreling with the suggestion. She had no wish now, or perhaps ever, to be included in the social life of this house.

"My father has returned early," Honora continued. "He desires you to join him in the library." Again her tone underlined delicate astonishment that anyone would *want* Saranna's company.

If Honora had come merely for the purpose of delivering that message, she showed no signs of departing now that her errand was completed. With a little smile which never reached her eyes she continued to study the younger girl.

"My father was most amazed to receive that letter from Mrs. Stowell—"

Saranna almost started in surprise. *Mother* had written to Jethro? But why had she not told Saranna? She could guess her mother's purpose—that she must have realized the seriousness of her illness and lowered her pride to ask for her daughter what she would not for herself.

"He had had no contact with his family for years," Honora continued and then paused.

Saranna made no comment.

"However, he was very concerned when he heard, after such a length of time, of his father's death and of the unhappy straits in which you were left as a result of that."

Saranna stared directly back. "We were not in dire want, Honora. Until my mother became ill we earned our living."

"As village dressmakers—"

Saranna kept tight control of her temper. It was never what Honora said, it was the insinuating way she said it.

"I helped her as much as I could. But I was also studying. My mother had arranged for me to be a pupil teacher this summer at the Female Academy in Boston. Miss Seeton had accepted me."

Honora looked thoughtful. "So you are bookish, Saranna. But a Bluestocking does not interest the gentlemen. However, in your case—" She allowed her voice to drawl away and Saranna grasped very well her meaning. For a portionless poor girl the question of any gentleman's interest would hardly arise.

"Now," Honora continued with that sprightliness which set Saranna's teeth on edge, "it is best not to keep one gentleman—my father—waiting." She spoke as if Saranna had been the one causing the delay. "Down the stair, the second door to the right. You had better hurry if you wish to avoid meeting an early guest."

Saranna hurried. Not, she assured herself, because of what Honora had said, but because she honestly wanted to get past this first interview with her unknown brother. She had heard so little of Jethro (though her mother had never set the blame for the long estrangement on him) that she did not know what to expect.

She paused for a second before knocking at the library door, her hand up to make sure her prim cap was tidily in place. Then she entered in answer to a kind of growl to which the thickness of the door reduced a low-pitched, masculine voice.

II

Chun *Initial Difficulties*

So this was Jethro! Somehow, though Saranna had always known he was even older than her mother, she had still pictured him in her mind as one of her own generation. But this man was gray-haired, thickened at the waist, seeming as old, if not older, than her father as she last remembered him. Though Captain Stowell had been youthfully vigorous on the day they had waved the *Spindrift* out of the harbor for the last time.

"Well, m'dear, with that fox-brush hair, there's no denying you're all Stowell."

An odd greeting, but delivered with a warmth Saranna had not expected to hear in this house. That this could be an awkward meeting, she well understood. Being strangers who shared a kinship of blood but no family memories in common, how could either look for instant acceptance? And the Jethro she had half-resentfully held in her mind was not one to welcome an unknown half sister except grudgingly, as a duty he could not escape.

Now he advanced from the hearth and caught both of her hands before she was aware.

"Feel off course, don't you, m'dear? Like as not you fear to fetch up against a reef somewhere, needing a chart to steer you right. That's as it would be. I can't deny that your mother's letter came as a surprise. She said she had written without you knowing. Only wish she had written sooner. But I could tell she was a proud woman, not one to ask anything for herself. Am I right in reading her so?"

Saranna nodded. His seaman's terms recalled her father's blunt heartiness. The brisk, no false sympathy way in which he spoke touched her more deeply than the conventional condolences she had had to face since her loss. She swallowed, fighting tears.

Jethro accepted the past, acknowledged its claims, but then dismissed the years behind as unimportant now.

As he stood so close to her she noticed that, though his hair had a powdering of gray, its original shade must have been red, perhaps even as bright as her own. And the eyes regarding her so kindly from beneath his bushy brows were green like hers.

"Pity is," he continued, "we won't have long to get to know each other. I'm new to the coffee trade, you see. Means I have to learn it—up from ship's boy to captain all over again. So I'm off to Brazil on the *Tern,* sailing the day after tomorrow. Have to be down there a good while—visiting the plantations, getting to know the exporters—all the rest of it. May be gone near a year.

"But Honora will look after you, and when I'm home again—then we'll have a good amount of time. Your mother said you were a book lover, that you want to be a teacher. There's no need now to earn your living, mind you that, m'dear. But if you want learning, then you've a right to it. Most females don't care. But I learned early, Saranna, all people are not alike. Had to learn the hard way, from the Captain himself."

Jethro glanced from her to the small fire banishing the spring chill from the high-ceilinged room. Though there was no shadow of expression on his face, Saranna thought he did not see those low-burning flames, but rather memories.

"Sorry you don't want to dine with us, m'dear. But Honora understands. Hard to meet a lot of new people all at once. Honora's good at understanding. She'll be fine company for you. Feed you up—make things easy. You just trust Honora."

Saranna suppressed the answer she would have liked to give. Trust Honora was the last thing she was inclined to do. Honora had already proven her deviousness in allowing her father to believe that Saranna had requested to be excused from dining with the household tonight. And Saranna was certain of one thing, the Honora Jethro knew did not in the least resemble the Honora she had met. There were no protests she could now make against being left in his daughter's care which would not seem both rude and ungracious to this man whom she was beginning to like very much.

She was in the midst of expressing her thanks (which he waved impatiently aside), when there was a rap at the door and Honora appeared.

"Father—Judge Crawford has arrived. He is most anxious to have a few words with you before our other guests come. Saranna, my dear, I know you wish to escape notice. Millie will show you the back way to your room."

Saranna felt as if one of those brisk sea winds she had met on the trip to Baltimore had swept her up and whirled her away. Without knowing just how it happened, she was back in her chamber with Millie lighting a lamp on the small table. She became aware that the maid watched her shyly when she thought Saranna did not notice her. And, though she knew very little about the girl, Saranna decided that Honora's estimate of the servant was prejudiced. Millie moved with grace and a dignity all her own about the small tasks she had taken on without any orders.

"Miss, you want your dinnah soon?"

Saranna was suddenly aware that she was hungry. The cold lunch they had had on board ship just before docking seemed very far away now. And there had been no tea (such as her mother and she had always shared during an afternoon) offered her.

"Yes, please."

When Millie had slipped out, Saranna unhooked her tight basque. Since she was going to dine alone in her chamber she might as well be comfortable. And she saw a tall copper jug by the washbasin on the commode. By the time Millie returned with a tray, she had washed and was wearing the matinee morning sacque her mother had made for her as a birthday gift. It was not mourning, but she felt closer to her dear lost one with it about her, her fingers touching gently the frills her mother had so patiently and skillfully embroidered, than she did in any show of black.

Millie set down a tray which looked far too heavy to be carried up the stairs by her slender arms. The maid raised the covers of the dishes displaying a cup of soup, lobster patties, a roasted pigeon, a boiled potato, hot bread, and some fruit. Then she poured a cup of coffee from a small silver pot, proffered cream and sugar.

"We have coffee, Miss. The Master, he likes for us to serve it—"

Saranna tasted the new beverage gingerly. She had heard tales of its bitterness and strength, prophecies that it would never replace the genteel tea, the satisfying chocolate. But she decided that, with the cream and sugar added, it was palatable. And if Jethro wished his household to make popular the product in which he dealt, then he had a right to see that it was served under his roof to all comers.

"My, that there do be a pretty coat, Miss—" Millie was gazing with open admiration at Saranna's loose sacque.

Saranna's lips quivered in spite of her firm resolve to keep her inner feelings strictly to herself.

"My—my mother made it—for my birthday—" She was sorry that her voice sounded so unsteady. Taking tight rein on her emotions, the girl added more firmly, "She was noted for her embroidery. I learned a little. But I can't do it as well as she could—ever."

"So pretty—" Millie repeated. "Wish I could learn me how to make such a pretty thing."

"No reason why not," Saranna said. "I have the patterns—and I know the stitches—I could show you." She did not know why she had made that offer so impulsively. But once made, she knew that this was another way in which she could lose herself in the present, without the nagging sorrow of the past, the uncertainty of the future ever in her mind.

Jethro had been cordial, more than she had dared to expect. But he would not be here. And she would be left to Honora's whims, which she did not in the least trust.

"I don't know, Miss. Miss Honora, she don't like us to do what she ain't told us. But she says I'm your maid, maybe so I could learn me a little. Then she won't—" Millie stopped short and Saranna was sure she saw a shadow of fear on the girl's childish face.

"She won't what?"

"She won't send me back *there*. She gets mad sometimes, Miss Honora does. Then she say I'm clumsy and lazy. After she talks about sending me back there—"

"Where is there?"

"The Manor—upriver. Tiensin they calls it—the white folks. Old Cap'n Whaley, he come back from China and he build it. Brought some queer folks with him to make it the way he wanted it. Then, when it was all done, she send those queer people back where they belong. But there's a haunt there—shut up behind the hedges. Jasper, he saw it once—'cause it comes out sometimes. She—" Millie's eyes turned toward the door as if she feared someone might suddenly appear there, and Saranna guessed that "she" referred to the girl's mistress, "don't go there much. She thought it was all goin' to be hers, but Master Richard, he died before the Old Cap'n, and now little Miss, she got it. Mrs. Parton, she lives there with little Miss, and the hands what works the fields. Me—I don't want to go upriver!"

Saranna knew that it was the worst of manners to listen to servant gossip. But she needed to know all she could discover about the family into which she had been so unexpectedly dropped.

"Who is little Miss?" she asked bluntly, waving aside the haunt story which was, of course, sheer superstition.

"Miss Damaris—she be Master Richard's own daughter by his first wife. Old Cap'n say she is real Whaley; Miss Honora ain't. So he make will, give everything to her. Miss Honora plenty mad. Poor Miss Damaris—she—they say as how she ain't always right in the head. How can she be right—a child livin' where a haunt can get at her?"

Millie shivered. Her lips parted as if she would say something else, then she turned and fairly ran from the room. Perhaps, Saranna thought, she was regretting her indiscreet speech and believed her words might be repeated to Honora. But the maid had left Saranna with a small mystery to muse over while she ate.

When she finished the last of her dinner, she arose from the small table to go to the near window. Double drapery and curtains there shut out the night. Saranna drew them aside to form a chink through which she could watch the gathering darkness.

A carriage drove up to the door below. She caught a foreshortened glimpse of a man's silk hat, the lacy evening hood of the lady assisted from the carriage—more guests.

The carriage pulled on to join the other vehicles in the street. Through the closed window, Saranna could hear the muted hum of the city, see lanterns and lamps marking the buildings beyond. She remembered her short interview with Jethro. He had done all the talking—his spate of words had swept her along. She could not recall now any pause which had given her a chance to speak. It was as if what she might have said was of no importance.

She had not been really aware of that at the time—only now. He had dismissed her so easily into Honora's care, Saranna frowned. At least he had mentioned Mother's plan for her as a teacher, and seemed to think that her desire for an education was praiseworthy. But—could she depend upon his help? Suppose he would agree to allow her to return to Miss Seeton's this summer, give her funds enough to pay her way? Surely he might be eager to be rid of his responsibility for her. Would she have a chance to suggest that before he left? The time was so short.

Now that Saranna had time to examine his words without his presence, she was a little chilled. He had seemed so friendly in his manner. But he would soon be gone, leaving her to Honora. And of Honora's lack of friendliness, she had no doubt at all.

What was she going to do? All her pride stirred. To stay on here as Honora's pensioner, that would be like being a prisoner. If she could just see Jethro once more, this time have him listen to *her*— Impatience possessed Saranna. She wanted nothing more than to confront her brother tonight, get this matter settled. And yet she knew she had no chance at all.

Though the bed was soft, the covers above her warm, she could not get to sleep. Plans formed in her mind, only to be discarded as useless. She was caught in the trap of her age and sex—a young female had to listen to her guardian, which in truth, Jethro now was. She had no resource but to obey his wishes. The realization of that aroused again the deep anger within her.

At last, she fell into an uneasy sleep and a dream. Before her loomed a hedge, untrimmed or curbed, which rose far above her head. The green of the leaves on those close-packed bushes which formed the barrier was dark, close to black. Yet there was no somberness or menace in its shadowy length. Instead, Saranna was filled with an excitement which made her heart beat faster; an eagerness to see what lay beyond moved her. She raised both hands to catch at branches, force them aside so she could see—what? She did not know, save that it was wonderful and waited just for her.

From that dream she aroused to see an edge of sunlight around the close-drawn drapery of her window. Millie stood beside her bed holding a small tray on which was a covered cup.

"Miss," her soft voice drove away the last of that dream, "Miss Honora, she says can you come see her soon—"

"Why?" asked Saranna before she thought. Naturally, Honora would not tell the maid.

"She mighty pleased about somethin', Miss Honora is," was Millie's oblique answer. By her tone, Saranna could guess that what pleased Honora might not be entirely acceptable to others. But that she had already deduced.

There was little choice she could make in clothing. But she dared to wear a white chemisette with fine muslin inner sleeves, instead of the dead black in which she had traveled. Her gown was so shabby that she needed the extra sense of support that vestee would give her. However, she scrapped her hair well back under the black cap she had so hurriedly fashioned, hoping that might balance her small defiance of true mourning dress.

She drank the chocolate Millie had brought in the cup and glanced once more in the mirror. Primish looks, very proper, perhaps she should also assume, she thought bitterly, a subdued expression suitable for a family pensioner? No! They must take her as she really was. She intended to play no meek role merely to gain anyone's good graces.

"Saranna, good morning—" Honora still wore her favorite half mourning, but this time her matinee robe and skirt were of lavender, bearing creamy white lace ruffling and banding. She was settled before a silver coffee service as hostess in the breakfast room to which Saranna had been directed.

Jethro was eating a slice of ham with the gusto of one who thoroughly enjoyed the excellency of the dishes set before him.

"Good morning," he swallowed visibly before he echoed his daughter's greeting. "What will you have, m'dear? The ham is choice. We have to thank Honora for that—comes in from Tiensin, the Whaley Manor upriver.

Potatoes, biscuits—" He did not look directly at Saranna, rather enumerated the contents of the various serving dishes. Then, again not waiting for any word of preference from Saranna, he carved a plate of ham, spooned the potatoes he had recommended, together with a square of light bread, and handed the plate to the hovering serving maid who placed it before the girl.

"Time—" Jethro shook his head. He had pulled his large watch from his waistcoat pocket, snapped open the case, to frown at the dial. "Never enough time. I will have to be going, a long, long day for me. Must make sure all is well before I leave. My dear, Honora has an excellent plan which she suggested to me only this morning, one which I think you will find most advantageous in every way. She will explain it all to you—"

He was already on his feet, heading for the door. As it had been the evening before, her half brother gave Saranna no chance at all to answer or protest. She watched the door close with a finality which definitely left her in Honora's dubious charge.

"Poor Father—before he sails it is always this way." Honora shook her head, sending the long lace streamers of her cap floating gently beside the most carefully arranged curls of massed hair. "There are so many matters he must make sure of that he is quite fatigued when he finally goes aboard. The voyage will give him the rest he needs. Now—Saranna," she spoke more briskly. "As you are in deep mourning—" her eyes flicked at that white chemisette as she spoke, "you will want peace and quiet. Father has certain social obligations which I have agreed to carry on during his absence. Thus, I do not think you would be comfortable here where there will be a goodly amount of entertaining.

"But at Tiensin, it will be very different. It is most quiet there, and Mrs. Parton is an excellent housekeeper and will make you very comfortable. She is a quite genteel sort of female, and one in whom I have placed a good amount of trust. You see—" Honora hesitated, "I

do not know what you may have heard of my own obligations, Saranna, but I do have one which is enough to
make anyone heavy-hearted.

"I was Richard Whaley's second wife. His first wife,
Laura, died when poor Damaris was born. Laura was a
Hampton, and, unfortunately, there is a weak strain in
that family—an excitation of nerves which has affected
several of the women. In the past, it has been necessary
that at least two of them live in seclusion with suitable
companions. Do you understand—?"

That she must be hinting delicately at some type of
mental derangement, Saranna guessed. And she nodded.

Honora apparently accepted that as encouragement
for greater confidences.

"Richard's father doted on Damaris—he would not
ever acknowledge that, young as she then was, she
showed already some signs of this nervous disorder. And
after Richard's death, his own followed within a year. It
was then we discovered just how blindly foolish Captain
Whaley had been, how he had refused to accept those
signs which were so plain to us. He had left Tiensin and
most of his other wealth to Damaris. Luckily, he had ap-
pointed a guardian, of course—my father. And I have
the overseeing of her upbringing and education. But,
poor thing, that she has any future, we doubt—nothing
beyond a very quiet life, well supervised, at Tiensin. We
must make very sure that she is not taken advantage of as
she grows older, and that she is guarded from a world in
which she would be utterly lost.

"Now you have planned to be a teacher—and Damaris
has no governess at present. The woman on which we
have been depending proved to be a superstitious fool,
listening to slaves' gossip. It was necessary to get rid of
her on very short notice. Thus I am deeply concerned
about the poor child. If you would be obliging enough to
be her companion until we can find someone able to give
her the care she needs—"

"I have had no experience as a nurse." Saranna took
advantage of the first pause in Honora's flow of words to

object. Like her father, Honora apparently cultivated the art of talk to the exclusion of any real give and take of conversation.

"Oh, I have given you the wrong impression," Honora shook her head as if aghast at her mistake. "Damaris is not ill. She is only one who needs to be talked out of the strange fancies which she clings to. She has a very odd belief about a derelict portion of the garden which we try not to allow her to dwell upon. In fact, if you can keep her from roaming about there and persuade her not to believe in her own imagined people, then you will succeed mightily. Who knows, perhaps you may even work the miracle we have so long hoped for and banish Damaris' fancies entirely.

"Much of her difficulties I truly believe is the fact that her early upbringing was too much under the control of Captain Whaley. He had lived in China for many years as a representative of a large shipping interest there. When he rebuilt Tiensin—" Honora actually shivered a little, "well, he brought in all sorts of queer heathenish things. He even imported servants from China—though he sent them back again years ago when the house was finally completed. Richard always said the Manor was full of what he called treasures—

"Unfortunately, Damaris believes, too, that these strange old things are precious. She has become very upset on occasion when some have been moved, or stored away. And it has been necessary to watch her if this happens, for she flies into an actual screaming rage. But I know that you will be most careful, now that you have been warned.

"Really, you have nothing to fear. Mrs. Parton has reported that Damaris has been very settled and docile since the governess left, and I know that you will find her eager to learn. She does have a quick mind. Too quick at times—especially when she builds upon something she hears or thinks she sees and then swears that her dreams are true. Now—very luckily, I have been able to arrange a way for you to reach Tiensin with the least trouble. Mr.

Fowke is going upriver on his private sloop taking some supplies and workmen for the rebuilding of his own manor which is next to Tiensin. He very kindly offered to let you travel with him. I believe he plans to leave at ten. I am giving you Millie—she has not settled down well here in the city. I think it is better that she be under Mrs. Parton's supervision for a while again—"

As she spoke, Honora rolled her napkin and inserted it into the silver ring near her plate.

"Such a busy morning—I have shopping to do—" Once more her gaze rested for a deprecating second or two on Saranna's dress. "By the way, you have said you can sew—there are some of my dresses in storage. Mrs. Parton will show you—feel free to make good use of them. You will have time in plenty on your hands upriver."

"But—" To have her immediate future so finally and abruptly settled had left Saranna astounded. However, Honora was already on her way out of the room. If she heard that first word of intended protest, she was not going to admit it or wait for any refusal Saranna might utter.

And how *could* she refuse, the girl admitted glumly to herself as she was left alone to face a now fast-chilling plate of far too heavy food. She had to depend on the Stowells, and both Jethro and Honora knew it. She had now no choice at all. Moodily she cut off a small bite of ham and chewed it relentlessly, wishing she had an efficacious way of dealing with Honora.

III

Lü *Treading Carefully*

Afterward, Saranna thought that the cottony fog into which Gerrad Fowke's river sloop plunged had been, in a way, a warning of the murky paths which lay before her. The thick tendrils gathering about the small boat were like a spider's web meant to entangle them past escape. And with the coming of that fog, the warmth of the spring vanished. The day was darkly chill. Moisture beaded the deck planking and the rail against which she stood, dampened her shawl, made her bonnet veil hang limp and heavy. Yet she shrank from going into the cramped cabin below.

The deck, save for a very small portion through which the crew moved, was piled high with stacks of lumber, barrels and boxes, as was the hold, so that the sloop rode low in the river. Since the sails could not be used, the crew were out with sweeps, three men to a side, walking back and forth to give them a very slow headway. While Mr. Fowke himself took the wheel post.

Millie, her eyes swollen from crying, huddled on one side of the boxes, a small figure of misery. The maid had shown such fear ever since Honora had decreed that she accompany Saranna to Tiensin that Saranna had not been able to get anything coherent out of her. Now Millie appeared as if facing a doom from which she had no hope of escape, displaying no interest in her surroundings.

For all Saranna's relief at escape from the house over which Honora had full command, her own uneasiness grew. And the heaviness of this fog did not dispel any forebodings. Though Mr. Fowke showed no signs of being aware that anything out of the ordinary was happening, his complete air of self-confidence and self-assurance drew her now to edging past the deck cargo and approaching his place of command.

The blacks at the sweeps chanted in rhythm with their swings of the sweeps. She could not understand a word and there was a strange, eerie note to that song (if song it was) which disturbed her so much she wanted to cover her ears with her hands. When she peered into the heavy mists, she could imagine that something or some things lurked within its folds, ever watching them evilly—

Saranna forced a rein on her imagination. Of course, there was nothing there! And Mr. Fowke knew this waterway as well as she knew the lanes of Sussex. Unlike its neighbor Virginia, since the earliest days of settlement, Maryland had used as roads those rivers which cut and sliced into its lands. The manors had their own wharves and landings, their own sloops. Neighbor visited neighbor via the water, and it was only since the beginning of this century that roads had come to link town and city. Still, the many rivers remained the easiest transportation by which to reach most of the manors.

"This will delay us," Gerrad Fowke's voice broke through the monotonous song of the scullers. "Unless it lifts, you may not reach Tiensin, Miss Stowell, until well past moon rise. I am sorry your introduction to the river had to be so unpromising a one."

"That you can move at all through this," she ventured in return, "is surprising. What if another boat comes—?"

He laughed. "We'd hear and so would they. We don't need fog warnings with Jason leading the chant." He nodded to the powerful man at the nearest scull.

"I can't understand what they are saying—or singing—"

Mr. Fowke shrugged. "Probably it's some juju petition

to the dark powers. They have their own way of thinking
and believing."

Saranna glanced at the sodden lump of misery which
marked Millie. Even in the short distance between them
now the black girl was half-hidden by the mists.

"Millie—she's badly frightened. She did not want to
come. She claims there is a haunt at Tiensin—"

He no longer looked amused. There was a firmness
about his mouth which reminded Saranna that he had
captained ships much larger than this sloop, and that air
of command he wore was his by right of experience.

"They are superstitious, and they cling to old gods.
What else have they to give them hope?" That was not
quite a question, but he turned a sudden searching gaze
at her. "They are slaves in a strange land; much has
frightened and left them defenseless. So they have perhaps a right to see menace in shadows, enemies all
around them."

"You do not believe in slavery—" Saranna glanced
from him to the men straining at the sculls. She had
thought that he would accept the customs of his home-
land without questions. Men usually did.

"I have no slaves," he replied flatly. "Queen's Pleasure
has its people, these men among them. None of them are
slaves. You will discover that that makes me somewhat of
a misfit here." Again that expression of assurance firmed
his harsh features. "Luckily I am also successful in my un-
dertakings. And since I have come back home with my
pockets well lined, I have a measure of acceptance—"

Now he did smile again. "Gold is a mighty way to back
one's opinions, even if they are unpopular ones. And I
am not the first to cause talk. Captain Whaley did not
own slaves either, at least not until his latter days. He had
real heathens—Chinese!"

"Chinese?" Saranna remembered some of Mr.
Sanders' explanation of what might lie before her.

"Yes. He was long in Canton, you know, being one of
the first to carry our flag to the East Indies. And he settled in his own factory there, had an excellent rela-

tionship with one of the Hong merchants. For about fifteen years he was the representative for several American companies. When he came home to Baltimore, he was accompanied by quite an entourage. All Chinese.

"They helped rebuild part of Tiensin, and lay out the gardens. But after about ten years, he bought passage for them and sent them all home again in style. But then Whaley was considered distinctly eccentric. There was the matter of the foxes, too—"

"Foxes?" repeated Saranna, completely bewildered by the introduction of this new subject.

Once more Mr. Fowke laughed. "Now I have surprised you. But the subject is somewhat of a serious matter all the same, and it adds to the queer stories surrounding Tiensin. You see, some of our back-country squires have delusions of introducing what they consider to be the customs of English aristocracy. Just as their grandfathers fought to break ties with the old country, so do they now think of aping some of the amusements from overseas. In short, they have a hunt, their blooded horses, all the rest.

"But not over Tiensin land! There is a strict rule there, no fox is to be hunted, shot at, trapped, not at Tiensin. Captain Whaley was determined about that, and he made enemies over his orders. At his death, half the parish was not speaking to him, not that he cared."

"But why foxes?" Saranna had forgotten the fog now. He had captured her full attention with his story.

"The odd part about it is that no one knows. But so adamant was his decree that he even left a solemn warning in his will that if his orders were broken in the future, there would be a penalty paid by his heirs for that mistake. And foxes do flourish at Tiensin. There are tales of exceptionally large ones walking boldly in the garden, even during broad daylight. The blacks call them haunts and are afraid of them. They will give way as if the foxes were their masters. But there are other things which set Tiensin apart—" he continued as if he wished her to know what might lie ahead and had a concern that she understand.

"There is the lost garden—"

He was watching her closely, Saranna did not understand why. Did he expect her to show some signs of dislike or fear such as Millie displayed since the news of her exile from Baltimore had been broken to her? Was he—could he—be telling some old tale partly born of his own imagination to see if she were one of those easily alarmed females who saw only dark menace in the unknown? If he was, the disappointment would be his. Captain Whaley's attitude toward foxes might be termed peculiar, to be sure, but Saranna could see little alarming in it. And a lost garden—if Mr. Fowke were in some manner baiting her, she was not in any way going to rise to the bait, even by asking a question.

After a very short pause, he continued. "There is what must be a goodly third of the land first set out for a garden cut away now and well walled off by the hedges which have been allowed, even encouraged, to grow as high as possible. The common notion is that there is no way in—and the ignorant say that it is to protect the Captain's treasure."

Now Saranna smiled. Did he expect her to be moved by that most childish of hints? "There is a treasure, of course?" she asked a little mockingly.

"Oh, the Captain had treasures all right." Mr. Fowke nodded. "You will see those in plenty at Tiensin. He had a love for China which few of those in the Canton factories ever possessed. Most merchants were content—are content—with their exports to build up their fortunes. But he loved beauty—precious things—not for their value in dollars and cents—but for the pleasure they give the eye. During the years Whaley spent in those waters, he bought many such. Perhaps some not legally. There are coast pirates which prey upon sections of China where the 'foreign devils,' as they so pleasantly term us, cannot ever hope to visit. The loot from those forays comes in time to markets where a canny man may have an agent bargain for him.

"There are rebellions which even the Banner Princes, those who are near the Dragon Throne, lose. And the price for rebellion in China is grim. Not only does the rebel suffer, but his whole family clan can be sent to follow him into death. Then their possessions are plundered, so bits and pieces find their ways into strange hands.

"Look well about you in the rooms of Tiensin, Miss Stowell. What you will see there is not the ordinary gleanings of an India merchant—but objects of far greater value. However, as to any great treasure laid up in any special place—no, I do not believe that Whaley left that. What may lie behind the growing walls of that garden no one really knows. Just that it is strictly forbidden territory to all. And the blacks fear it even more than they fear those bold foxes. They say it contains a ghost whom the Captain brought home with him—a very potent and heathen ghost."

Again Saranna smiled. She was sure that Mr. Fowke was trying to tease her a little.

"A Bluebeard's garden then. But since I am not wedding Bluebeard, I do not think I have anything to fear. And if there are rules at Tiensin, I am fully prepared to keep them."

"See that you remember that." His tone was so serious that Saranna was a little surprised. Had he really not been teasing at all? Could he have *meant* that there was some particular danger at the Manor? But such a suspicion was absurd, of course.

The thick fog was breaking, stirred by a wind which twanged the lines of the sloop's rigging. Within what seemed to Saranna a very short time—sails were raised to catch that wind, and they scudded forward at a pace which suggested that Mr. Fowke's pessimistic estimate of their time of arrival might be wrong.

But dark had come and they had eaten a cold meal from a basket the master of the sloop provided before the sloop did nose in to a wharf on which hung a pair of lanterns. There was a woman, with a hooded cloak about her shoulders, standing well to the fore, to welcome them; behind her, several blacks, one with an empty wheelbarrow. As Mr. Fowke helped Saranna onto the wharf, and then swung Millie bodily up and over in her wake, the woman moved forward to drop a stiff curtsy of an earlier day.

"We had word from the headlands you were coming," she said in a low, emotionless voice. "Mr. Hangton's man brought it. I am Mrs. Parton." Again she bowed.

In the dark, which the lanterns of those about them did little to break, Saranna could see nothing of Mrs. Parton's face, which was hidden in the shadow of her hood. There was something, however, forbidding in her manner—in the stiff way she held herself. Though perhaps, Saranna thought, again she was imagining things.

At the present, she was far more aware of her own fatigue and an overwhelming desire to reach whatever bedchamber was assigned her, then to bed.

"I am Saranna Stowell," she replied wearily. "And I am very pleased to meet you."

The woman gave no response, merely stood waiting, her very attitude expressing impatience. Saranna turned a little from her, and perhaps it was the forbidding stance of the housekeeper of Tiensin which put an extra shade of warmth in her voice as she thanked Mr. Fowke for his assistance in her journey.

Nor, in spite of her fatigue, did she turn her face from the river until the sloop cast off and was on its way farther northwest. Her sea chest had been lifted into the wheelbarrow, and now she walked with Mrs. Parton, one of the men servants carrying a lantern just ahead to light their way, Millie scuttling behind. Saranna was presently aware of a small twitch at her skirt and knew, without turning to see, that the maid had dared to seize hold there, as if such contact with Saranna was all that gave her the courage to follow.

Mr. Fowke had mentioned moon rise. However, there

was no moon tonight. Though the fog had lifted, lowering clouds remained. And they walked a narrow path between shaped and trimmed hedges toward the bulk of a building where there were enough lights in windows to suggest that it was of an imposing size.

They were perhaps a third of the way toward that house when Saranna sighted small glitters, sparks of green, which were near ground level along the hedge. There were so many that her curiosity was fully aroused.

"Please—" she broke the silence which Mrs. Parton had maintained since her self-introduction, "what are those—?"

Whether the housekeeper had seen her gesture toward the sparks, Saranna could not be sure. But she did feel the sudden jerk at her skirt which betrayed Millie's agitation. Then the woman beside her spoke in the same even tone:

"Those are the foxes. You see their eyes reflecting the lantern light."

"Foxes!" Saranna did not add as she wished—in such numbers? But she was truly astonished. She did not believe that foxes ran in packs as their more-to-be-feared cousins the wolves did. And in spite of Mr. Fowke's story, she had not been prepared for any sight such as this. It was almost as if the animals were so highly curious that they crowded to watch her arrival. They did not venture into the open, of course, but still they were close enough to the small party making their way toward the house to suggest that the animals had little or no fear of the human beings who claimed ownership here.

"You will become used to them, Miss Stowell," Mrs. Parton continued. "They have been long protected by Captain Whaley, and are still so by his decree. Though the blacks are alarmed by them, they have never been known to be vicious or to attack anyone. Now, if you will just step this way—"

They were at the house and Mrs. Parton glided ahead to open a door and usher Saranna and Millie in. There she threw back her own hood, allowed the enveloping cloak to slide from her spare shoulders.

Though her skirt, of a small indigo-and-black sprigged print, was wide and full, her narrow shoulders, long neck, tightly netted hair beneath a plain cap, added to her height and to the suggestion of stern repression. Her hair was gray above a pallid face, with unnaturally plump cheeks bracketing a very small mouth. The nose separating her small eyes with their scanty lashes was a mere dab of a button, as if, Saranna thought, her whole countenance was fashioned of the kitchen scraps of dough, such as her own mother had given her to play with on baking day when she was small.

"This way, please, Miss—"

The survey Mrs. Parton had made of her in turn had been a very quick one. In fact, even when she faced Saranna squarely, her eyes seemed fixed on a point over the girl's shoulder. As if she had dismissed Saranna as unworthy of any notice, and so searched behind her for some more important visitor.

The housekeeper picked up a lamp from a nearby table. Holding this in a firm grip, she turned to the stairway not far behind her. This had none of the wide grace of that in the town house. And, Saranna recognized a moment or so later, they must not have entered through the main doorway of the Manor at all, but were now in a humbler portion of the Great House.

If this were the servants' stairs, the treads were meticulously dusted. There was the faint odor of wax and polish to be sniffed, making quite certain that Mrs. Parton ruled her own domain well and with energy.

The flight gave upon a hall where lay a carpet of dark red patterned in buff, yellow, and dull blue, while the paneled walls were broken at intervals by white doors. The lamp, as they passed, caught framed, glass-protected strips of embroidery mounted on those panels like pictures. Faded creamy silk provided backgrounds for exotic birds, flowers, and sometimes queer stiff animals, none of which Saranna could identify so swiftly did Mrs. Parton whisk them along.

At last the housekeeper paused to set hand to a door latch. Someone spoke out of the dusky shadows beyond the reach of her lamp.

"So she's come—"

The voice was clear and young, but it was not childish. Then the speaker moved into the light with a quick dart as if she feared Saranna might vanish before she reached her. Though her eagerness was perhaps not meant to express pleasure in the visitor's arrival; rather the reverse.

"Miss Damaris—" Mrs. Parton began.

The child hunched a shoulder, not even glancing at the housekeeper, her attention fixed solely on Saranna. She was very thin, her arms, within the knitted lace of her undersleeves, scarcely rounded at all. Her dress was an unhappily chosen drab green which made her skin look sallow and yellowish, as if she were recovering from some dire illness.

For so young a girl (she might perhaps be twelve, Saranna decided), her features were strongly marked, too much so for any claim to the rosebud prettiness which was the youthful ideal. Straight dark brows lined over eyes which rested on one with a disconcerting and piercing steadiness, as if Damaris wanted not only to see the object of her regard, but beneath the surface into the bargain. Her nose was as marked as Mrs. Parton's was self-effacing, her mouth nearly as straight as her brows, with more than a shade of stubbornness in its setting.

Dark hair had been bundled up into a net, but not very tightly, so that a strand or two had come loose to stray over her shoulders and around her thin neck. She was plainly not the sweet and biddable child so often idealized by those who know very little of children.

Saranna held out her hand:

"I am Saranna—"

"I know," Damaris spoke fiercely. "*She* said you would come. *She* wants you here. But you're not going to keep

me in order. You can't, you know, not if you want to
please *her,* you can't. *She* wants me bad—I know—" The
words poured from her lips in a passionate burst of
specch. "*She* hates me. *She*'s sorry 'cause Grandfather
gave me Tiensin. *She* wants to make *me* sorry, too. You
needn't think I'm going to let her or you or anybody in
the whole world do that! 'Cause you can't—you can't ever
do so!"

She whirled about and was gone with a flap of skirt, a
bob of uncoiffed hair, disappearing into the shadows.
Without a word of comment, Mrs. Parton opened the
door and proceeded with unruffled calmness into the
room, placing her lamp on a table.

"Sarah will bring you tea and hot water," she said.
"Millie is to have the trundle bed." She shot a single,
quelling glance at the maid. She might have been noting
her presence for the first time. Saranna saw Millie shrink
back as if the last thing she wanted was to attract Mrs.
Parton's attention.

To her own surprise, the housekeeper continued to
make no comment on Damaris' dramatic arrival and retreat. And Saranna decided to ignore it also for the moment. She sensed that beneath the outwardly ordered
surface of life in this house, there must be many whirl-
pools. Those she must chart before she launched into any
hurried speech or action.

As the door closed behind the housekeeper, the girl
untied her bonnet strings, to lay that and her shawl aside.
Millie still stood near the lamp table, her eyes shifting
fearfully from side to side.

"Did you see them, Miss? They was a-watchin' us.
They was—all them foxes. They goes an' tells about us
comin' to the haunt. All they sees, they tells." She shivered. "Then the haunt, it knows an' it can—" She was crying again, her voice rising in a wail.

"It can what?" Saranna went to the girl, laid her hands
on the bowed and shaking shoulders. "Millie, you are
quite safe here—look around you. Do you see any foxes?
They don't come into the house ever, now do they?"

"Never so far, they ain't," the girl admitted.

"Well, then, do you have to worry about them here and now?" Saranna was not yet sure what steadying words she could best use with Millie. She would have to discover the best way of soothing the maid when she was not quite so tired, nor worried over Damaris' reception.

"I guess so—" Millie concluded, reluctantly.

Should she question Millie about the situation here? Ask her about Damaris? Maybe in the future, but not now. Saranna's one thought as to how to handle the situation for the present was to ignore that scene by the door as thoroughly as Mrs. Parton had done. To discuss the young mistress of Tiensin with Millie was not a good way of beginning. Honora's comment concerning Damaris' excitable temperament and the sad family heritage behind the girl was a warning.

A maid almost as young as Millie brought in a can of hot water and a little later, a tray with a pot of tea, some biscuits, and a small china dish of jam. Millie went with Sarah willingly enough, after Saranna's urging, to get some food for herself.

When they both had left, Saranna went to the window to look out, wondering if she could see any of those foxes that had watched her coming. That the animals' behavior was unnatural, she could admit. Why had Captain Whaley seemingly made pets of such woods creatures? Had his sheltering really tamed them so? There was surely some reason—

Though the night was still cloudy, she could see, now that her eyes were turned away from the lamplight and adjusted to the gloom outside the pane, something of the land beyond the house. But there was only a short clear stretch here. Then there arose a tall hedge thick and overgrown enough to form a stout wall. The lost garden!

Its untended brush showed inky black in this less than half light. In the gloom, that growth had a threatening look, as if it were a portion of some awe-inspiring fortress. Saranna could now understand those who believed what it guarded was evil. Now there was no sparkle of eyes along its edging. If foxes still paced there, the loom of the hedge kept their ways well secret.

Saranna let fall the curtain and began to inspect the chamber. The room was well sized, but not as luxuriously furnished as that which had so briefly been her quarters in the Baltimore house. However, there was, on the mantel above the fireplace, something which drew her attention the minute she sighted it.

Picking up the lamp, she carried the light closer to see it better.

A carving of some smooth brownish substance. Saranna drew a breath of wonder and delight. A patient craftsman half the world away (for she had no doubt that this was indeed one of the treasures from China which Mr. Fowke had mentioned) had wrought in delicate and detailed miniature a tiny landscape with towering mountains and lower lands. That artist, who had brought some dream of his own so to life, had most cleverly utilized the natural mottling of the stone to enhance the effect he desired.

Saranna knew very little of art nor of the timelessness of such creations. But she recognized utter beauty, and she wanted to hold the piece in her hands. Returning the lamp to the table she went to pick up that wonder, run fingertips over the minute indications of tempest twisted trees, the gnarled faces of rocks less in size than the span of her own fingernail. One could never tire looking at this because there was always something new to see, some later discovered wonder to astonish.

"Give me that! You're just like *her*—grab, grab!"

Saranna had heard no door opening. She was totally unprepared for the coming of the hand which fiercely snatched the carving, wrested it from her own grip in an instant.

Damaris, her face ugly with a black scowl, clasped the carving tight against her flat chest.

"It's mine! Every one of them are! Grandfather said so. *She* wants to get them, she always has. I heard her lots of times, always talking to Father about how they were no good buried out here. But she never liked *them*. She only wants them because they're worth lots and lots of money. Grandfather told me so. He said I must never sell them— just keep them to look at—to learn how to know beauty. And you're not going to get a one of them!"

The child backed toward the door, one arm holding the carving very tight to her, her other hand outstretched with the fingers crooked a little as a cat might show unsheathed claws in warning.

"You just try to get this—anything else—" she hissed. "You just try—"

This action must not be allowed to finish so, Saranna knew. If Damaris left now she might never be able to establish any proper contact with the child. She moved more swiftly than Damaris now, dodging around the child so that she stood with her back to the door.

"I did not want your treasure to keep—" She tried to make her words as emphatic as she could. "I only wanted to look at it closely because it is the most beautiful thing I have ever seen."

Damaris still scowled, but she slowly lowered that threatening hand.

"*She* sent you—and she wants it—"

Saranna decided this was time for the truth, what she believed to be the truth.

"Honora sent me here," she said, "because she wanted to get rid of me."

IV

Hêng *Perseverance*

Damaris eyed the older girl searchingly, as if by the very intensity of that survey, she could gauge the truth of what Saranna had said.

"Old Poker—I heard her talking. *She* was to send you to keep me in order, that was what Poker said!" She spat. "After Prune Face left, because she was too nosy for her own good, then *she* said that they would find somebody to keep me in order! So *she* sent you."

Saranna shook her head. "I was sent because Honora did not want me in Baltimore." And because she was certain that that was indeed the truth, perhaps her words made some impression on the child.

"Why?" was Damaris' bold demand.

"Why? Well, because I am in mourning." Saranna indicated the limp spread of her black skirt. "Because I do not fit in—"

"Then who are you? If you're not one to keep me in order?" Damaris demanded. "They never tell me things, you know." She pointed with her chin toward the door behind Saranna as if to indicate the rest of the household. "I have to listen to learn anything at all. Old Poker— when Grandfather was here—she'd never dare act this way. He would have sent her packing. That's what he used to tell me. 'Never allow insolence, girl. Send 'em packing if they don't give the Captain his due.' I'm like the Captain—but they won't admit it—they listen to *her* and—"

Saranna saw the quiver of the child's mouth. "I do wish Grandfather was here," she ended. Then the scowl came back.

"I got rid of Prune Face all right. And I'll get rid of you—if you try to spy on me." Once more her tone was fierce. "If *she* sent you, then you don't belong here."

"No, I don't," returned Saranna as bluntly. "But just now I have no place else to go. So you will have to bear with me until I can find one. I am not a governess hired by Honora. I am Jethro Stowell's half sister from Massachusetts."

"But—" Damaris said slowly, "Mr. Stowell's old, real old. How can you be his sister when you're so young?" She was plainly wary, not in the least convinced.

"Because his father—my father—was married twice. I was born long after Jethro was a man."

"You look a little—just a little—like Jethro," Damaris conceded. "You look—foxy!" For the first time she smiled. "That's what I'm going to call you—Kuei-Fu-Lu-Li—" The strange syllables came easily from her lips. "You didn't know I can speak Chinese—real Chinese, did you?" Her head tilted a little to one side. "I can, you know. I learned, Kuei-Fu-Lu-Li—that means Fox Lady. What do you think of that!"

Her scowl had faded, and there was a change in her attitude. The defiance she had earlier shown was ebbing.

"I think you are a very clever girl, Damaris," Saranna returned. "From what I have heard, Chinese is a very difficult language."

"It is. Grandfather said most of the traders talked just 'pidgin.'" Now there was the sharpness of scorn in her voice. "But he said 'pidgin' was an insult to his intelligence. He hired a scholar to teach him the real Chinese talk and then he taught me—a little anyway," she corrected herself with honesty.

She hesitated a moment and then held out the carving. "I guess you weren't grabbing after all. If you want to look at this, go ahead. You know what it really is?"

Saranna shook her head as she accepted the peace offering.

"It's a rest for a writing brush. The Chinese, they don't write with pens the way we do, they use brushes. When Grandfather left Canton, the scholar who had taught him Chinese gave him that. It's brown jade, and there's even a name for it—the Mountains of Peaceful Contemplation. That means that you can look at it and feel peaceful, but you have to think about what it means."

"The Mountains of Peaceful Contemplation," Saranna repeated, running her fingertip down the flank of the tallest of those carved mountains. "Thank you, Damaris, for telling me that. It *is* like looking down into a small world, isn't it?"

The girl nodded. "Grandfather, he used to take one of the treasures 'most everyday—put it on the table and just look at it. He told me that was the way to learn. So I do it—sometimes—unless I'm made to do something else—" That scowl flitted across her face again.

"Old Prune Face, she wanted to lock everything up, saying I might break things. Break them! Grandfather taught me to be very careful. She said no child ought to be allowed to handle things—and that they were heathen things anyway and bad for the young mind." It was apparent Damaris was quoting. "She used to slip around spying—until—"

Damaris stopped almost in midword, her face suddenly blank.

Saranna was greatly tempted to ask, "Until what?" but at that moment, intuition strongly advised her to let it go. Damaris might reveal more of this extraordinary household if she were not questioned.

"But Old Poker said you were going to come to keep me in order—"

The inflection of that was not that of a statement, but a question.

"And who is Old Poker?" Saranna asked then, thinking that this much might not be resented.

Damaris laughed. "Mrs. Parton—don't you see? Grandfather always said she walked as if she had an iron poker for a backbone." Her face clouded a little. "She never talked too much when he was here. Grandfather gave the orders at Tiensin! Her husband—he's the over-seer—Collis Parton. He can give orders out in the fields. But here, inside, Old Poker, she tells *him* what to do. Then there's Rufe—"

For a moment all Damaris' assurance was quenched. "Rufe, he's Old Poker's son. He's been away—to school. Old Poker thinks he's God on earth—"

"What!" Saranna was startled out of her well-maintained calm by that expression.

Damaris nodded. "That's what Grandfather said when Rufe was just little. Now he's grown up, she'll probably be worse. And he's coming back here. I don't want him—he's a *wu lai*! *She* likes him 'cause he pretends to want to do just what *she* wants. So I hate him!"

"Miss Damaris!" There was a rap on the door startling Saranna. But Damaris' eyes only narrowed, her jaw set stubbornly as she looked over the older girl's shoulder at the shut panel.

"Miss Damaris, I know you are there. It is long past your bedtime—"

Saranna turned and grasped the knob, opened the door to find Mrs. Parton standing there. In spite of the odd plumpness of the housekeeper's face, her very stiff carriage did suggest the thin, unbending rod of a poker.

"Miss Stowell, this hour is long past Miss Damaris' bedtime." The small mouth opened and shut on the words. But the housekeeper's eyes roved beyond Saranna's shoulder, manifestly seeking Damaris.

"Of course, Mrs. Parton. We will come—" At that moment, Saranna had no intention of turning Damaris over to this woman. The outpourings of the child might have been highly colored by her suggested nervous temperament. On the other hand, Saranna believed that Damaris had now at least half-accepted her, and she had no inten-

tion of allowing the fragile bridge of implied understanding between them to be broken.

"You will let me come with you, Damaris?" she asked.

For a moment, it looked as if the child were going to
object, then she caught at Saranna's hand, her grip hard
and tight as if she wanted to be sure Saranna kept her
word. If Mrs. Parton had thought to object, perhaps their
united front kept her silent.

Instead, she turned back along the hallway, a small
lamp in her hand, leading the way to a door which was
nearer to those back stairs up which Saranna had come
earlier. There she stood like a sentry on duty, pushing
open the door to let Damaris, tugging a little at Saranna's
hand, past her.

"You must go to bed, Miss Damaris," she stated in her
monotonous voice, "at once."

"I will see to it, Mrs. Parton," Saranna returned. It
was better, she believed, that she establish as soon as possible that Damaris was supposed to be her charge. What
influence that fact might have on this woman, on the rest
of the household, she did not know. But it might be better for Damaris herself.

She closed the door on the housekeeper. There was a
single candle glimmering in a holder on the washstand.
And, though she peered through the shadows of the
room, Saranna could see no other light, no lamp.

"Why did you come?" Damaris was unbuttoning her
dress, but her attention was more for Saranna than her
task.

"Because I was asked to watch over you—"

"By *her*! And you promised to spy—to—" Again indignation flared.

"Not at all!" Saranna raised her voice and put into her
words all the firmness she could summon. "I was not
asked to come. I was told. Do you understand?"

Damaris considered that. "You aren't going to tell *her*
all about me—"

"Why should I?" asked Saranna.

Damaris again studied her closely. "I don't know, but I'll wait and see. At least you don't look like Prune Face—"

Saranna supposed she ought to suggest that using of such names was not proper for a young lady. But she had no desire to take on the role of a governess, not in that direction. Damaris, she now believed, could be more reasoned with than bluntly ordered about. And she was still close enough to the child's age to remember how it had seemed with her when she was being molded to the pattern of young ladyhood. Though luckily, it had been Keturah Stowell, with her wise and tolerant knowledge, who had done that molding.

"I am glad that I am Kuei-Fu-Lu-Li," she tried hard to remember the phrase Damaris had used, "and neither a Poker nor a Prune Face—"

Damaris laughed. "You don't say that right, you know. But—I can teach *you* if you like."

Saranna echoed her laughter. "Good enough. You teach me Chinese and I'll teach you whatever I can. Is it a bargain, Damaris?"

But the other was still wary. "Maybe."

Having seen Damaris into bed, Saranna groped her way back to her own room through the thick dark of the hall. She wished she had brought a candle with her. There was something about this darkness—twice she paused to listen. Was it only her skirts brushing against the wall as she felt her way along which had evoked that faint whispering? She had to believe that. But she found her heart beating faster and she whisked around her own door and into her room as if some presence she did not care to meet had been following her along.

Millie was there with a fresh copper jug of hot water. She had pulled the trundle bed from its place beneath the four-poster and spread it up, while Saranna's gown and nightcap were laid out ready and waiting. Seeing those, the whole fatigue of the day settled upon the girl and she willingly made ready and crawled into the bed, seeing Millie light a small shielded night candle as if this need for some assurance against the full power of the dark was accepted as a matter of course in Tiensin.

For the second time, Saranna had the dream about the wall which was a living hedge. But this time, she thought she recognized it for the one she had seen from her window, that which closed off the hidden section of the Tiensin garden. Now, along the foot of those somber-leaved bushes were pairs of eyes. Not as small as those which had caught the lantern light on her entrance to Tiensin, but large, glowing, trying to fasten and hold her own gaze. That she feared above all, that she would become prisoner to the eyes.

She tried to run, yet her feet would not obey her, rather they moved of themselves, carrying her nearer to the hedge and the waiting eyes. Somewhere a voice imperiously uttered a command she could not resist—called the strangely accented words Damaris had spoken:

"*Kuei-Fu-Lu-Li*—" And then added another. "*Mei—Mei—Mei—*"

Saranna awoke. The dark was broken by shafts of gray light from the two windows. The night candle had burned out. She could hear the heavy breathing of Millie from the trundle bed. But somehow she could also still hear that echoing "*Mei—Mei—Mei—*"

Slowly she repeated the strange word to herself, trying to fix the alien accent. This was only a dream, of course, yet she had a longing to know if she had carried out of it a strange word which did have a meaning.

Saranna sat up in bed. Furniture looked out of the shadows, the bulk of the pieces taking on an alien appearance in the early hour. Not threatening—just strange. As if in the night hours, bed, dressing table, wardrobe, all the rest, had played other roles.

She shook her head. Imagination—fancies—very wild fancies— Perhaps this was the type of fancy which Damaris voiced, which made Honora speak of her as being too nervously excitable.

Excited the child had certainly been last night. But there had been nothing really hysterical nor fantastic in any of her talk. That she hated Honora was plain. And also that she had had a strong tie with her grandfather. Perhaps Captain Whaley had had little liking for his son's wife and had communicated that too frankly to an impressionable child. Though Saranna tried to be neutral and just, she had to admit that her sympathies lay, in any such dispute, with those opposed to Honora. Her own dealings with Jethro's daughter had not been such as to foster any close ties between them.

Then the light touched the small table beside the lamp, and there Saranna saw again the Mountains of Peaceful Contemplation. She slipped off the wide expanse of the bed, tiptoed past Millie and stood, shivering a little in only her nightgown, fingering the piece.

Brown jade—a brush rest. She had always thought jade was green. And writing with brushes instead of a pen—yes, others had spoken of that. How odd it would seem. But this—this was truly a treasure. She must ask Damaris—

Not wanting to light the lamp, Saranna carried the piece to the window to study it more closely, but when she got there, she stood instead looking down at the hedge. It *was* the one of her dream! She almost found herself hunting the eyes which had shone so brightly along the roots of those bushes. Though those were not there.

But there *was* a flicker of movement. Saranna leaned so close to the pane that her forehead touched the chill of the glass, striving to see better. Movement indeed. A small cloaked figure edging along the thick brush. Some servant's child—but why so early? And Millie had said that they all feared a "haunt" having connection with the closed-off space of the garden. Surely no black child would dare to go so close.

Then—Damaris! But why— And—

Saranna blinked.

The figure was gone! But—surely she *had* seen it! She was no longer dreaming. Damaris—if it were Damaris—

where had she gone? For the girl had vanished as quickly as if she had been snuffed out like a candle flame.

Saranna turned back into the room and looked about her for clothing. In her haste, buttons refused to slide easily into their proper holes, tapes became exasperatingly tangled. But at length, she was properly covered. Though she did not stop to do more than bundle her hair loosely into a net.

Snatching up her shawl, she ran out of the room. The hall was dark, but up the stairwell came not only light but faint sounds as if, early as it was, some members of the household were already awake and about their duties. Saranna had no desire to be seen or questioned. Until she knew more about Damaris' activities she had no idea of destroying any possible friendly relationship by such betrayal of the child's actions. Somehow, without realizing it, she had crossed a line of neutrality in spite of her wishes and found herself allied with Damaris. At least until she learned that the little girl might have been drawn into some folly.

The sounds came from what Saranna decided must be the kitchen, but that she avoided, reaching the door through which she had been ushered the night before. The latch gave easily, and then she was out in the open, though away from the hedge.

She must round the corner of the house to see that. Dew soaked the hem of her skirt, wet the stockings above her low-heeled slippers. Saranna gathered up her skirt and ran, seeking the place where she had seen Damaris disappear.

Only when she reached the hedge, she discovered it was another matter to locate the exact spot. Seen from ground level the growth had a different appearance than it did from the second story window. She could not even be quite sure at this moment, looking back at the house itself, just which window was hers.

Thus she had to go slowly, studying the hedge and the ground. There was light enough now to show some tracks—small smudges in the dew-dampened soil and grass. Heartened by that sight, she trailed along, watching as carefully as might a woods hunter.

The tracks ended abruptly, and Saranna could discover no other indication that the one she tracked had gone beyond this spot. But neither, she was almost certain, had the child returned to the house. Then—where had Damaris gone?

There was only left the hedge wall itself!

With that answer, Saranna began to study the growth with care. She allowed her shawl to flap free, using her hands as well as her eyes to explore. A portion of bough gave. Now Saranna faced a break in what had earlier appeared an impenetrable wall. Low and narrow—meant much more for the passage of a child. Could she, in her full skirt and petticoats, her bigger body, squeeze through? Saranna was determined to try.

Branches raked at her, her hair net caught, and, when she tugged to free herself, it was scraped off so that long strands fell free across her shoulders. But, somehow, she wriggled and pushed until she did reach the clear space beyond.

Straightening once more to her full height, Saranna swept her hair from her eyes to look around. At first glance, it would seem that she had entered a tangled wilderness which bore no relation at all to the well-tended, mown, and pruned section about the Manor House. Then she saw that she stood, not on a gravel path such as she might have expected to find, but a curving walk made up of small pieces of stone set in no pattern but roughly together. This wound and turned so that, within only a few feet, it rounded a stand of trees and disappeared.

Saranna was tempted to call Damaris, yet there was such a quiet in this place that she shrank from breaking it. The longer she gazed at what lay about her, the more strange this world beyond the hedge seemed. As if she had passed through a door into a country unlike that she had always known.

Hesitatingly, the girl moved along the path, rounding

the growth of small willows which veiled the further section from the hedge. Again she paused with a deep drawn breath. Before her now was a perfect round gate buttressed on either side by rough rocks and beyond that was—

Saranna might have been looking once more at the Mountains of Peaceful Contemplation. For here, on a much larger scale, but still in miniature, more rocks had been set up in such an uneven design as the artist had carved in the jade. The water of a pool reflected them in part, and the pool, in turn, fed a stream over which was a narrow, humpbacked bridge. This gave on a small terrace of dull red stone on which stood a very small building. In the wall of that, facing her, was a window fashioned in the form of a four-petaled flower which was filled with a lattice tracery of oddly angled branches and a bird all of stone, yet as delicately worked as might be a piece of fine embroidery.

The roof of the building had sharply slanted sides falling from a center ridge quite highly raised. And the eaves up-curved at the four corners. As a breeze stirred the early morning air, Saranna heard a faint chime of bells, as if they had been set a-ringing by the wind itself.

Just as she was about to move forward to the bridge, drawn by a need to see more of this fantastic place, Damaris appeared around the side of the flower-windowed building. Catching sight of Saranna, she stopped, and there was no mistaking an utter dismay, which speedily became fear, on her face.

"No!" Again she flung up her hand in much the same gesture she had used the night before when she believed that Saranna threatened the brown jade carving. "No!"

She ran over the bridge, coming straight to the older girl.

"You spy!" she cried out. "I'll tell the Princess. She'll make you sorry—sorry—sorry!"

She flung herself at Saranna, her face flushed, striking at the older girl with both fists.

Saranna was nearly thrust off balance and had to

struggle to catch those small fists while Damaris kicked at her in a frenzy.

"Damaris!" Saranna wondered if the child was gripped by some kind of a hysterical seizure. So thinking, she was frightened in turn. She had never seen such rage, if it *were* that emotion which now filled Damaris, and she had no idea how to control the younger girl. Perhaps, the idea flitted across her mind, Honora had not been so wrong in her estimate of her stepdaughter's nature after all.

"Damaris!"

The child was sobbing and still struggling, her eyes wild, her expression near that of a trapped animal. Saranna gave her a hard shake.

"Damaris, listen to me!" She tried to reach some point of reason which was not dominated by that wild response to the mere fact that she had entered the hidden garden. "I mean you no harm. I was curious when I saw you come in here—understand? I was just curious. Just as you might have been had you suddenly saw me disappear. If you wish it, I will tell no one about your being here—"

Damaris stared up into Saranna's face. Some of the distraught look faded from her own.

"I mean no harm—I am not spying—" Saranna repeated. "This is a very beautiful and wonderful place, Damaris. If it is your secret, then I envy you. And I shall say nothing at all about it—to anyone. This I promise—"

Damaris now stood quiet in Saranna's hold, all the fierceness of her attack gone.

"You can't, you know," she said suddenly, in quite an ordinary tone of voice. "The Princess would know if you did, and then you would be sorry. And don't go ahead and ask me who the Princess is, because I won't ever, ever tell you!"

"All right," agreed Saranna swiftly. "I won't ask you any questions."

"And you'll come away right now and promise never to come back?" Damaris demanded. "I don't see why they let you in. They never have before. Nobody but me—and Grandfather— They watch—"

Her eyes darted right and left. Saranna found herself looking in the same direction, not knowing just what she expected to see. She was startled by a movement among the willows, but she did not catch full sight of what was in hiding there.

"They're waiting—" Damaris sounded triumphant. "You had better go. I tell you—go right now."

"But what about you, Damaris?"

"Oh, I'll come—this time. Maybe I had better. If they see me, they'll let you go. Only just never try to come back."

She tugged at Saranna's hand, drawing her back along the stone path to that hidden entrance. Saranna had no excuse to linger. Pushing her way among the stiff branches, she found and rescued her net and paused for a moment to tuck her hair back into it.

"Hey, there, Missie, now what are you doing?"

Completely surprised by such a hail, Saranna looked to her right. But the man who spoke appeared to be talking to Damaris, who stood scowling again, as he came farther into view from a walk formally walled by clipped and tended box.

"Oh, it's you, Rufe!"

"Yes, it's me, Missie. And where've you been? Don't you remember about going off by yourself—what Miss Honora said would happen if you did?"

Saranna moved out, to put her arm about Damaris' thin shoulders.

"Damaris was not alone," she eyed the newcomer narrowly. "She was showing me the garden."

V

Ko Change

He was, Saranna decided upon survey, not much older than herself—perhaps only by two or three years. Though he wore clothing with some pretense to fashion, it did not fit his stocky body well. And above a creased stock his round face, with its blubbery lips and small eyes had, in her estimation, no claim to be even a mildly pleasant countenance. He was grinning now, his stare at her bold enough to make her uncomfortable, though she trusted she did not reveal any sign of her uneasiness.

"Well, now, ain't you the spitfire!" The young man spoke with what Saranna found to be odious familiarity, such open rudeness as she had never met before in her life. As if—as if she were a serving maid in some tavern.

If Mrs. Parton possessed an iron poker for a backbone, in that moment Saranna developed a steel rod along her own spine. She gazed back at this stranger with all the quelling hauteur she could summon.

"Yes, now, a regular red-headed spitfire," the impossible young man continued. "Me, I like 'em with a bit of fire—makes it more fun like—"

Was he out of his mind? Saranna could not believe that she really had heard his freedom of speech. No one in her whole life had ever so dared step across the boundaries of good manners. She thought of Mr. Fowke. Friendly, he had been, but always a gentleman. This— this creature was manifestly not!

She would not answer him. To speak was to admit he was on a level which could even be noticed. Instead, she caught Damaris' hand.

"Come—"

For an awful moment, she thought this fair-haired lout was actually going to step into their path, physically restrain them from escape, and her heart beat faster. However, instead he laughed slyly, and made an ill-formed bow.

"See you again, spitfire. Miss Honora, she's a-waitin' up to the house. Best get along, she's a lady as doesn't like to be kept a-waitin'—"

Honora—here? Saranna felt Damaris jerk back against her hold, as if the child would have willingly run back into the hidden garden. But Saranna looked down at her.

"We must go," she said.

Damaris nodded. "He better not go poking around where he isn't wanted," she glanced back over her shoulder at Rufe. "Or he'll find more than he knows."

She had spoken in a voice hardly above a whisper, plainly meaning her threat to be heard by Saranna alone. While Saranna made up her mind firmly that she intended to demand Honora not allow her—or Damaris—to be again exposed to the insulting behavior of the housekeeper's son.

As they hurried back to the house, she once more contrasted him in her mind with Mr. Fowke, even with the common seamen who had, in the not-too-distant past, sailed with her father. There had been rough, untutored men in that company, but never had one ever addressed her with such familiarity, as if he were fully her equal and intended making her aware of that and of himself.

This Rufe was supposed to be away at school (though he looked well overgrown and certainly not a schoolboy), but what kind of a school? And how *dared* he use that tone of voice, such words, to her?

It was as if Damaris could read the thoughts passing through the older girl's mind, for the child said suddenly:

"No use you ever complaining about Rufe, you know. *She* likes him. He never talks that way around her. Just is always ready to do what she says. *She* doesn't ever believe people who try to tell her things she doesn't like to hear—"

Saranna's anger was still well aroused, too much so to accept that warning.

"She will hear what I have to say!"

"Better not. If she gets mad at you—" Damaris looked very sober, "she can make you a lot of trouble. I always just listen. Then I plan how to do what *I* want in spite of what she says. The Captain always told me—'Let the storm rage, but just ride it out—then go about your own business.' "

Saranna had dropped Damaris' hand since they were now in the hall away from the bold gaze of that—that creature! She was trying to order her hair, draw on the net which confined it. But the wise comment Damaris had just uttered made her pause. That the child had been encouraged so to circumvent her stepmother was another inkling of how Honora had been regarded in this house while its master was still alive.

Only that rancor he had encouraged now lived on, past his own demise, and might be a worse trouble for his beloved granddaughter than any help. Why had he not seen that? Saranna could well believe that Honora was one who would have her own way, either ignoring any obstacle, or disposing of it ruthlessly. And if Damaris were considered an obstacle to anything her stepmother truly wanted— Saranna tucked in a last wandering lock, more intent now on what might be the situation here than her own disheveled appearance.

Honora's tales of an unhealthy inheritance, her hint of mental instability where Damaris was concerned— Was there some dreadful purpose about that, not just reaction to perhaps some such outburst as Saranna had faced in her chamber? If so—then how could she herself warn the child—?

"Good morning, Saranna, Damaris. What have the

two of you been doing—grubbing about in the garden?"

There was amusement and distaste blended in that voice. Once more Saranna met the lady of the house (and her complete ease here established her in a role which poor Damaris was as yet too young to play) descending the staircase.

This time Honora did not wear her mauve silks and laces, but was dressed for riding, the long skirt of her habit held up in one hand as she descended. Her fair curls were displayed to the best advantage under the brim of a leghorn hat with the rim looped up on both sides, and from that a feather drooped nearly to her shoulder. The habit was of lavender cashmere (it seemed even in such matters Honora kept to her half-mourning), but it was enriched by needlework in black of vines, flowers, and arabesques, its bordered sleeves slashed to reveal under ones of black net, the same material forming her chemisette.

"You had better wash—thoroughly—" Now the distaste had the upper hand in her tone. "Breakfast is on the table. Have the goodness to remember that Mrs. Parton has many duties and do not delay over long—"

She waited for no reply, having set them on an equal basis, as naughty children. Saranna, to her own inner anger, found herself obediently climbing the stairs to make a hurried correction of the many faults of her morning toilet. When she issued forth from her chamber again, Damaris was waiting at the head of the stairs.

"You won't tell?"

Saranna shook her head. "I promised," she returned.

Honora was seated behind the coffee service with the same accustomed ease of manner as she had displayed in the Baltimore house. And Mrs. Parton stood before her replying to searching questions concerning provisions.

"I, of course, shall have supplies sent from the city," Honora was saying. "After all, country fare is hardly what we would wish to place before such guests. When Mr. Fowke settles in at Queen's Pleasure, we may expect more select society here. I have promised him to ride over today and give my opinion of what is necessary to enhance the great parlor. Ah, there you are, Saranna, Damaris."

She nodded to them as they slipped into their chairs, managing to convey that they were both lacking in manners, burdens which she must bear.

"Who is coming here?" Damaris demanded bluntly.

Honora smiled. "Friends, my dear. There will be a party of ladies and gentlemen out from Baltimore. You must strive to make a good impression. Though of course, you will not be seen very much. Little girls do not enter into company—"

"I did not invite them!" Damaris' thin face was flushed.

Honora paused in filling a cup from the silver coffeepot. Her smile was not in the least diminished by the interruption.

"Of course not, Damaris. You are hardly of an age to invite company to Tiensin—"

"And this is not *your* house!" Damaris concluded as if her words were meant to drown out any answer from Honora.

"Little girls," Honora accented the *little*, "who are rude are also punished. I fear that your nervous health is not very good, my dear. We shall have to have Dr. Meade come down and see you—"

Saranna could hear the gulp Damaris gave. The child's eyes, fiercely bright, were centered on Honora who made no attempt to meet that steady gaze, but continued to center her attention on her cup, the waiting pot, as if the graceful transference of hot liquid from one container to the other was all that mattered in the world.

Danger! Saranna was as aware of that troubling the atmosphere of this sunny morning room, which should be so tranquil and restful, as if someone shouted a word of warning. Damaris must remember to follow her own advice—not give Honora the least chance to prove that she was excitable, perhaps unstable.

"Now, Saranna." Having silenced her stepdaughter,

Honora turned to the older girl. "Naturally, being in deep mourning, social festivities will not appeal to you. We shall all understand that, and Millie will serve your meals in your room while we have company. But there is a pleasant surprise. Rufus Parton is here. He will be very glad to take you boating on the river if you wish, or escort you riding—"

Saranna only just managed to suppress an outburst of indignant anger. Rufus Parton—to take her boating— riding—that—that lout—that insulting lout! But, with Mrs. Parton standing still at Honora's side, she discovered she could not protest.

There was an odd look on Mrs. Parton's face, a kind of gloating smugness. Saranna could not be sure of that entirely, but she was sure that the housekeeper was pleased.

She was able to contain her protests. The advice which Captain Whaley had given his granddaughter could also be applied to her own present situation.

"We shall plan it then, Mrs. Parton," now Honora had dismissed Saranna from notice as well, "for the twentieth. The wisteria will surely be in bloom by then. And Parton must have the garden room well cleaned out for dancing. The food will be down from Baltimore by the fifteenth. See that it is kept on ice. We will need all the strawberries which are in the orangery—and any other fruit which can be forced there—"

"Yes, ma'am."

So the company was not to arrive at once. Which would give her, Saranna, time to reason with Damaris so that the child would make no outburst. She shifted uneasily in her seat. Her present position seemed far too much like that of a captain who recognized storm warnings ahead but could not alter his course.

"Oh, Saranna," Honora once more addressed her, "my father was unhappy that you did not say good-bye to him, but he understood your need to be quiet after your sad loss. He shall be gone so long—" Honora's eyes were still on the fragile coffee cup she turned about in her white hands, studying the design thereupon as if it were an important letter she must read. "Six months—perhaps a year. You may have made other plans by the time he returns—"

That there was a suggestion in that, Saranna was sure. Honora meant her to be gone before Jethro's return, though she was unable as yet to guess the reason. Very well, if she could, she would be, the girl determined. Though as yet she had no idea how her escape from Tiensin and all the crosscurrents under its roof might be managed.

"Yes, John?"

It was as if Honora had eyes in the back of her head, for she had not looked around when the door opened and a houseman stood there.

"Mr. Fowke, ma'am—"

Honora put down her cup in a hurry, was out of her chair, with a rustle of skirt, to face the man who entered.

He, too, wore riding clothes, his boots shining, with small silver spurs to jingle as he walked.

"Gerrad—" Honora held out both hands, her face alight. "But you are early! Will you not have coffee then before we go, and some of Mrs. Parton's biscuits? I vow she bests even your Aunt Bet when it comes to biscuits! Naughty man, you have quite surprised me. It is lucky that I was ready early, not playing the lie-abed city belle. Do sit down. Mrs. Parton, send Elvira for the biscuits and some of our mint honey— And fresh coffee—hot coffee!"

Mr. Fowke laughed. "Honora, your hospitality overwhelms me. Very well, I shall judge Mrs. Parton's biscuits, and I shall taste your coffee. I must confess that I should serve it also, since I am now an associate of the firm bringing it hither. But so far, Aunt Bet refuses to try it, and one does not argue with the genius who presides over the kitchen."

"But you are master," Honora replied. "It is *your* wishes which should be carried out. You are far too lenient with her, Gerrad. Sometimes she acts as if Queen's Pleasure is *her* domain and not yours."

He laughed again. "Maybe in some ways it is, Honora. She has certainly been within its walls, and trying to keep it running, far longer than I have. I owe her much for those lost years. But I am forgetting proper manners— Good morning, Miss Stowell, Miss Damaris—" He had disengaged himself from Honora's hold on his hands, bowed in the direction of Saranna and Damaris, giving the younger girl the same deference he would if she were truly grown-up.

Saranna murmured something, feeling ill at ease in the way Mr. Fowke always affected her when he noticed her in company. On the fog-enshrouded boat, she had not this sense of being weighed, compared to Honora. But Damaris, smiling, arose from her seat and went to him.

"There are lily buds in the pool again," she said, her eyes alight, "and I think there are going to be more. They *do* look like those in the water painting!"

"You must show me. Has Horace shown up lately? Does he still look like Judge Pryde?"

"More like Fa Kuan Chiao Lao Te," Damaris answered. "Yes, he is back on his own special rock again. I think he must really be one of the Honorable Old Ones— among toads—"

"Damaris," Honora still smiled, save for her eyes, "do let Mr. Fowke have his coffee. John is bringing a fresh pot now. And I think you had better not chatter in that heathen tongue. It is not at all polite when the rest of the company does not understand you. I have spoken about this matter before."

Saranna expected the girl to flare up at Honora's interruption. Instead, she regarded her stepmother calmly.

"I am sorry. I forgot you do not know Chinese. Pray do excuse me." Her self-possession now was as unusual to Saranna as her early outburst had been. But she returned to her seat sedately, as if every point of good manners had been drilled into her.

Only, Saranna, watching her, caught that wink, and a swift glance showed that Gerrad Fowke returned it, un-

seen by Honora who was supervising the placing of fresh
plates, a cup, saucer, and all else Mr. Fowke might need
to share their breakfast.

"And you, Miss Stowell, what do you think of Tiensin?" he asked.

"What I have seen of it has been most interesting."
Under Honora's gaze, her answer could be nothing but
formal and remote.

"Has Damaris shown you all the treasures?" Mr.
Fowke continued to turn his attention toward her,
though she wanted to escape his notice. Added to that
self-consciousness she continued to feel in his presence
was the firm conviction that Honora was less and less
pleased when any of his interest strayed from her own
person.

"Not yet." She knew that her answers sounded almost
rude in their brevity, but she longed for nothing more
now than to escape from this room.

"But she must. Captain Whaley knew perhaps more
about Chinese art than anyone now in this country. He
was a remarkable man in many ways," Gerrad Fowke continued. "When I was a boy, hardly older than Damaris
here, I came once when ashore to visit at Queen's Pleasure and chanced to meet the Captain. When he discovered I was interested, he brought me here for a grand
tour. But I was too young and ignorant then to know
just what I was seeing, except that it was wonderful. It
is indeed just what the Captain declared it—a treasure
past price."

Now Honora was regarding him intently. "Heathen
idols and the like? Why, who would want such things?"
she asked.

"A good many collectors, nowadays, Honora. Merchants in the Indies trade are beginning to know the difference between the bright trash the Chinese make for
the foreign trade and that which they cherish for themselves. Yes, I think the Captain did leave a real treasure at
Tiensin. I hear you have invited Henry Walsworth here,

Honora. You'll find it hard to get rid of him again once he sees a little of what the Captain gathered together."

"Mr. Walsworth—" Honora repeated the name as if to fix it more firmly in her mind.

"Now—" Mr. Fowke pushed back his plate a little, took a last sip from his coffee. "I freely admit that Mrs. Parton's biscuits match Aunt Bet's best. But don't you tell her so. She will then try to outdo her record, and I shall be inundated with biscuits for weeks to come. If you are ready, Honora, we had best be on our way. I want to be sure that the new mantles are carefully handled, and you must tell me what you have decided concerning the Great Room draperies—"

"Oh, I will. And I have a surprise, Gerrad. Mrs. Parton has packed a hamper—we can picnic by the river—"

She rested her hand on his arm as they went toward the door. A moment later it closed behind them, but not before Mr. Fowke had looked back and said good-bye to each, a gesture which Honora completely neglected.

"He shouldn't have said that," Damaris glanced about as if to be sure that both Mrs. Parton and John had left them alone.

"Said what?"

"About the treasure. *She* listened, didn't you see it? Now she'll be thinking about it— And it belongs to Tien-sin!"

"Of course it does." Saranna was ready to agree. "Will you show it to me, Damaris?"

For a long moment, the child regarded her in silence. As if she were weighing Saranna in some balance of her own. Then she nodded.

"You understood—about the Mountains. Come on then—"

For the next two hours Saranna wandered, amazed. Here Damaris was no child. She spoke with authority about screen, bowl, carvings, vase, lacquer work, jade, bronze. She pointed out this or that quality which made the piece in question unique of its kind. And Saranna grew more and more in awe of all Damaris had absorbed and was able to recall. Nor did she parrot these facts as one who had learned it all by rote; rather she spoke as one who knew exactly what each disclosure meant. Now and then she used a Chinese word or expression, which she would translate when she realized Saranna's complete bewilderment.

The older girl believed that her own education well exceeded that of those girls her own age whom she had known in Boston and Sussex. She had taken to book knowledge eagerly from the time she had learned to read at four. But at least in this one subject Damaris far out-stripped her, and spoke with the authority of a collector of many years standing.

"Captain Whaley taught you all this?" she asked at last, her amazement leading her once more to questions.

"He and the Princess—she knows—" Damaris flushed. Her hand flew to cover her own mouth, as if to smother the words. But she had already uttered them. Now she looked frightened, almost as if she were ready to burst into tears. All her authority was stripped from her. Again, she was only a little girl, suddenly fearful. "I—you must not ask me! Please, don't ask me!" The face she turned to Saranna was piteous, and Saranna restrained her curiosity.

"It's all right, Damaris. I won't ask you anything you do not want to tell me," she said quietly, soothingly.

"I—I remember things very well. Grandfather always said I did," Damaris obviously was trying to regain her self-confidence. "He said I had a quick mind. And he taught me how to learn with my fingers. He would tie his handkerchief around my eyes and give me something to hold—a piece of jade, or a bowl, or one of the bronze horses. Then he would tell me to feel it all over, so my fingers would learn how it should be. Afterward, he would bring out things—things like Mr. Fowke called trash—those the Chinese make to sell to foreigners who don't know about the real treasures. And he would have me feel those, too. So I would get to know the difference. It was a game we played. I was good at doing it, Grandfather said."

"Do you still do it?"

Damaris' eyes slid away hurriedly. "Sometimes. Maybe I can show you—but you have to be real careful."

Saranna looked around her at the delicate porcelain, the carved jade, the burnished lacquer. She was not quite sure she wanted to take the responsibility of that game. To handle such exquisite pieces was a danger.

"I like Mr. Fowke," Damaris changed the subject, "even if he is probably going to marry Honora. I wish he wouldn't, he's too nice for her—much too nice!"

She touched a fingertip to the edge of a shallow bowl of a soft green shade, across the surface of which was spread a single flowering branch in white.

"Honora is a *Nu Wu*," she added.

"And what is that?"

"A witch. She witches people so they do what she tells them. She witched my father so he wouldn't listen to anybody but her. But she couldn't ever witch Grandfather—he knew what she was. He said she was a *Nu Hsing Kuei.* That's a kind of demon. The Chinese have big screens at the doors of their houses so the demons can't get in. Demons have to fly in straight lines, you see," Damaris continued seriously, as if the lore she now recited was as authentic as that she had known concerning her grandfather's collection. "So if you have a screen, they just strike against that and can't ever enter. It was too bad we did not have one of those here at Tiensin when Honora came."

"Damaris, there are no such things as demons."

The younger girl shook her head. "You don't know, Saranna, really you don't. My grandfather said there were a lot of things in this world that men laugh at until they meet them face to face. I've—" Again she paused, flushing. "Anyway, maybe you're right that Honora isn't any ghost-demon. But she can make a lot of trouble."

They went out of the last of the rooms which held the collection and Damaris closed the door carefully behind them.

"Damaris," asked Saranna suddenly, "what does the word *mei* mean? Is it Chinese?"

She tried to give the word sound the same accent as it had held in her dream. But she was not sure that she had succeeded.

"*Mei?*" Damaris repeated.

Saranna recognized the slightly different inflection.

"Yes, that is it!"

"It means Younger Sister! But where did you hear it?"

A Chinese word, why had it come into her dream? Surely it was not one which Damaris had used in her hearing. Before she thought, Saranna answered with the truth.

"In a dream—a dream about the hedge wall, and the foxes' eyes shining there. Then a voice called that word."

Damaris moved away from her with a jerk. The child's face was contorted with the same scowl she had shown when she had found Saranna examining the brush rest.

"It's a trick!" she cried. "You couldn't have heard that! You wouldn't be allowed— Only me— Only me—" She whirled around and before Saranna could say a word, she ran down the hall, banging through the door at the far end.

"Missie up to her tricks, eh? She's touched in the head, she is."

Saranna looked over her shoulder. Rufe lounged in the doorway of the breakfast room, one shoulder supported by the door frame. He grinned at her lazily.

"Miss Honora, she said you might fancy a turn on the river, or maybe a walk in the garden. Says I'm to make myself agreeable. That's no hard thing, Miss Saranna. I just have a likin' to be agreeable to a pretty girl like you now—"

With some of the same speed Damaris had shown, Saranna reached the stairway and started up, making no answer. Surely Honora could not intend for her to show

this loutish boy any encouragement. There was something about the way he watched her which made her
shrink—but not visibly, she hoped. She wanted never to
let him think that he had the power to frighten her.

But that he did, Saranna could not deny as she found
herself in her room, shutting not only the door, but turning the key in the lock before she was thinking clearly
again. She must make Honora understand that she would
have nothing to do with Rufe Parton. In the meantime,
Saranna put her hands to her flushed face—what was she
going to do? She could not remain locked in her room,
letting Rufus Parton believe that he had penned her
there. What was the matter? She could not even understand her own aversion to him. That emotion was so
much deeper, and therefore more frightening, than any
dislike she had known before in her serenely ordered life.

VI

Chien _Difficulty_

Saranna settled in a chair near one window. She forced herself to think calmly; that her situation was going to be uncomfortable, she knew. Honora's horrifying suggestion that Rufus play her escort was even a threat. She could not stay forever in her own chamber, though when Honora's company arrived that apparently was just what would be asked of her. And why did Honora want to keep her out of sight?

Saranna glanced around at the mirror of the wardrobe door. By that painfully accurate witness, she was indeed a shabby, poor relation, yes. But she had a suspicion that Honora, if she pleased, might easily remedy that. And certainly Saranna's looks, or lack of looks, were such that Honora could have no fear that this stranger in her rusty black could outshine the beautiful and accomplished daughter of Jethro Stowell.

She sat up straight now, her shoulders squared back. No, she would keep out of the way of Honora's guests, that was a small matter. But that she should be kept captive in her room because of Rufus Parton—that she must not allow!

What she should be considering with her full attention was means of escape from a situation which at best was disagreeable and at worst— Saranna shivered. She could not put into words what she felt beyond the fact that fear lay at its core. And she was so alone. There was

66

no one here at Tiensin to whom she could appeal for aid. Millie was friendly, but in a timid, helpless fashion. And certainly Damaris might be as much a victim as herself—

Victim? Why did that word come into her mind? Why *was* this shadowy feeling of danger so much a part of her now, as if it enwrapped her with a visible cloud of darkness?

She arose abruptly. Whether she liked it or not, she was aware that her mother's daughter could not dismiss the problem of Damaris as none of her concern. Was Jethro Damaris' only guardian? Did Honora have full control over the child's future during her father's absence? With the way Damaris talked so wildly of Honora being a witch, or a demon—let anyone hear that and they might readily believe Honora's own estimation of her stepdaughter's condition.

When she thought of Damaris, Saranna could forget Rufus Parton's sly, leering grin, and push off her uneasiness. She unlocked the door with defiant purpose, went down the hall to stand before Damaris' chamber where she tapped gently on the closed panel. Even though there was no answer, Saranna felt her mission important enough to try the knob. It turned easily under her hand.

"Damaris," the older girl called softly from the threshold.

By the clear light of day she could see the contents of the chamber much better than she had on her earlier visit. The fingers of sunbeams touched upon wall panels of the same aged and exotic embroidery as lightened the walls of the hallway without. What Saranna had taken to be a four-poster bed on her first visit, she now perceived to be something else. The piece had four posts to be sure, but carved work built around three sides in screen fashion made it appear more a small inner room than a bed, now that the curtains which had veiled it were looped up for the day.

All the furniture was set out in odd formality, mainly paired pieces back against the walls. Twin wardrobes of a dark, heavy wood, showing golden threaded fibers when the sun touched the second on one corner, the well-polished surface reflecting the light, stood parted by a small square table on which were carved boxes. The next wall was broken by a dull red chest, its outer surface painted with a time-dulled and fanciful scene. By the bed was a table on which rested a number of smaller boxes, a slab of worked stone, and a small vase in which was a single sprig of green at an angle, the arrangement very simple but somehow attractive, far more so than the crowded vases of flowers Saranna had always been used to. There was a stool on the opposite side of the table from the bed.

But of Damaris herself there appeared no sign.

Saranna would have withdrawn, uneasy at her own intrusion. Then the child she sought moved out from behind the shadowed corner of the bed.

She held a bunch of what appeared small, thin wands in one hand, as if she had been interrupted at some task, but her expression was no longer hostile. Instead, there was a measuring watchfulness in her eyes.

"Kuei-Fu-Lu-Li—" The strange words might have been a greeting. "I knew you would come—you had to," Damaris stated almost impatiently. She might have been awaiting some tardy guest, ready to begin a ceremony—

Ceremony? That word flitted through Saranna's mind. She was now aware of the scent, elusive, but still to be noticed in the room—spicy—different— Not a flower— What?

"Why did I have to?" That simple question came to her lips first.

"Because—because—it is willed. I know that now. You—somehow you are a part of it. I—I'm going to throw the wands. Of course—I'm not a real *hsueh che*, a scholar who knows all the readings. But—well, I'm going to try."

She turned to the table by the bed, and quickly shoved all the objects on it to the far side, leaving bare that portion of it which was in the clearest light. With both hands then she caressed the small wands she held, closing her eyes, muttering words so faintly that they reached Saranna only as unintelligible sounds.

Suddenly, she tossed the wands from her so that they fell on the table. She hastened to move them so that they made a pattern in six horizontal bars, one above the other. Completely mystified, Saranna moved closer. Now she saw that while some of the wands were of a uniformly dark color, others were broken in two by light bands.

"*Chien*—" Damaris leaned over the wands, her attitude one of reading. "Struggling with great difficulties—yes, but friends come to help— Oh," the child's expression changed as if she were not angered, nor intent on what she was doing, but rather as if she were distressed at some inability of her own. "I cannot read—not like—" She shook her head. "There is so much to learn, and I don't know enough."

She swept the wands back together in her grasp. "I must ask—" Once more her gaze swept toward Saranna and she stopped short.

"What—what are you trying to do?" Saranna thought she dared ask that question, even though, with Damaris, she must be very careful indeed.

"I was trying *I Ching*—to find out— To find out what is going to happen. Only," her answer now held a note of despair, "I don't know enough. Not how to read the Yarrow sticks, maybe not even how to toss them properly. I've only watched it before. I've never really tried to do it myself."

"*I Ching*—?"

Damaris nodded vigorously. "It's an old, old way of telling one's future. Grandfather—he knew how—a little. The Princess, she—"

Her eyes went wide with what Saranna could only read as pure fear. Once more, as she had done before, Damaris clapped one hand over her mouth. "I said it! I told!" her voice was near a wail.

As much as Saranna wanted to pierce the mystery which Damaris cherished, she could not press the child further, her distress was far too evident.

"I won't ask you any more questions," she said. "But, Damaris, surely you know that no one is really able to read the future—"

Now that look of distress changed to one which mingled scorn and pity.

"There's a lot of things you don't know either!" Damaris returned with her usual self-confidence. "You'll learn—if you stay here. Know what I heard *her* say?"

She rolled the wands into a tight bundle and slid them back into a bag of scarlet silk embroidered with gold thread. That the "her" she spoke of meant Honora, Saranna had no doubt.

"She wants Rufe to beau you around; she told Mrs. Parton that!"

Saranna betrayed, she hoped, no reaction on that statement.

"I am sure Honora made no such remark before you."

"I told you," Damaris continued. "I listen—I have to. With *her* around one must. She always gets her way, or thinks she is going to. Do you want Rufe to beau you?"

"Listening is wrong, Damaris," Saranna gave lip service to her own training. But she was in no doubt at all about the truth of what Damaris had blurted out. Honora must have made just some such statement to the housekeeper. Her own suspicions, thus reinforced, brought about real inner dismay.

Only this was the enlightened nineteenth century. Girls, in spite of the disadvantages of being much under the control of relatives and guardians, could *not* be thrust into some situations against their wills. And if a strong will were needed to protect herself against such an encroachment upon her own privacy, Saranna could certainly summon such.

Damaris laughed. "That made you think, didn't it? I could see you didn't like to hear that. It was good of me, really, to tell you, you know. Now you can be ready when *she* tries some of her tricks. And she will, she always does—"

"Damaris," Saranna spoke with what she hoped was emphasis enough to make the younger girl listen and heed. "You must remember your grandfather's advice and not provoke Honora. I do not know how much power she has over your future, but—"

"Jethro Stowell is my guardian. He says what is done here, until I am grown up."

"But Jethro is in Brazil. He will be there a long time," Saranna reminded her. "Is—is there someone else—besides Honora—who can decide your way of living here?"

Damaris regarded her with a long, searching look before she answered. Her tongue tip swept over her lower lip as if her mouth had gone suddenly dry. Then she nodded.

"There's someone—someone who can take care of the *Nu Wu*—"

"Who?" Saranna demanded.

Now Damaris shook her head with the same vigor as she had nodded.

"That's a secret. Grandfather's own secret. Only I know now—"

"It may be important for me to know too, in the future." Saranna was exasperated.

"I know. That's all that's important. You'd better think of Rufe and what you are going to do about him." She laughed a little maliciously. "Me—I'm going to dust the porcelain. Mrs. Parton and the maids—Grandfather said never leave it to them. Butterfingers—that's what most of them are!" She skipped past Saranna to open the door and slip out. The older girl had no recourse but to follow her. Before she could even call to Damaris, the child was already halfway down the stairs and Saranna felt it wiser not to try to follow her at that moment.

Saranna had no idea how she would handle the problem of Rufus Parton, but she was not going to let him intimidate her, she made up her mind to that. She was going to walk in the garden. If he appeared there, to again make himself objectionable, she would snub him in a manner which would pierce even his thick skin.

But it was the sharp cry of pain which led her to Rufus. That the cry came from an animal, Saranna never doubted and she hurried toward it, certain that some poor creature was in great trouble. So she ran, from one of the alleys of clipped box which walled the garden path, into the open.

There were two figures before her, intent upon a fox which was struggling wildly to escape from a net, the ends of which were held by a black youth. While Rufus Parton, his face flushed, his small eyes shining with a kind of greedy delight, rained blows with a riding crop on the animal. Its yelps of pain were echoed by laughter on Rufe's part, and, as the crop rose and fell with a horrible regularity, Saranna could only believe that he was engaged in a slow and horrible process of beating the poor beast to death.

She did not hesitate to rush forward, and Rufus did not see her, so intent was he in making sure that the animal could not evade the crop. Thus her grasp upon his arm was so forceful and determined that he actually swung part way around, unable for an instant or two of surprise to break free.

Saranna shouted at the black boy, "Let it go! Let it go—at once!"

The fox, seeming to realize her support instantly, lunged, though still within the net, snarling at the black. With a cry of fear, he dropped his hold, and jumped back. Out of the meshes which had held it for that outrageous punishment, the creature won—and was gone, slipping under the box hedge where no man could possibly crawl to track it.

Saranna, herself, stumbled back, Rufe having flung her away to free himself. He swung up his arm again, the crop ready, as if she were about to share the beating that the fox had been enduring. Then that horrible glistening of pleasure faded from his eyes, his mouth twisted in the smile she had detested from the first time she had seen it.

"You got a right hard grip for a little girl like you,

Miss Saranna." He rubbed his arm with his other hand as if she had indeed been somehow able to bruise both flesh and muscle. "Fiery temper, too. Some men would be mighty put out at your interfering when they were handlin' such vermin like they ought to be handled. But me, I'm all soft with a pretty girl—"

"You know," she put as cold a note in her voice as she could summon, "that foxes are neither mistreated nor hunted at Tiensin."

He still smiled. "That was what the Captain always said, yes. But the Captain, he's gone. Gone where he can't come back to give any more orders about pamperin' vermin and such. Mrs. Whaley, now she understands proper. You can't go coddlin' beasts, you got to keep 'em down—teach 'em to stay away and act proper—not like they own this here place. Mrs. Whaley, I guess she's the one to give the orders here now. The Captain's day— that's all over."

Before she thought, Saranna blurted out a denial of that.

"Mrs. Whaley does not own Tiensin—" she began, and then stopped short.

"You mean it all belongs to Missie?" Rufe laughed. "Maybe the law says so. But no little girl's goin' to have her say about this here manor—that ain't the law. Them in charge of her, they do the talkin', seein' as how they know best.

"Now then, I don't want to have you mad with me, Miss Saranna. I told you, me I like red hair, I rightly do. Seems like you kind of have a foxy look your own self. Not that I mean that in a bad way. You don't find me down-speakin' a pretty girl like you. We're goin' to be good friends once you get over your stiff ways. I can show you a good time—"

Saranna swung away and stalked off, fighting the desire to muffle his voice out of hearing with her own hands over her ears. But she would not give him any satisfaction of knowing that he had made such an impression on her that she loathed every word he said.

If Saranna had shrunk from Rufe before, she detested him twice as much now for the nasty scene she had interrupted. His pleasure in the pain he had caused the captive fox was so shocking. At least the poor creature had escaped. She only hoped that the treatment it had been accorded would warn it away.

But the boldness of the foxes at Tiensin was a matter of fact. They had never been exposed to ill-treatment. Surely some of them would come to a painful death if Rufe was allowed, even encouraged, to continue as she had seen him in action today.

In the meantime, she must not let Damaris know what had happened. Saranna was convinced of that. If the child exploded into open rage against either Honora or Rufus, her outburst would be held against her. Whether she wished or not, Saranna now knew she had somehow assumed responsibility for Damaris' future—to the best of her ability.

Her resolution was sadly tried when she re-entered the house. There were voices—raised—and one shrill one which could only be that of Damaris. The clamor guided Saranna to the best parlor where she found the child behind a table on which lay a pile of soft cloths. Another was wadded into Damaris' hand as she faced Mrs. Parton.

"Get out!" Damaris' face was flushed, she fairly spat the order at the housekeeper. "You know I dust these, that Grandfather would not let you lay a finger on his treasures, ever!"

"It is you who had better go, Miss Damaris," the housekeeper answered stolidly. "Mrs. Whaley has given orders you are not to handle the porcelain. There is too great chance of it being broken by carelessness—"

"Carelessness!" Damaris was fairly screaming now. "I *know* how to handle these. Grandfather taught me. He never allowed *her* to touch a single piece of it! You know that! And *she* has no right to say anything about it anyway. It belongs to me, not to *her*!"

"Miss Damaris—you're upset." There was a faint curve to Mrs. Parton's lower lip.

Saranna shuddered. Though the woman retained an almost masklike countenance, there was a faint hint now of that avid cruelty which had marked her son far more openly.

"Damaris—"

Saranna moved forward with the same speed she had shown when she had ended the torment of the fox. Her hand fell on the child's shoulder, not in restraint, but as an attempt at warning.

"My dear, of course Tiensin's treasures are yours." As she spoke through a sudden silence, she eyed Mrs. Parton over Damaris' shoulder. "And, Mrs. Parton, I think since Damaris has been handling these pieces for years and very cautiously, there can be no reason for suggesting that she has suddenly grown careless. Perhaps Mrs. Whaley does not understand the very great interest Damaris has in her grandfather's collection and her concern for it. Damaris," she now spoke to the child, "no one would presume to deny your ownership. Since everyone knows the truth of that, it is not necessary to stress such a truth so vehemently." Her hand, still resting on the girl's shoulder, pressed gently. She hoped that Damaris would understand and heed what she meant as a warning.

If Mrs. Parton would have pursued that matter had she not come in, Saranna did not know. Now the housekeeper shrugged and turned away, moving with her usual silent walk, going out of the room as one who has performed her duty in giving an order, but would leave to others the consequences of that order not being obeyed.

"She—" Damaris once more scowled, her eyes watching the door, "she does everything *that* one tells her. I want her to leave, Saranna. Maybe—" The scowl lightened; there was a strange expression taking its place. "Maybe there is a way to get rid of them both!"

"Damaris." Tightening her grip on the child's shoulder, Saranna urged her around so that she could look straight into her face. For a long moment, it was as if Damaris was so lost in some secret thought of her own that she was not even aware of Saranna's presence.

"Damaris!" the older girl repeated with force enough to make the other at least return her gaze. "You must be careful. You are only a little girl as far as Honora and most others are concerned. Everyone considers it perfectly proper for her to give orders in this house. With her father away, she is, in several respects, your guardian. I am afraid with such outbursts you will only make trouble for yourself—"

"You mean she'll send for the doctor. That he'll say I don't know my own mind—"

Saranna was startled. She had not guessed that Honora's estimate of her stepdaughter was known to the child herself.

Damaris laughed, a harsh sound with no lightness in it. "Oh, I know what she says. I told you—I listen. Last winter she had a doctor here. They did not tell me he was a doctor even, but he talked to me a lot. I knew what *she* was trying to do, make him believe I didn't know enough to own Tiensin. But that time, it didn't work. I showed him some of the treasures. And I told him about Grandfather and all. He didn't give *her* any satisfaction. *She* was mad, I could tell that.

"And—" again that shadow of a strange look crossed the girl's face. "I have something—something you—no one knows about. Something I can use if I really need help."

Saranna had a sudden suspicion. "Damaris—the *I Ching*! Is that what you mean? But, child, you cannot depend upon anything like that! It isn't true, you know. You can't foretell the future, or use any—any kind of magic. That is all a falsehood."

Damaris twisted out of her grasp.

"I don't know what you mean, I am sure," she said stolidly. "What kind of magic would I know? That's all foolishness—"

Her quick agreement puzzled Saranna. She had been so sure that Damaris, after her solemn play with the wands earlier that day, had really shown herself a believer in some strange knowledge. Yet she now denied the fact as firmly as if that scene in her bedroom had never occurred.

Instead, she was busy folding together her store of soft dust cloths with the air of one who had successfully finished a morning's labors.

"I'm finished in here anyway," she announced. "And I won't touch the library pieces until after lunch. You—" she nodded toward Saranna, "better get ready. Mrs. Parton won't hold back dishes for anyone. And if you're not there on time, the food gets cold—"

As if no scene had ever occurred, Damaris marched out of the drawing room, leaving Saranna to meekly follow, not quite sure of either the situation or her designed part in it. Damaris now was no child to be protected; she had the air of someone far older than her years who was in complete charge of affairs.

VII

Kou *Meeting*

If Rufe was a favorite of Honora's, at least he did not presume to attend family meals as Saranna had half-feared that he might do. She faced Damaris across the table they had shared with Honora and Mr. Fowke that morning, eating, in some state, a very good meal. No matter what Mrs. Parton's shortcomings might be in the field of manners, no one could deny that the house of Tiensin ran smoothly and well under her direction.

However, Saranna made a point of joining Damaris after the meal while the child carefully dusted those pieces of her grandfather's collection which were on display in the library. She persuaded the child to discuss the "treasures" while she worked. Once more Damaris was completely lost in the realm into which Captain Whaley had so carefully initiated her. For whole long moments of time, Saranna, herself, could forget the unpleasant scenes of the morning, charmed by Damaris' explanations concerning this or that piece she was handling.

When she had done and wadded her used cloths into a bag for washing, she smiled straight at Saranna.

"You like these, don't you?"

"Very much indeed."

"Wait!" Damaris turned around to survey the shelf where she had just finished replacing the last piece. "This!" Her hand closed upon the figure of a cat wrought in pottery, the whole a delicate yellow shade, the eyes open holes—a night lantern Damaris had told her. "For you—" She held it out to Saranna. "Take it!" she ordered abruptly. "I want you to have it, truly I do. You can use it tonight—put a candle in it—"

Saranna hesitated. Damaris' gift was impulsive. She did not doubt in the least that the child meant it, but it was an act which could be questioned. If she took it though, she could always return it later. And Saranna had no wish to arouse Damaris' opposition to the state of affairs now at Tiensin by pointing out that she might not be allowed to give away any of Captain Whaley's collection.

"Thank you—very much." She put all the warmth she could summon into her voice. "Indeed, I will do just that tonight."

Damaris nodded eagerly. "A night light is good, you know. I have one. *She* tried to say once I was afraid of the dark! I'm not, truly I'm not. But it makes one sleepy to lie and watch the candle glow. This is old. And it's yellow. That was a color only the Emperor or the Empress could use. Maybe this came from a palace a long time ago. When I'm older, I guess I'm going to China and see—"

Again she broke off sharply, as if she were about to say something which must not be mentioned. Her quick glance at Saranna underlined her suspicion that she might have said too much. But the older girl asked no questions.

"That would be wonderful," she commented. "To see such pieces in their own surroundings would be even better than looking at them here. And I shall feel very grand watching the candle flame tonight burning in a lantern which might have once belonged to the Emperor himself!"

She carried the cat lantern to her chamber unobserved by any save Millie who was bringing in an armload of newly washed clothing. The maid's eyes grew round as she eyed the piece Saranna placed with care on the table near the bed.

"That's a haunt thing!" She made a wide circle about

the table. "Why for you bring it here, Miss Saranna?"

"Miss Damaris wants me to use it for a night light."

Millie shook her head determinedly. "Me, I don't want no haunt thing near me, no, I don't—"

She cast such a look of aversion at the yellow cat that Saranna was troubled. Millie would certainly talk below stairs and that talk would be picked up by Mrs. Parton, and relayed to Honora. Yet the girl felt sure if she returned the cat to the library secretly, as she had intended, Damaris would speedily discover the rejection of her gift. Then the sympathy between them would vanish and Saranna might not be able to influence the young girl again.

"Move your bed to the other side tonight, Millie," Saranna suggested. "Then you won't be near it."

"Better I sleep in with Rose. She's been after me to come—"

Millie glanced at Saranna and then away quickly, as if she were suggesting something she felt would be instantly refused. But Saranna was relieved. She had never welcomed the idea of Millie sharing her chamber, for she felt that unwittingly Millie would relay to the servants every small action of her new mistress. She had a suspicion that that was what Millie had been set to do, though not perhaps with the girl's own knowledge.

"Of course you may go with Rose," she answered at once.

Millie beamed. "No need tell Old Miss?" she added.

"Old Miss?"

"Mrs. Parton. She don't never come where the gals sleep. Never know I ain't here—'less you say so."

"There is no reason for me to do that," Saranna replied.

When that afternoon Honora returned from her visit to Queen's Pleasure she was in an excellent mood, well pleased with herself. Her constant flow of talk throughout their dinner was of her own perfect suggestions as to the furnishings and decoration of the derelict Manor

House which Mr. Fowke was fast bringing back into re-
pair, and of how grateful he was for her interest and aid.
She was so intent upon her own affairs that Saranna did
not believe Honora noticed that Damaris was entirely silent during the meal, or that Saranna, herself, made only
short murmurs of assent at long intervals.

When the meal was finished, Honora did speak directly to her two listeners:

"Gerrad needs me again tomorrow, so I must get a
good rest. It is so necessary that no mistakes be made now
by the workmen. And, of course, I have the time free
now, which will not be true when our guests arrive. So I
shall be gone most of the day."

If she expected either of them to show dismay at her
promised absence, she would be disappointed, Saranna
thought. By all the signs, Honora apparently cared for
nothing now but her friendship with Gerrad Fowke,
which was certainly approaching the culmination she desired—what appeared to be her forthcoming marriage.

Saranna, on her way upstairs a little later (she had
borrowed a book from the library and maintained she intended to read in her room), considered that marriage.
To her mind, Gerrad Fowke was not only a sensible man,
but one of some authority. Though he had chosen Honora, there might be a hope that he was not altogether
under the dominance of the widowed Mrs. Whaley. His
politeness to both Saranna and Damaris at their breakfast
that morning, when Honora had clearly expected all his
interest to be centered only on her, was a promising sign
for Damaris' sake. It might be that in Mr. Fowke, the
child would find the protection from Honora's schemes—

To go directly to him with hints and suspicions—no.
Saranna could not do that. He might well question her
own motives, decide that she was only a malicious trou-
blemaker.

She must wait upon chance, or a greater understanding, to approach Mr. Fowke. Yet the thought of him
provided her with a vague comfort for Damaris' sake. He
was not a man easily fooled. And, though his connection

with Honora was still a matter for Saranna's private wonder, she did not believe that he would be a party to any threat against the very young mistress of Tiensin.

Her thoughts turned and twisted, and she could find no easy answer to many of them. Suddenly she remembered Damaris' remedy for sleeplessness, watching the candle night light in the cat lantern. Saranna arose, made her preparations for bed. When she was ready, she struck a match and lighted the candle.

The round spots of radiance which at once marked the figure's eyes made her think once again of the fox eyes which had lined the hedge on the night she had arrived at Tiensin. That fox which had suffered at Rufe's hands, at least the beast had escaped! And she hoped it was far away by now, also that its fellows took warning.

Had the cat she still eyed as she lay back now upon her pillows really been once the property of an Emperor; had it lighted some palace chamber half the world away? Saranna wished there were some way one could learn of all that cat had seen as it crouched for centuries, ready to beam out light from its hollow eyes.

The slight flickering of the flame within the cat made those eyes seem to change—to watch first her and then another corner of the room. No longer did it seem just a piece of exquisitely wrought pottery; rather more like a living creature—on guard—

Her own eyes closed, her tangled thoughts seemed smoothed, were fading, as if nothing that had alarmed her during this day could now trouble her night—not with the Emperor's cat watching—

Saranna must have slept, for she awoke as if from a slumber so deep that her mind was a little bemused. She realized that she was sitting up in bed, listening. Listening as intently as if she expected to hear the footfall of some intruder creeping close.

But it was no footfall that she heard now. No—it was—music! But such strange, uncanny music. The sounds were like nothing she had ever heard before, shrill, with a scale of notes totally unfamiliar—weird—

Yet—

She must follow it, discover who—or what—made that sound! Saranna was being drawn to it as surely as if some leash lay on her, governing her freedom.

Slipping from her high bed, the girl found her slippers and thrust her bare feet into them. Then she caught up her shawl which lay across the chair. In the Emperor's cat, the candle had burned low, its eyes were not as bright as they had been. Now they rested upon her as if in imperious order. Yes, she had no choice—she must go!

Though the hall was dark and she had no lamp, Saranna sped down it unerringly, hardly knowing where she went. All that really mattered was what lay ahead— Now the stairs. The garden door, but that was bolted! She tore at the stiff bolt in a kind of frenzy until she shot it back to be free on the garden path.

There was no question where she was bound. The music drew her around the corner of the house, straight to that hidden opening in the hedge where Damaris' tracks had earlier led her. Saranna fought a passage through, into the moonlit secret garden beyond. This time, however, she crossed the bridge, went around the tiny house with the flower-shaped windows, pushed by a tall thicket, until she paused at the edge of a large, open space.

Before her was the bulk of a building far larger than the tiny one at the bridge side. Though in style, this one also followed that same general pattern of sharply peaked roof, upturned eaves, and oddly shaped windows. Now it formed a background, of which Saranna was but vaguely aware, for the scene on a terrace which stretched from the rounded moon gate of the house into the full rays of the moon.

Against the wall of the house, on low stools, sat three figures, who were shadowed from light. Their faces Saranna could not see except as whitish blurs. But it was they who made that music which had drawn her. The instruments which they played were also so deep in the shadows she could not see them clearly.

While out on the terrace in the full light—

She heard her own gasp even through the wailing chords of that playing.

For, drawn up in ordered rows, facing the three musicians were—foxes!

Large and small, even differing a little in color. For some were plainly darker in shade than their neighbors. And two were an amazing silver-white. Yet all sat in nearly the same position, as if they were listening—or waiting—

She thought the last only when there was movement within the circle of the moon door. Someone came out of the house, advanced into the open where the moon's radiance caught her plainly.

It was a woman wearing a long robe, the sleeves of which covered her hands, being of such a length they swept to the pavement of the terrace. She came dancing, weaving a graceful pattern with the fluttering of her overlong sleeves. Her hair was dressed high in stiff formality, and in those rolls, gemmed pins caught the moon, reflected that light with small glitters like the sparkles on frost-rimmed snow.

But—

Her head had turned a little as she wove her airy design with the fluttering sleeves before the foxes. Her face—

A fox! A fox's countenance on a woman's shoulders, beneath that high piled hair!

Saranna's hand flew to her mouth, in somewhat the same gesture Damaris used, to suppress a cry. Her first astonishment did not give way to any fear. She felt nothing now but wonderment. There was an unreality about the whole scene which brought not terror but interest. As if this was something to be cherished, that Saranna was in a way privileged to be a witness here and now.

She never knew how long she stood there watching the intricate steps of the dancer, bewitched by the eerie music, the sight of that motionless, fascinated pack of foxes watching with her as their fur-visaged mistress swayed gracefully in the full light of the moon.

Then the dance halted; the woman's arms swept out in a gesture of command. From the furred throats before her came a loud yapping chorus. At once, the foxes scattered, melting away from the terrace. The music had also stopped, but the Fox Lady did not return to her house.

No, her muzzle pointed in Saranna's direction. The girl knew without any doubt, that her presence had been detected; yet again, the knowledge brought her no fear. Instead, as one of those sleeve-muffled hands raised to beckon, she went forward to answer the unvoiced summons, moving across the terrace toward the dancer.

Before she quite reached the other's side, a light flickered to life within the moon door itself, and then a second, sending yellow fingers out to dispute the paler radiance of the moon. As the dancer half-turned from Saranna to that doorway, she beckoned a second time.

With an odd confidence that this was right, the girl followed the other into the house where five lanterns on legs sat around a room, giving vivid life to its furnishings.

A woman with the seamed and wrinkled face of age, yet who moved with some of the spring of youth, had just put light to the fifth and last of the lanterns. She wore a short black satin jacket, embroidered with red, over black trousers. Her hair was drawn so smoothly back from her face, that it lay against her skull as if painted in black strokes of ink. The bulk of it was knotted at the nape of her neck with two gold pins through the knot.

But the dancer wore a loose robe of a brilliant rust which was also the red of an autumn leaf or a fox's coat. It was tied by a sash high under her arms in a fashion such as Saranna had seen pictured on a lacquer screen among Tiensin's treasures—a screen many centuries old.

The gemmed pins in her high piled hair were her only ornaments and her fox face was very obvious, the upper lip lifted a little to show the gleaming of teeth. Yet Saranna felt none of the astonishment which had first gripped her at the sight of the dancer.

In one corner was just such a bed as Damaris had in

her chamber, giving the impression of being an alcove of the room, rather than a piece of furniture. Two lanterns stood at either end, affording more light at that point. Screens and the drapery of brocaded curtains of a yellow-red shade afforded privacy, and there was a low railing about it which opened in the center of the side nearest them.

A pile of what might be quilts was folded lengthwise in place at the back along the wall. And on a brocaded padding a very short-legged table sat on the surface of the bed. With graceful ease, the Fox Lady drew her long skirted robe about her and seated herself on one side of that table. Again, she gestured to Saranna to join her at the opposite side of that board.

In the air hung a spicy scent whose like Saranna thought she remembered from her visit to Damaris' room. But she was far more interested in the fox woman herself than in her surroundings. As if, when the dancer were present, nothing else mattered.

As Saranna, suddenly conscious of her disheveled hair (she must have lost her nightcap among the bushes), her snagged shawl, and her heavy muslin nightgown, all appearing in painful contrast to the elegance of her strange hostess, settled herself on the edge of the huge bed, she felt very insignificant, very much an intruder. The Fox Lady's sleeves fluttered back away from her hands which she clapped together.

Her flesh was like carved ivory, there was no hint of a fox's paws here, rather fingers, long and slim. And, covering the nails on each hand, sheaths of gemmed and filagreed gold protruding far beyond any natural length.

At her signal, the older woman pattered forward, carrying a tray on which rested two covered cups of jade, but a jade so different in color that Saranna only knew it to be that precious stone from Damaris' tutoring. For this was cream-white, a flowered branch carved in high relief on the side of each. The Fox Lady gracefully slipped the top from her cup, held it to her muzzle. At the inclination of her elaborately coiffed head, Saranna followed her example.

This was tea before her, but with the addition of some herb, the girl believed. At least, she had never sniffed such an aroma rising from any tea she had had poured from a New England pot.

For the first time the Fox Lady spoke, though her jaw did not move to shape the word.

"*Mei*—"

Her slim, nail-sheathed hand moved forward so that she nearly, but not quite, touched one straying lock of Saranna's long hair which had escaped down the girl's shoulder.

Damaris had said that word meant "sister." Was it because her rust-red locks did resemble a fox's coat that this dancer thought to call her so?

"*Mei*—" the other repeated and then, which seemed very strange indeed, she added a word in Saranna's own language:

"Drink!"

Saranna found that the contents of the jade cup were not too hot to drink after all. The taste was odd but she liked it. There was something so refreshing in the liquid that she swallowed eagerly again and again, until the cup was indeed empty.

The eyes of the fox mask regarded her steadily. Yet Saranna sensed that this person, whoever or whatever she might be, meant her no ill. There was a drift of scented smoke rising from a brazier beyond the draped curtain of the roomlike bed. That smoke appeared now to be growing thicker—like a fog or mist—like the mist which had folded in upon the sloop which had brought her upriver.

Through the mist came sharp glints. From the gemmed pins in the dancer's hair? Or were those eyes—the eyes of foxes gathering within this room, padding through the moon door out of the night to join their mistress? Saranna blinked and blinked again, striving to fight a new languorous apathy which gripped her.

Fox eyes—gems—moonlight—a dancer with the form of a woman, but a sharp pointed, red-furred muzzle for a face— Fox face—fox eyes—

"Miss Saranna!"

Far away a voice calling. Then nearer, nearer—more urgent.

Saranna stirred. They must be hunting her. Would they come into the hidden garden—through the moon gate—and—?

She opened her eyes. Her lids seemed so heavy; she did not want to look around her, to take up the burden of knowing again. To drift in the scented beauty of the dancer's room— To—

But—this was her own bed! Her own bed, with Millie leaning over to shake her shoulder a little timidly. She was in her own bed. She had only been dreaming! But so real a dream—so very real a dream!

Only, of course, it could only be a dream. There could not possibly exist any exquisite figure with a woman's body, a fox's face! But never before in her life had Saranna dreamed in such vivid detail. She could, at this moment, still somehow feel the smooth jade cup within her hand, list the number of lanterns, describe the hangings, the folded covers of that bed, the sweep of the dancer's long sleeves as she turned and twirled until those ribbons of soft material had whirled out—

"Miss Saranna—it do be breakfast time—nearly—" Millie was staring at her.

"Oh." The warnings of Mrs. Parton's demand for promptness came to mind. Saranna got out of bed.

For a moment, she felt a little dizzy and queer. She put her hand up. No, her hair was not straying free. It was decorously tethered beneath her nightcap. Of course, she had not gone running out through the night.

"I'll hurry, Millie. Put out the sprigged cotton, please."

There was a can of hot water waiting by the washbasin. With her face cloth, she rinsed the last remnants of the dream from her. And it was not until she hooked the bodice of what she knew was a hideous and out-of-date dress (drab black with very small and faded sprigs of off-color white) that she saw what lay on the dressing table.

A loop of silken cord of the same rust-yellow as the dancer's robe coiled around what must be a pendant of jade, the same milk-white jade of the tea cup. Only this piece of that imperial stone was wrought in the form of a fox head, and the eyes were small yellowish gems which held a glow, as if, in their depths, there was indeed a spark of actual, knowing life.

Saranna glanced around. Millie was bustling about, splashing the water from the basin into the slop bucket. She put out her hand quickly, her fingers closing about the pendant before, she hoped, the maid had noticed it.

Surely Damaris had not shown her the like of this. Saranna would have remembered such a piece. Unless there were some of Captain Whaley's collection which his granddaughter had not thought, or remembered, to display. There had been some jewelry—kept in a locked case. But this pendant had not lain there. Then where—?

Not out of her dream? It could not have come out of her dream! Not possibly!

But that it was precious, a piece of great value, Saranna was sure. And until she could question Damaris, no one must see it. There was only one really safe hiding place—her own person.

She swiftly slipped the cord over her head, pushed the pendant well down under the prim collar of her chemisette, assuring herself by a searching survey in the mirror that it was entirely hidden. Against her skin it felt cool, very smooth, and she was strongly conscious of it as she hurried toward the door that she might not be late to breakfast.

VIII

T'ung Jên *Companionship*

"Miss Stowell—"

Startled, Saranna paused in her descent of the wide staircase. The outer door was a little open; Mr. Fowke stood just within. He smiled up at her.

Why had she ever thought his strong face unhandsome? When he smiled in that fashion she was surprised at her own past blindness.

"I'm late—" she said in what she knew must seem an idiotic way. But again she was flustered by having his full attention turned on her.

"And Mrs. Parton cannot be kept waiting," he added, as if he were repeating some oft-heard admonition. "Yes, Mrs. Parton is ruled by the clock's inexorable tick, isn't she? I wonder if ever in her life she has longed to break the bonds of time, just wander freely outside minutes, hours, and perhaps days."

Saranna found the courage to smile in return. "I really don't know her well enough to venture an opinion," she replied, her uneasiness subsiding a little.

Suddenly he looked almost stern, forbidding, his glance at her so intent Saranna wondered for a moment if the jade pendant could be seen. She raised her hand hurriedly to press against the hidden gem. Why was he watching her with that strange measuring look, as if she presented some problem, and one which he found at least a little distasteful.

"You will doubtless be given plenty of chance to learn and understand Mrs. Parton's quirks in the future." His tone was now remote and Saranna was at a loss. It was almost as if she had offended him in some fashion. Yet when she recalled her words they were certainly harmless enough. She could not in any way see why such a commonplace observation had brought about this change in his manner.

"Gerrad! You are already here—"

The door to the breakfast room had opened to let Honora, again in riding dress, bustle out.

"But why did John not announce you? I vow these house hands grow lazier every day. Saranna—" Her attention, for a moment, rested on the girl. "My," her nose wrinkled as she surveyed her, "we simply must do something about your clothes! Such a figure as you do cut this morning! And you do want to appear your best these days, don't you?" That ice-tinkle of laughter sounded, the eyes above the chilly smiling mouth were hard as polished stones. "I must have Mrs. Parton look out for some things to be altered. But," the gem-hard eyes swung from Saranna's discreetly capped head to the hem of the girl's limp skirt and back again, "you certainly must be prepared to make some alterations. We are not of a size at all."

Saranna did not reply. She could feel the warmth come into her cheeks at this contemptuous appraisal. That Honora would reveal such pettiness in her own nature so clearly before Gerrad Fowke must mean that she was indeed betrothed to him, whether or no any such announcement had been made public. The girl longed to raise her eyes to his face, to judge by his expression how Honora's behavior moved him. But that she would not allow herself to do.

"Yes," Honora was continuing with her usual overbearing stream of words, "you must have a new dress or two. With your prospects it is only right. Gerrad," in an instant she turned back to her waiting escort, "I have had a wonderful idea concerning the garden. It came to me in the night and I wrote it down lest I would forget it. Oh, do let us get on to Queen's Pleasure so I can show you just what I have been thinking of—"

"Miss Stowell." Though Honora's hand was now on his arm, he still lingered, making a bow in Saranna's direction. Only his face was still tight and closed in the forbidding way.

Saranna inclined her head in return, feeling forlorn now instead of angry as she had a moment earlier. She would probably never know what had made Mr. Fowke act suddenly so different toward her. It was with a sense of oppression and loss that she watched the door close behind the two, then walked slowly into the breakfast room.

Damaris stood at a window, her hand pulling aside the edge of the lace undercurtain so she could see the curve of the drive beyond.

"There *she* goes," the younger girl reported. "Well, she won't be back soon, we can depend on that. You should have heard her this morning, you really should have, Saranna!"

Coming back to the table, Damaris revealed the old scowl which caused a most unpleasant twist of eyebrow, lift of lip on her young face. "*She's* going back to Baltimore tomorrow to do some shopping for her wedding things. Though she can't be married yet, not until her father comes back. However, she and the Poker have been having their heads together—they were whispering when I came in this morning. *She* needn't think she can keep any secret—I'll learn sooner or later!" Damaris appeared a little more cheerful, and began spreading a biscuit with an overload of strawberry preserves.

Saranna, without much appetite, assembled some of the half-cold food and picked at it. The depression which had closed on her in the hallway seemed now a dark cloud. She felt that she must learn one thing—had Damaris left that jade pendant in her room? If that were true, Saranna must make certain the precious thing was returned at once to the safekeeping where it had once lain. She had no intention of allowing the child to make any trouble for herself, as well as perhaps Saranna, by her impulsive gift. The porcelain cat could be easily returned. Perhaps Honora or Mrs. Parton, if they discovered that piece in her room, would not realize its full value. But a piece of jewelry was a far different matter, and Saranna had no doubt that Honora would be well aware of the worth of any treasure which was an adornment for the person.

"You are awfully late." Damaris had crunched her way through her biscuit and was not watching Saranna. "Did you oversleep?"

"Yes."

Damaris smiled. "That was the fault of the cat light. You tried it, didn't you? I told you that you can watch it and sleep well."

"But I had better not do so again," Saranna commented.

"Not if you want a hot breakfast," Damaris agreed frankly. "And here's Rose to clear away. Take some fruit—we can go outside. It's a very nice day, warm so you won't need a shawl."

Saranna did reach for another biscuit, chose an orange. She was eager herself to get away from the house, where there might be listening ears, and have Damaris to herself.

"We'll explore," the small mistress of Tiensin announced firmly as they came out into the full sun of morning. "You haven't had a chance to see the outside. Of course, Rufe would be glad to show you—" She shot a sidewise glance at Saranna, a faint trace of that malicious amusement in her eyes.

"I think you know better," Saranna refused to allow herself to be in the least ruffled.

" 'Course I do," Damaris agreed. "I was born here, you know. And when Grandfather couldn't get around on his feet much he used to send me out to see how things were kept. He said he could trust me—"

Here was another undercurrent. If Captain Whaley

had sent his granddaughter, young as she was, to check upon that part of his estate he could no longer supervise, his action suggested he had reason to believe that there might be trouble.

" 'When a man is at peace, he ought to be as alert as if he were in trouble; so he can forestall an unforeseen contingency. And when he is in trouble, he ought to be as calm as if he were at peace; thus he can bring to an end his crisis'—" Darmaris recited the words as she might some set lesson. "That was written down by a sage. Do you know what a sage is, Saranna? The Chinese believed that some men could learn to control their bodies and their thoughts so that they were not men any more, but something else, that they could then live for hundreds of years. But I don't think I can really believe that. Grandfather learned a lot of sayings like that. There's another one he explained to me and that I do believe—'Whether time is long or short, and whether space is broad or narrow, depend upon the mind.' That's right. If you're very interested in something, then time goes fast. But if you have to do something you don't like at all—the time is very long. Now—let's start here—"

With some of the same competence she had used when introducing Saranna to the resources of the house, she marched along the curve of the drive to the back of the Manor.

There the various outhouses, the older girl discovered, formed what was like a small village of their own. Damaris indicated the milk house, corn house, hen house, cheese house, meat house, ice house—the stables, and, farther yet beyond, the orangery where both fruit and out-of-season flowers could be forced at a time not normal for their development.

The blacks in service at the various buildings bobbed curtsies, "made their manners," but Damaris did not speak to any of them. In fact, she gave but a very superficial tour of this portion of the estate.

It was not until they were beyond that cluster of buildings and walking between the orchards of morello cher-

ries and peaches, which she said in passing were grown to
make brandy, that the younger girl slowed pace.

"They don't like me," she said then. "The Poker—she
gets them to watch me sometimes. But they don't dare do
that too closely." Now she smiled. "They just don't dare.
They know what would happen if they did—"

"And what would happen?"

Damaris did not look up. She scruffed her slipper on
the path.

"They'd just be in trouble, that's all—a lot of trouble."
Her answer was evasive and Saranna knew better than to
push at this moment. "There is the pergola—" Damaris
pointed to a structure beyond which curled the river.
Wisteria and vining roses had been trained up its side,
hung in heavy festoons. The walls behind those were latticed, and there was an upper deck with a balustrade
about it.

"It's for parties—they dance there—" Damaris explained. "*She's* going to use it. See, Seth and Ralph are
fixing it up."

Saranna halted. The two black boys were not alone.
Rufus Parton stood watching their labors. Perhaps he was
supervising. She had no desire to catch his attention. But,
neither, it seemed, did Damaris either.

"We can go this way!" Her hand thrust into the older
girl's, pulled Saranna to the right. They pushed under
the low hanging limbs of a tree and out around some
flowerbeds to where a bench was backed by a wall of box.

"He can't see us here," Damaris announced. "You
don't really like him—?"

"No." Saranna was blunt.

"*She* wants you to," Damaris observed. "But I haven't
found out why yet. Though I think she told Mr. Fowke
yesterday— She said something to the Poker about making *that* clear to him. *She* always has a reason for things,
you know. And sooner or later I do find out. When I do,
I'll tell you—"

Saranna knew that she should not encourage Damaris's chronic eavesdropping, even by her silence now.

Yet weakly, she did not try to reprove the child. She *did* want to know why Honora was so intent upon suggesting that Rufus Parton be friends with her father's half sister. Even if she deemed Saranna so far beneath her notice, surely any such condition of affairs would be a matter of surprise to Honora's friends. Saranna was as much a Stowell as Jethro and Honora herself.

At least she now had a time in which to discover about the pendant. Once more she raised her hand to her basque, pressed the cloth tightly enough against her breast that she could feel the full weight of that gem.

"Damaris," she began, "some of your grandfather's collection are pieces of jewelry—"

The younger girl nodded. "You saw them," she returned.

"Are those *all* the pieces of jewelry you know about?" Saranna interrupted.

"Yes. Why?" Damaris swung about sidewise on the bench so that her watchful eyes were able to meet Saranna's. "Why do you ask me that?" she repeated.

"Because—" Saranna's hand went again to the front of her chemisette. She could see no other way of gaining her knowledge but with a straight question. "Because this morning, when I woke up, I found this lying on my dressing table. Are you sure, Damaris, you did not leave it there to surprise me?"

She had found the cord, now she jerked the pendant up into the light. The purity of the jade carving was even clearer out here under the sun, and the small inset eyes flashed boldly.

"A white fox—an auspicious omen—" Damaris repeated those words as if again quoting some precept she had learned from Captain Whaley. But her complete surprise could not, Saranna believed, be counterfeit.

Then, almost instantly, her surprise vanished. She shrank away from Saranna along the length of the bench.

"No!" Her denial was a protest. "No, it is not true. You didn't see the Princess—you couldn't have! She doesn't let anyone come to her but me—never, never, never!"

Saranna swallowed. Her dream— But it was not true, it could not be!

"Damaris!" She spoke the name sharply, demanding the child's full attention. "Damaris, you will have to tell me the truth now. Is there someone in the hidden garden, someone living there?"

Damaris' head turned from side to side slowly as if she refused to answer. "I can't—I promised! I can't break my promise ever. Grandfather told me so. He did—he did that just before he died!"

Saranna drew a deep breath. "All right, Damaris. I won't ask you to break your promise. But I want you to listen to me. Last night—" Slowly, and summoning every detail she could draw from her memory, she described her dream—that vision of the Fox Lady dancing before the company of those who appeared her four-legged kin, of the room beyond the moon door—and of how she had drunk scented tea from a white jade cup and awakened in her own bed—with only the pendant lying there to be explained.

Damaris, her face going blank of any expression, as if she had been able to set some strange curb on her emotions, listened without interruption.

When Saranna finished, there was silence between them for a long moment, then the older girl added:

"It must have been a dream. I could not have seen a dancer with a fox face. Only—here is the pendant—" She looked to Damaris in appeal. Their position might have been reversed from what she had felt yesterday when a need to protect the child had moved her. Now she wanted reassurance from Damaris—some reason for the pendant.

Once more Damaris shook her head slowly. "I can't tell you, really I can't, Saranna. I promised. But," she pointed to the pendant, "that is yours, you would not have it if that were not so. And it is not part of Grandfather's treasure. Only I wouldn't ever let *her* see it. *She would find a way to get it from you. And that she musn't. That's a thing of power. It is of jade which is the Heaven stone, you know. And it is a white fox, which means very good luck. You keep that hid, never let anyone know. And—Saranna—"* She had slipped from the bench, came to stand directly before the older girl. "I would tell you if I could, honest I would!"

Saranna managed a smile. "Yes, I believe that, Damaris. And I know that this is a precious thing that is better hidden." She tucked the pendant carefully out of sight. "I only wish that you might tell me more. But I shall ask no more questions." She sighed.

Damaris' action left her prey to bewilderment. Maybe she *had* been in the hidden garden last night after all. Saranna had heard some talk of a man named Mesmer who had been able to make people believe that they saw things which did not exist by sending them into a kind of sleep and impressing on their minds orders he gave. The fox-headed dancer could—must be an illusion of sorts. Only *who* had so impressed the memory of her on Saranna's mind? That this could even be done was a frightening thought, one she did not want to consider.

"Miss Damaris, Miss Saranna—" Millie had come upon them. "Mrs. Parton, she do want as how you should come, Miss Saranna. She do have some clothes, Miss Honora do say you should have—"

For a moment Saranna was glad of the interruption, galling as it might be to her pride to have to accept Honora's bounty in the way of clothes. Damaris came with her, on up to Saranna's chamber where the housekeeper was watching Rose turn out a bundle of dresses on the bed. They were all black, of course. No doubt, Honora's discarded full mourning. Saranna had no wish to turn them over or examine them with Mrs. Parton watching.

The housekeeper had picked up a crumpled skirt, was shaking out the creased folds. She ran her hand along the breadth with appreciation.

"Excellent material—the very best," she commented,

glancing at Saranna, perhaps as if to see the girl properly grateful for such munificence.

But the material she so admired was heavy satin, and entirely unsuitable for the warming weather of the season. However, Saranna summoned pride.

"How very kind of Mrs. Whaley," she returned. "I have had a great deal of sewing experience, Mrs. Parton. It will be unnecessary for me to ask for any aid in making the needful alterations. I appreciate your kindness in having these brought to me."

Mrs. Parton's expression did not change. She gave a nod and accepted her implied dismissal, leaving the room. Damaris caught up the satin skirt the housekeeper had draped across the chair before she left and took it closer into the light of a window.

"Look here!" she demanded indignantly. "I thought I recognized this. Look at this! It's the dress *she* spilled wine down, the stain is all over the front." Contemptuously, she tossed the offending skirt back toward the bed, but it landed instead in a heap on the floor. "I wonder what else she gave you. Things no one could use—"

Saranna made herself examine the clothing. Most of it was either as damaged as the skirt about which Damaris had been entirely correct, or else unsuitable for the season. She did manage to find a black cambric which could be worn with an underskirt, put together from one which was ripped but could be repaired. And there was a poplin one which Damaris greeted with a laugh.

"I know that one, too. *She* only wore it once. Mrs. Langtree had one made almost like it and *she* was very angry when she came home from the tea. Most of this stuff, Saranna, it's no good at all! Just what she would do—"

But Saranna now began to look at the jumble of cast-offs with a new idea dawning. Honora had skimmed from her wardrobe what she considered to be worthless. But Mrs. Parton had been right in one way, the materials were of the best quality. And the girl had not watched her own mother contrive and plan to get the most out of comparatively nothing without learning quite a lot. There was no reason to turn aside because of resentment. She could better be engaged in proving to Honora that in spite of her present shabbiness, she was not devoid of either clothes sense or skill.

"You're thinking about something," declared Damaris. "I can tell—when you get that funny little wrinkle right there"— She pointed a finger to a spot between Saranna's eyes—"that means that you're thinking. What are you really going to do about this mess?" She indicated the tumble of clothes— "You ought to go right and throw them back at her."

"On the contrary," Saranna said blandly. "I shall thank her very much for her generosity—"

Damaris made a sound not unlike a snort.

"I shall thank her," Saranna repeated. "And then—I shall get busy."

"Doing what?" Damaris wanted to know.

"Cutting out, putting together, sewing—"

"You mean, use *these*?"

"Of course. You see, Damaris, for some years my mother had to make her living as a dressmaker. I helped her a lot—though I was also studying to go to school and become a teacher. But my mother had excellent taste, and she was very clever with her fingers. Perhaps what she taught me then will be now of more service to me than any book learning."

"Ladies don't make dresses—" Damaris said dubiously.

Saranna flashed around to face the younger girl. "Ladies, Damaris, do any honest work which comes ready to their hands. Has no one ever taught you sewing?"

Damaris laughed. "Well, Prune Face tried. She gave up after a while. I was too much for her."

"But, Damaris, you so admire the beautiful panels of embroidery. That's needlework. Haven't you ever wished that you could copy something like that?"

"That wasn't what Prune Face wanted. She talked about hemming dusters—and sheets— But—" the younger girl studied Saranna speculatively, "if you want me to learn how to sew. Well, maybe I just might do it. I'd learn if I could help you turn some of those old things into a dress to make *her* eyes pop out. I surely would."

Saranna smiled. "And Millie wants to learn, too. It will be excellent training for her if she continues as a lady's personal maid. Very well, we shall have a sewing class—right here—beginning tomorrow."

"Mrs. Parton has a real sewing machine. She doesn't run it much—she's afraid of it," Damaris volunteered. "And she won't let any of the maids touch it—'cause they might break it. Grandfather ordered it from New York—he meant it for me. But when it came, Mrs. Parton locked it away; she said no child could run it."

"We may even ask her for the use of that," Saranna promised. "Mother saw one demonstrated in Boston, and then had me go and watch, too. But we couldn't afford to buy one. We'll see."

With more purpose she began sorting through the castoffs for the second time, this time with the intention of guessing just how much could be salvaged from damaged, stained, or otherwise unusable garments. And she finally believed that it might be possible to squeeze out three completely new frocks. Of course, she did not pretend to her mother's skill, but the old fact of economy (well-known in Sussex where one penny was long made to do the work of two), that a bodice could be refurbished by a new chemisette and married to the skirt of another dress whose upper part was past hope, was in her favor. At the worst, she would be better clad when she was through than she was now with her skimpy and far too old dresses.

"Saranna," Damaris sat on the edge of the bed, fingering the stained satin skirt, "you—you talk about your mother as if you were just visiting—as if you were going back home to see her—not as if she were dead. You don't cry when you mention her—"

"No, I don't cry—" Saranna fought against that painful sudden pressure in her throat. "But that does not

mean, Damaris, that I do not think of her, want to—
Only that wanting, it is selfish; it is wanting what is best
for me, not what is best for her. You see, she was ill, very,
very ill, when she died. The doctor told me she could
never be really well again; she could not work. We did
not have any money except what we could earn. If she
had lived—she would have been very unhappy. Now I am
sure that she is safe. She does not go hungry; she is never
cold. I think of her being as I saw her once when we had
a precious day all to ourselves.

"We rode out in the country, away from the town, to
see an old school friend of Mother's. It was a wonderful
summer day and we stopped in a big field where there
was a brook—with flowers—and ferns—and the lovely,
warm soft air—the sunshine. Mother had to work so
hard, she sometimes never got out of the house all day to
even step into the garden, such as it was, around our cottage. But that day she looked around and told me that
she thought that Heaven must be like that field. And I
am sure it is—for her. So whenever I get selfish and think
I miss her so much—then I think of her in that field with
the flowers and the sun—"

Saranna had almost forgotten that she was talking to
anyone, she was so caught up in memory.

"I like that. Grandfather—I don't think he would
have wanted a field," Damaris observed softly. "He—
maybe he's in a place like China where there are a lot of
wonderful palaces full of beautiful things. And he's walking through them straight and tall—without having to use
his cane anymore—just looking and looking— Oh, Saranna, I'm so glad you've come to live here! I'm so glad!"

Damaris threw herself at the older girl, her arms now
about Saranna's waist, her head pressed tightly against
her breast right over the pendant. Saranna's arms went
out in turn to enfold the child.

"And I am, too, Damaris. I am, too!"

She was, she understood in a kind of wonder. For all
its strangeness and shadows, at this moment Tiensin took
on the appearance of home.

IX

Wei Chi *Not Yet Accomplished*

Saranna did make a point of thanking Honora, and her tone must have carried sincerity. For, no matter how Honora had intended the gift, Saranna was determined to make the best of it. And her own shabbiness had been a growing discomfort for her, surrounded as she was by the splendors of Tiensin which reflected her own dowdiness that much the more.

But she doubted if Honora greatly cared. She was far too absorbed in her own plans of returning to Baltimore to refurbish her own wardrobe.

"I shall be able to come out of mourning next month." She stared dreamily into the distance over her dinner plate as if able to envision the rolls of lace, the waiting bolts of material only a day's journey away downriver. And she spoke of her term as a grieving widow, Saranna thought, rather as if that period of time had been a cell to confine her. Perhaps that was so.

From what Saranna had deduced about Richard Whaley, the Captain's son, he must have been greatly overshadowed in life by his far more dominant father. That he had found two women to marry him might not have been due to any personal charm, but the wealth of which Tiensin was the symbol. Though, if she had married for position, consequence, and wealth, Honora had been sadly disappointed in the end.

For the first time Saranna realized that, though Damaris had spoken freely of her grandfather, and that her tie with the Captain had been very close indeed, she had never mentioned her father or mother. Perhaps the Captain so overshadowed all the household during his long life that they had not mattered to their child.

"Yes—" Honora was continuing, though she appeared now to be speaking her thoughts aloud, not addressing either of the others at the table. "Blue, I think—and one of those embroidered lawns— I look well in green, too. And those new bonnets with the blush roses under the brim." Her eyes sparkled, there was a delicate flush in her cheeks. Saranna had no doubt that Honora was mentally picturing herself in one gown after another.

She caught Damaris' eye and the child answered with a slight grimace. Since dressmaking seemed to be the subject for conversation, Saranna dared to break into Honora's delectable dreams with a blunt question.

"May we have the use of the sewing machine?"

"The—what—?"

For an instant, Honora was completely at a loss.

"The sewing machine. I understand Captain Whaley had one bought shortly before his death. Since I must make some alterations in the gowns you so generously gave me, use of it will make my task shorter."

"A sewing machine? But those are vastly complicated—"

Saranna continued firmly. "I have seen one, had it demonstrated to me in Boston. While they are not good for fine sewing—the matter of seaming and such is made very much easier."

"Where is it?" Honora had been drawn fully out of her own preoccupation with the delights of shopping to come.

"I believe Mrs. Parton has it in custody. She dislikes using it herself and rightly does not trust the uninstructed maids—"

"Oh, very well. Yes, tell her that you must have it." Honora nodded, her good humor very evident. "I know she will be most accommodating—to you, Saranna."

There was something in the emphasis of that speech which alerted Saranna.

"Why should she be any more accommodating to me, Honora? I am only a visitor here—" and, she added silently to herself, in all eyes, except maybe Damaris', a very unimportant one.

"You are no child, Saranna, but a young lady," Honora's smile was almost demure, though that was a difficult adjective to use to describe anything about Mrs. Whaley. "Surely you know of Rufus Parton's interest. He is a very estimable young man who has worked hard to raise himself above his class. It is his intention to go West where there are many opportunities for one of his ability. And—"

"And he might as well look elsewhere!" Saranna flashed hotly. "I am not interested in the least in Rufus Parton."

Honora's ice-tinkle of laugh rang out. "Oh, he is a little rough about the edges, to be sure. But a canny wife can smooth him down and show him more civilized ways. He is not penniless, you know. His uncle left him quite well off for one of that class; land, too—out in Tennessee—or some such place. He can well afford to marry a girl without any portion. Also, liking improves upon acquaintance, you know. You must give Rufus a chance for you to know him better. He will be an excellent *parti*—"

Saranna had fought hard to control her temper. After all—this was only the culmination of her fears put into words. Somehow, instinct told her, she must succeed in hiding from Honora the extreme revulsion the other's suggestion had raised in her.

"Gerrad agreed with me yesterday that this is an excellent chance for a secure settlement for you, Saranna. After all—what training have you had? No female who is respectable can hope for a better future than a prudent marriage. Surely your years of scraping and paring after your father died taught you that being a seamstress or such can barely keep one alive. Father said you had ambition to be a teacher—but is that any better a life? No,

Rufus is a coming man, with enough in his purse to establish himself well on the land his uncle left him. His wife might even be the grand dame of such society as that backwoods offers. You must be reasonable and sensible, Saranna. Rufus Parton is a chance such as few penniless girls in your circumstances can hope for—"

"And if I dislike him?"

Again Honora laughed. "Dislike him? You hardly know him. You must allow him to make his manners properly. *You* can not afford to be missish, my girl!" The last sentence was delivered in an entirely different tone of voice, one which held the snap of a whip.

Honora might urge this on her, Saranna thought, but she could not force her kinswoman to accept Rufus Parton. Never! Before that happened Saranna would leave Tiensin—she would find some way of supporting herself. Suppose she wrote to the Academy. There must be something she could do!

"My, what a fierce frown!" Honora was smiling. "You will have wrinkles far before you age, Saranna, if you continue to screw up your face in that petulant manner. Think about what I have said; you are rumored to have some intelligence. It should be easy for you to see now which is the better choice—to live on charity, or to be the mistress of your own establishment. Think it over. I believe you will see that we are not enemies but friends to wish this for you."

She sipped the last drop of her coffee and arose from the table.

"Gerrad will be coming this evening to discuss some purchases he wishes me to make for him."

Saranna needed no broader hint. "I have a book I wish to read." Her pride came to her rescue swiftly.

"Damaris—?" Honora for the first time spoke directly to her stepdaughter.

"Oh, I have a book, too," the younger girl mimicked Saranna's tone. "You need not worry that we do not understand that Mr. Fowke comes only to see you." There was no disguising the hostility in her voice.

Honora's color deepened a little. "Certainly not to listen to the rude trivialities of little girls!" When her voice
was that sharp it also gained a shrill note which hardly
was a tone for polite conversation, Saranna decided.

" 'Better to be kind at home than burn incense far
away'—"

Again Honora's flush grew stronger. "Don't you quote
your heathen words at me!" she flared. "I had enough of
that when—" She bit her lip. Damaris faced her squarely.

"You were going to say when Grandfather was alive,
weren't you? Because he isn't here any more you think
what he believed doesn't matter now. Don't waste your
hours—the sun sets soon."

Without waiting for any answer, Damaris turned her
back on Honora and marched out of the room. Her stepmother regarded the closing door thoughtfully. Then her
look shifted to Saranna.

"She is getting far worse in this obsession of hers! You
must see it. I cannot believe but that the Captain's mind
must have been affected by senility when he fostered her
learning of such heathenish ways. I really do not know
what we can do with her if she grows worse. My father is
her guardian, and he will be away so long. We may have
to take some steps in her behalf before his return. I so
fear that little can be done now to counteract this truly
pernicious knowledge in which she was drilled. Does she
talk to you of her dreams—of how much she knows of
this devilish belief or that?" Honora's study of Saranna's
expression grew even sharper as if she expected to draw
from her some agreement.

"Damaris has told me nothing except about the Captain's treasures. There she indeed amazed me by the
completeness and depth of her learning. I think even few
men on this side of the ocean could equal her special
knowledge of Chinese art—"

Honora shrugged. "Do not deceive yourself with such
nonsense. My father-in-law prattled of things he *said* he
had learned; she picked it up parrot fashion and uses it
to impress. She is only a child, and a willful, hysterical

one, with a poor heritage and a worse temper. I shall look to you to keep her out of the way when the company arrives. Last time anyone came to this house, she darted into the parlor and snatched a vase right out of the hands of Dr. Montgomery—having the audacity to declare he was about to harm it with carelessness. That I will *not* have happen again. Do you understand, Saranna? If Damaris cannot learn control and proper behavior, then she needs the discipline of some establishment intended to control those of uncertain intellect. It needs only another such outburst or two before company, and even my father, hearing such a report, will agree to such a step!"

There it was in the open—the thing Saranna had feared for Damaris. She had enough belief in the inflexibility of Honora's will to realize that this was more a dire promise than a warning threat.

There remained Gerrad Fowke. If she could only talk freely to him perhaps he could provide the understanding and safety for Damaris. Only—she herself might have been reading far more into Mr. Fowke's sympathy. As she went upstairs a few moments later, Saranna recalled only too well that other statement which Honora had uttered with her usual complete assurance—that Gerrad Fowke had discussed the matter of Rufus Parton and had agreed with Honora that the housekeeper's son meant an excellent match and a secure future for Saranna herself.

How could he! Suddenly that old pricking constriction was back in her throat and she fought tears. Mr. Fowke—how could he believe that she would be happy—or even safe with the man she had seen beating a helpless animal? One who, when he looked at her, made her feel as dirty as if she had slipped and fallen into a bog? How much did he know about Rufus Parton? Or was he only accepting Honora's own report on Rufus' character?

"Saranna—" She looked up, startled. There was no lamp lighted in the room. But the gray of twilight displayed Damaris standing between her and the window.

"*She* told Gerrad you want to marry Rufe—"

"Yes!" Saranna echoed a little forlornly.

"I heard her talking about it when they came back this afternoon. He wanted to know why *she* let Rufe hang around; he spoke sharp about it. *She* let him think you asked her to have him, that you knew Rufe before you came here, when he was away. I don't think Gerrad liked that. His face went stiff and his eyes stared at her. She was all laughing and fluttering," Damaris' voice was scornful, "like *she* always is when he is around. But I am afraid he believed her."

"Since it is not the truth, in time Mr. Fowke must learn that," Saranna answered without any confidence herself in that reply.

"Not with *her* around," Damaris stated. "'Water and words are easy to pour, impossible to recover.'" There was almost a note of smug satisfaction in what must be another quote from her grandfather's store of Chinese wisdom. "*She* 'most always gets her way. She couldn't with Grandfather, though—and she isn't going to with me!" Damaris' assertion had the fervor of a vow.

"Damaris, you must be very careful," Saranna warned. "She told me you made a scene when a visitor picked up a vase once before. If you do that again, before witnesses, she will have backing in—"

"In trying to prove I'm a crazy person? I know, I told you I know! A lot more than you do. For example, I know why she wants me gone from Tiensin—why she talked at first about sending me to a school up North, and now"—for the first time Damaris' voice wavered a little—"and now to someplace else—worse. She wants Tiensin. When she married my father, she thought she would get it. He had been sick for a long time. But she married him. And then she tried to play mistress here. But Grandfather soon put her to rights. *She* didn't like that, but she was afraid of Grandfather. You see—he knew what she was. She couldn't get around him with smiles and sweet talk, not at all.

"But she knew he was old and when he died, my father would be master. Then she could have everything her own way. Only my father died when the boat upset, he was going down to Baltimore to see a new doctor. And Grandfather was still alive. Then she thought she would still be able to give orders when he was gone.

"Only he called in Judge Ralestone and Squire Barkley and he talked to them a long time. After that, he made the will and she did not get anything at all—'cept a little money my father had left her."

Saranna seized upon the two names Damaris mentioned. "Judge Ralestone and Squire Barkley—where are they now, Damaris?"

The younger girl shook her head. "They're no help. The Judge—he had a stroke and has to stay in bed over at Bremeade. And Squire Barkley has gone West to see about some land claims out there."

Saranna sighed, for a moment it had sounded so easy—that there might be two responsible members of the community to whom she could appeal if Damaris were placed in any danger, two who knew her grandfather's desires for her.

"Saranna," Damaris put out her hand to touch that of the older girl, "don't worry so. Maybe I *can* tell you more. But I have to wait and see—for a while. And I promise that I won't do anything *she* won't like. At least not until I know more about what may happen."

"*I Ching* again?" Saranna asked anxiously. She did not want the child to depend on some superstition out of another world.

Damaris laughed. "Perhaps. Only this time, I won't be using the wands. Only—I do promise, Saranna. And—" she moved forward, putting out her hand to touch the older girl's sleeve, with some of that same outpouring of emotion she had shown when she had said she was glad Saranna had come to Tiensin, "please *don't* worry." She repeated earnestly, "There's—there's something here which Honora doesn't know anything about, something Grandfather said would protect me if I ever need help. We'll be safe—'cause I'm going to see that you are, also. That I promise, too."

There was complete confidence in Damaris' tone. However, when she had gone, the thoughts ran round and round in Saranna's head. She could not concentrate on her book, she had no wish to look at the clothes she had put to one side to deal with. Restlessness drove her from her rocker, set her to looking out of the window down on the high-grown hedge. There were no points of light there which might be eyes, no sign of any life beyond it. Dream—?

At last she dragged herself to bed. But this night the Emperor's cat had no influence on sending her any deeper into slumber. She had only broken snatches of sleep, and awoke in the morning with a slightly aching head and heavy eyes. At least Honora was leaving and to-morrow was Sunday. They were to drive to the small church for the service. Perhaps in the peace and quiet it offered, she could find some ease of mind.

Honora was in a bustle of leave-taking during their early breakfast which she interrupted several times to give further orders to Mrs. Parton concerning the preparations for the coming company, to ask about the whereabouts of various articles of luggage which she was sure had been, or promised to be, forgotten. Her attention was completely on herself and her own concerns—which was a relief Saranna had not quite expected.

Damaris, on the other side of the table, ate quietly what was offered her, said nothing. She did not even watch her stepmother with those sudden sidewise glances which always seemed to Saranna to be too measuring, too knowing for her years. She walked sedately down the box-walled avenue to the wharf and stood there beside Saranna, as if there had never been a rebellious thought in her head, while the sloop Gerrad Fowke had put at Honora's disposal pulled out into the current of the river.

But when her stepmother was well out of earshot and nearly out of sight, Damaris came to life.

"You have the use of the sewing machine," she caught at Saranna's hand eagerly. "You must show me how to use it, too. Then I can have it just as Grandfather always

intended I should. Come on—I want to show you something first!"

Tugged by that demanding grip, Saranna returned to
the house, was urged by Damaris into the upper hallway.
But they did not go to the younger girl's own chamber.
Instead, Damaris stood by the last door of all, and from
under her apron, she brought a large key which she had
tied about her middle with a length of somewhat grimy
string.

"In here! And you mustn't tell now—promise!"

"I must know what I am promising," Saranna ob-
jected.

"This—in here are some more things Grandfather
brought home. He told me they were to be mine when I
was a grown-up lady—some of them—others— Well,
those are part of the secret. But I can show you all—
'cause they are mine to have, or give away!"

She had turned the key even as she spoke, now she
pushed open the door. Saranna hesitated for a moment,
wondering just what new mystery lay beyond, but Damaris' hand on her arm again fairly jerked her inside.

"Come on! The Poker is never going to get in here.
And even *she* doesn't know anything about it. If she did,
she'd be pushing in in a minute. But it's not hers and
she's not going to take it."

There was an uncurtained window, and, from it, the
morning sun made a golden path across a dusty floor. Set
around the walls of the room were chests made of red
leather, decorated with golden cut-out ornaments.

"One for each season." Damaris relocked the door
firmly behind them. With a pointing finger she indicated
the chests in turn. "Spring, Summer, Autumn, Winter.
The Chinese people keep their clothes this way—folded
up ready for each time of year. Only it isn't clothes that is
inside them now. Look!"

She flung up the lid of Spring so Saranna could gaze
down upon a richness of fine brocade such as she had
never known existed. The material was a green-blue and
interwoven with gold thread in a pattern of a long-legged

bird in flight. Damaris quickly lifted the edge of its folds to show another such length below, this of a delicate apple-green shade, also with an intricate woven pattern. Below that was one which was neither coral nor true red, but between them in shade.

Around the room Damaris sped showing what lay in each box. There were not only brocades, but silks, some so fine to the touch that they seemed hardly heavier than a gossamer veiling—all colors except yellow—all like a garden of flowers released to the sunlight.

Carefully Damaris closed Winter when she had displayed the last of this woven richness. "No yellow— because that is the Emperor's color and Grandfather could not ever buy anything which might be woven for the Palace. But all the rest—they're to make dresses. And if you can teach me how to sew— I would never show these to Prune Face. She would have run right away to tell *her*. And think how *she* would want this!"

"Damaris, these are too precious, too rich for us to work with." Saranna was appalled at the thought of putting scissors to any of those shimmering, priceless lengths.

"Not now." To her relief, Damaris nodded. "I would have to learn a lot. But someday, yes. And you must choose a piece too, Saranna." She stood back and studied the older girl. "One of the greens, I think—maybe that lighter one in the Spring box. It makes one think of new plants pushing up into the sun. Yes, I do believe you must have that green from Spring."

"Not now—" Saranna denied.

" 'Course not. If you had a dress like that now, *she* would be right after us to know where you got it. But someday—you'll have it for your own self."

"We'll wait and see," Saranna temporized. She watched Damaris once more unlock and lock the door, return the key to hiding under her apron. In the finest shops in Boston, the older girl had never seen such lengths as Captain Whaley had gathered. That a man would buy such material and store it puzzled her a little.

Damaris had not been born, she understood, until long after his retirement from the Far East. Had it been the color, the texture, the sheer beauty which had so awakened the Captain's covetousness that he could not resist adding them to his collection? What had he originally intended to use them for? Curtains? The heavy brocades might have served well in that manner. But the light silks, no. It puzzled her a little as Damaris turned to her once more and said eagerly:

"Mrs. Parton has to let us into the sewing room now. *She* said you could use the machine. I'll bring my workbox. There, that's the sewing room." She pointed to a door just beyond that of the locked chamber of the four chests.

Two long steps brought Damaris to it and she turned the handle. The knob gave. She nodded triumphantly back over her shoulder at Saranna.

"Yes, it's open. I'm going to get my workbox and tell Millie to bring yours and all those dresses and things. Then you can start to show me—"

She was off before Saranna could answer, leaving the door she had tried a little ajar. The older girl opened it wider to enter.

X

Shih Ho *Criminal Proceedings*

Sunday, until midafternoon, was indeed a day of peace as Saranna had hoped it would be. They had driven in the carriage, accompanied by Mrs. Parton (with Rufus, together with the very taciturn and self-effacing Collis Parton, riding escort), to the church. Luckily, the Partons did not try to share the family pew which she and Damaris enjoyed in solitary splendor. Thus Saranna was relieved of her unwelcome admirer's presence during the service.

Saranna studied the vicar with close attention, more intent upon the personality of the man than his sermon. In Sussex, Pastor Willis had been a bulwark of aid to those in distress. She wondered whether this far more worldly appearing man might possibly be one in whom she could confide her doubts and forebodings. But there was something about him which she could not warm to, a certain loftiness of manner, as if he felt himself in a superior station of life, so assured of his own correct position that he would not welcome anything which might tend to ruffle the even tenor of his ways.

Mr. Fowke occupied another large pew to her left on the other side of the church, doubtless that belonging to his family. She sighted on the walls various memorial tablets to both Fowkes and Whaleys, already worn looking, though the church was less than a hundred years old.

When the service at last came to an end, Saranna was

eager to be on her way back to Tiensin. She had not been unconscious of those curious glances flashed in her direction from beneath the brims of bonnets and hats when she and Damaris had taken their seats. And, though no one ought properly to think of one's clothes on such an occasion, she had been painfully aware that hers were poorer even than those of the black servants who sat in the galleries above. That she must make such a distressed appearance on her first meeting with the neighborhood she found mortifying.

"Miss Stowell, Damaris—" It was Mr. Fowke, tall beaver in hand, who awaited them as they edged their full skirts out of the pew door, into the aisle. "A pleasant day—"

For a moment, Saranna could forget the poor figure she made under the sharp eyes of those who were undoubtedly Honora's acquaintances. It *was* a pleasant day. Though their drive here had been marred for her because Rufus had urged his mount (except where the road was mercifully too narrow) up-level with the carriage, watching her slyly. A surveillance she had refused to acknowledge in any form.

"Yes," she answered breathlessly now, once more aware that a large portion of the feminine section of the congregation were focused on their meeting, that ears were being strained to catch the slightest word of this exchange. She had no doubt that Gerrad Fowke was very much the subject of female speculation in the neighborhood. And there must be more than a little disappointment that he had already fixed his attentions on Honora.

"Pleasant enough for a short drive?" he asked.

"Where?" Damaris was not in the least shy and Saranna was very glad at that moment that the younger girl did have the tendency to forwardness.

"Past Queen's Pleasure," he said. "Even Mrs. Parton cannot demand that you be at the table before one, and I promise to have you back safely again before that hour. Since she shares your carriage, as I noticed, that will further delay her plans." He was smiling and Saranna smiled uncertainly back.

With Mrs. Parton to accompany them, there would certainly be no impropriety in such a small divergence from their path. And she had to admit to herself that she wanted to go, to see the old Manor Gerrad Fowke was slowly rescuing from the ruin into which his cousin had plunged the estate.

"Oh—I want to!" Damaris caught eagerly at Saranna's gloved hand. "We can, can't we?"

They had reached the door of the church and Mr. Fowke bowed slightly to the housekeeper who, in her stiff, bottle-green best, rustled up to join them.

"I have persuaded the young ladies to make a short detour on their way home—past Queen's Pleasure. I will promise not to delay your household arrangements for long. Perhaps your husband and your son can carry on to Tiensin any message you wish to give the cook."

Mrs. Parton's small mouth opened as if she were about to utter some protest. Did it close again because of Mr. Fowke's air of calm assurance? Saranna thought it unfair that no female could deliver such a quelling tone when she wished. At least no young female—

So it was Mr. Fowke who handed them into their carriage. Saranna was well aware that Rufus had moved forward. But Gerrad Fowke's complete indifference to young Parton's presence (as if Rufus were indeed invisible) was something Rufus could not prevail against. She saw his father put out a hand to his son's arm, draw him back. But there was a black look on the younger man's face.

"Queen's Pleasure, Sam—" Mr. Fowke gave the order easily and clearly to their coachman, mounted himself on a powerful looking gray horse to rein in, keeping pace with the carriage as they moved off at a sedate amble suitable for the day.

"The Manor has a romantic name—Queen's Pleasure—" Saranna observed.

Damaris nodded vehemently. "That's because a real

Queen gave the land to one of her favorite ladies-in-wait-ing. Later, that lady married one of the Fowkes, the one who built the first Manor House. Of course, that has been added to a lot. The first house was kind of small. But you can see Queen Anne's name carved over the door with a crowned lion. 'Cause she was the Queen who gave it at her pleasure."

When they pulled to a stop before the door, Mr. Fowke, who had trotted his mount ahead once they turned into the driveway, had dismounted and was wait-ing to hand them down from the carriage. Glancing up beyond his shoulder Saranna did indeed see that deeply cut name of the royal Anne and the weathered lion play-ing sentry.

Inside there was the smell of paint and freshly sawed wood, but the stair leading to the second floor was un-touched save by years of careful polishing. While the pan-eling about the walls glowed with the same patina pro-vided by age.

"Let me show you the drawing room. It is my inten-tion," Gerrad Fowke said to Saranna, "to retain as much of the original fittings of this room, of all the house at that matter, as I can. You see—the extra width of the wall provides window seats—" He gestured. "This center block which was the original house is united with two pa-vilions, one of which provides me with a library-office. The summer veranda is on the north facing the garden—cooler during the hottest weather. We Marylanders have a liking for our northern verandas, Miss Stowell."

"Miss Saranna, Miss Damaris—" Mrs. Parton had not advanced any farther into the room than just within the door. "It is getting on nigh to one o'clock."

Saranna was a little surprised that the housekeeper had had the audacity to interrupt them with a reminder of the time. Perhaps, in spite of her chaperonage, they had been forward in coming here. The girl was too igno-rant herself of the manners of the countryside to be sure. Though certainly Damaris had every right to accept such an invitation from her stepmother's betrothed, and she, herself, saw no harm in what they had done.

For a moment there was a shadow of a frown on Mr. Fowke's rugged face, as if he found Mrs. Parton overstepping the bounds of her position. Then he shrugged and turned to the door.

"I am sorry that it is so late," he said. "I would have liked you to see the rest of the house, all that is being done to render it comfortable after long disuse. My cousin kept to one room largely in the last years of his life. I do not think he even looked into the others. Perhaps another time we can arrange that—"

Mrs. Parton, her object achieved, had turned her back on them and was hurrying out. Damaris had wandered off to run her hand along one of the window seats.

Mr. Fowke inclined his head closer to Saranna's beveiled and out-of-fashion bonnet.

"Miss Stowell," his voice was so low that it hardly escaped the pitch of a whisper. "Is it true that you know young Parton—?"

He did not quite finish that sentence. It was as if he feared he had taken a liberty as a gentleman should disdain to use.

Before she thought, Saranna blurted out the truth.

"I know him only as Mrs. Parton's son."

"Then he did not—"

"You know," Damaris was back at their side, "this is the kind of house which ought to have a secret place for treasure—like Grandfather's—only maybe not as much." She shook her head determinedly, unable to admit that anything could ever eclipse the wonders of Tiensin.

To her despair, Saranna had no chance to hear the rest of Mr. Fowke's question. Did she dare to believe he was testing the truth of what Honora had told him? And that, if Damaris had given them only a moment or two more, she could have made plain her dilemma and perhaps even gained enough of his sympathy to enlist his influence with his bride-to-be on her behalf so that the

threat of Rufus Parton's interest in her would be less-
ened? If he had meant it so, they had no further chance
to go into the matter, for Damaris continued to chatter
on about treasure and secrets until they were once more
in the carriage.

Then, at Mrs. Parton's quick order, the carriage
moved off, leaving Gerrad Fowke on his doorstep and
hardly giving them a chance to thank him for their small
expedition away from Tiensin and all the shadows which
hung to obscure the future there.

"I like Mr. Fowke," Damaris announced as they went
along at a much smarter pace, suggesting that Sam was
properly influenced by the housekeeper to make their return as short a trip as possible. "But I like Tiensin better
than Queen's Pleasure. I think *she* does, too. Tiensin's
bigger and more important."

After lunch Saranna sought the parlor, which appeared to be one of the areas forbidden to Rufus. She
settled herself thankfully therein, her mother's worn
Bible in her hands. For a while she thought of the time
past, of the good days when Keturah Stowell had not
been driven by poverty to constant labor with her needle,
and there had been Bible stories on Sunday, the singing
of hymns to the music of the harpsichord which had been
Saranna's grandmother's prized possession. Then memories became too painful, and Saranna resolutely applied
herself to blocking away those which hurt the most.

She had been staring idly, more intent upon her own
thoughts, at the massive twelve-pannel teak screen which
stood half-concealing the door into the hall. It was at least
seven feet high, and a large portion of it was made up of
blue and white porcelain tiles; those in the upper panels
pictured landscapes, the lower ones contained figures.
Between these were carved characters which Damaris had
informed her represented the Five Blessings—counting
them out on her fingers as she had recited them.

Long life, riches, good health and peace of mind, love
of virtue, an end fulfilling the will of Heaven. Over only
two of those perhaps did mankind have control—the

third and the fourth; maybe only the fourth. The rest were certainly a matter of chance, fortune, or perhaps divine will. But one could *choose* to love virtue.

Her attention shifted from those deeply graven characters, looking so odd to the Western eyes, so difficult to see as true writing, to the fancifully pictured panels set below them. First, tall mountains in queer full humps, and dwarfed beneath them, three horsemen on a lonely road. For all its strangeness of line one sensed the barrenness, the threat of that country through which the horsemen pushed. Next came a garden, a man sitting under a flowering tree before a table on which were set out a scholar's tools, inkstone, inkstick, brush, paper, brush rest, seal—and a little behind him another man crosslegged on the ground, his back against a rock, a flute in his hands.

The third— Saranna's gaze became fixed. She sat upright as if jerked. How could she not have seen that before? Or maybe she had seen it without really remembering, until it came to life in her dream.

Because this was, in some ways, the very core of her dream!

There were three musicians to one side, a drum player, a man with a flute to his lips; the third, a woman cradling a long-necked stringed instrument against her knee as she plucked upon it. In the center of the tile postured a dancer, her long sleeve ends aflutter, the swirl of skirts about her as if she had only this second come to the end of her dance. Her hair was dressed in the same looped and puffed fashion as the Fox Lady's had been.

There were only two things missing—the circle of foxes watching, and the fox's mask. For this dancer in blue and white had entirely human features. That was it! Saranna must have seen this tile, some unremarked portion of her memory had stored it away as an impression. Then the stories she had heard about the foxes of Tiensin had released that memory in the form of a dream!

Only— Her hand went to where she still wore in hiding the jade pendant. Where had *that* come from then? If it had been the gift of the Fox Lady, why was it given? But, of course, there was no Fox Lady! She was a dream taken from a screen tile and—

"Saranna!"

Damaris whipped around the screen. Saranna had seen the younger girl defiant, she had seen her rebellious, and even in the grip of some fear she would not explain. But she had never seen her so distraught as she was at this moment.

"Saranna—it is gone! Out of the desk—it is gone!" Her words were scrambled together so it almost seemed she was stuttering in her distress.

Saranna held out her hands and Damaris caught them in a hold so tight that her nails made painful impressions in the older girl's flesh.

The child gave a great gulp. Then tears spilled from her eyes. She was shaking, clearly in a near-hysterical state. One which awoke fear in Saranna, remembering all Honora's hints of Damaris' heritage.

"Now then," she tried to speak calmly, in a way which would reach through whatever emotion had been so aroused in the younger girl, give her a sense of security so that she herself might discover what had brought on this perilous attack.

"What is gone?" She drew Damaris closer until the child half-perched on the sofa behind her. Damaris could not loosen that fierce grip she had on Saranna's hands. "What is gone?" the older girl repeated in as even a tone as she could, fighting the inner foreboding which made her want to shiver in turn.

"The book—Grandfather's book!" Damaris spoke with impatience, as if she expected Saranna to know at once and share with her that frantic sense of loss which plainly filled her.

"What kind of a book—?" Saranna continued. That this was plainly some volume Damaris valued highly there could be no mistake.

Damaris shivered. Her voice was as unsteady as her body when she answered:

"The book—the book Grandfather had made! The one about his treasures." Perhaps Saranna had had some calming effect upon her for now she lifted her eyes and stared imploringly into the older girl's face.

"He—he made it about his treasures. It had drawings in it—of all the best things. The names of those written in Chinese. And then *he* wrote descriptions of the pieces in English. All about who might have made them, how old they were—everything the scholars and artists could tell him. He had the book specially bound with tribute silk—a piece which was supposed to come from an Emperor's own storehouse. It was so important. Grandfather never, never allowed it to be taken out of the library. He had a special drawer in his desk and he kept that locked. I was the only one—the only, only one with a key to open it!

"But, Saranna, when I went to look for it just now—the drawer was empty. It was gone! Who could have taken it?"

"I don't know, but we shall find out!" Maybe she was promising more with those words than she could deliver. But at least Damaris needed all her support at this moment. "Show me where it was; perhaps there is some sign there—"

"Of who took it?" Damaris' despair had changed now to eagerness in a mercurial fashion which Saranna did not like. But that she had accomplished this much in reducing Damaris' reaction to the loss was perhaps good.

The younger girl held on to one of Saranna's hands, hurrying her out into the hall, across that to the library. There the curtains pulled completely across the windows, the drooping drapes gave the room an austere gloom, which even the rows of richly bound books did nothing to lighten.

The desk stood in a commanding spot not far from the fireplace and indeed, one drawer stood open. Saranna saw, as she approached, that the drawer itself had been lined in velvet. As if it were meant to act as a jewel case to enshrine and guard some irreplaceable gem or gems. It would appear from the safe Captain Whaley had had fashioned to protect his book that he considered it also one of his treasures, equal to those others whose descriptions it contained.

Saranna knelt down by the desk as Damaris freed her hand. She pushed the drawer closed. It ran very easily and smoothly until the lock edge touched. Then she could see the marks there. Though she was no expert, she was sure that this had not been opened by any key such as the one Damaris had said was in her possession; no, plainly it had been forced.

Rising she went to the bell cord, gave a resolute pull. This was one matter concerning which she certainly could ask questions. And she intended to do just that right now.

XI

K'uei *Opposition*

When the houseman John came in answer to that summons, Saranna, rather than Damaris, was in command of the situation.

"John, please ask Mrs. Parton to come here. It is of the greatest importance."

His eyes dropped from meeting her gaze. "She— Miss Saranna, she don't like never to be called on Sunday afternoon. She never likes—"

"I said it was important, John. I will take the responsibility. This is a grave matter. Please tell her that we must see her at once!"

He went reluctantly. Damaris gave a sudden laugh which was almost as sharp as a fox's bark.

"She's going to be very angry, you know. She takes a nap. What do you want with her, Saranna? Do you think she took the book?"

"Since Mrs. Parton is in charge of the staff, she must be informed before we question anyone," Saranna explained. "Who is responsible for cleaning the library, Damaris?" Though she was sure the theft was not the work of any of the servants. There was plainly a purpose in taking such a book, which in itself could have but little value, no matter what the Captain had thought about it.

"John, he does some, and Emily. But what would they want with the book, Saranna? They can't even read. And they know that they aren't ever to touch that drawer.

Why would anyone want it—?" Damaris had calmed down from the agitation that had gripped her when she found the drawer empty.

"I don't believe any servant took it," Saranna returned frankly. "Not unless they were ordered to do so. As you say, such a book would have no meaning for them."

Once more she knelt to examine the drawer lock carefully. She believed from the gouges in the wood that some slender but strong instrument had been used to pry until the lock gave.

"Was it open when you found it?" She glanced up at Damaris.

"Just a little. I had the key and I put it in the lock before I really saw that it was pulled open just a little." Damaris plumped down beside her. "Then—when I pulled it all the way out—I saw that the drawer was empty."

"When was the last time you looked at it?" Saranna asked.

"Three days ago—I wanted to find out about something—" Damaris had leaned forward to stare down once again into the velvet-lined space. Her tone was evasive, but there was no need to demand from her why she had wanted the treasure list. Not now at least. "It was there. And I locked the drawer when I put it back—"

"What has happened?" Mrs. Parton had come into the library so quietly that Saranna was startled to find her standing beside the desk, observing them both with her usual unexpressive countenance.

"We have just discovered," Saranna arose to confront her, "that a book belonging to Captain Whaley, one which was always kept locked in this drawer, is missing. It was here three days ago, but when Miss Damaris came to get it this afternoon she found the lock broken and the book gone—"

There was no change in Mrs. Parton's expression. "I'm sure that there must be some mistake. A book is of no value. And there has been no stranger in this room.

None of our people would touch that which did not belong to them."

"Nevertheless, the lock is clearly forced, as you can see for yourself." Saranna refused to be quelled by the housekeeper's manner. "Miss Damaris has the only key to the drawer, and the book was of concern only to her. She would not force this to steal from herself; there would be no need. Will you question the servants concerning who has been in this room, or shall I in your presence? This is not a matter of no import. And the book does have a value of its own. It is a complete listing of all the pieces of Captain Whaley's collection."

The lips of Mrs. Parton's too small mouth twitched.

"You have no authority in this house, Miss," she returned with a boldness which approached insolence. "I shall inform Mrs. Whaley when she returns. Then, if she thinks it right and proper, questions can be asked."

"*She* has no authority here!" Damaris pushed from behind the desk to stand before the housekeeper. "This isn't *her* house! It is *mine*. And if Saranna wants to ask questions, then I say she can."

That twitch of the lips had become a malicious smile. "You do not give orders here either, Miss Damaris, not until you come of age. Mrs. Whaley, she's in charge until her father returns. And you had better not forget that if you know what's good for you. Also, you had better not go accusing people of taking things. How do we know that you have not hid this book yourself and made up a tale—like all those other wild ones—just to get someone into trouble? The Captain, maybe he would stand for your stories, but Mrs. Whaley won't. I warn both of you to keep quiet if you don't want trouble—"

With that she moved out of the room, leaving Damaris flushed of face, and Saranna, shaken at this display of the woman's assurance, speechless for the moment. Mrs. Parton would never have dared answer so, the older girl thought, unless she were certain that her own position was entirely secure. And her warning meant that indeed Honora had taken the reins at Tiensin and intended to hold them.

"I know—" Damaris burst out. "I know now who took it!"

"Mrs. Parton? But why?"

"No—not Poker. *She* did! She must have! But I don't know why—unless," Damaris' thin shoulders hunched as if fearing a whiplash across them in a punishing blow, "unless, she wants someone to know—to know all about the collection! I won't let her! I will never let her take any of it! Never, never, never!"

"But you have no proof of this," Saranna felt bound to say, though Damaris' suggestion made logical sense.

"Who else would want it?" demanded Damaris bitterly. "It would be of no use to anyone except a person who wanted to know all about Grandfather's treasure. I think she took it to Baltimore with her to show to someone there. If she has—" her hands doubled into fists and she beat on the top of the desk, her agitation increasing again, "I'll—I'll—"

"Damaris," Saranna moved quickly to the child's side, put an arm around her shoulders. "Listen to me very carefully. This is so important—did your grandfather have any friend, any man of business beside those two of whom you spoke to me—someone he trusted very much?"

For a moment it seemed she was not getting through the cloud of Damaris' impotent anger. Then the child's scowl became thoughtful.

"Grandfather didn't visit anyone. The Judge—Squire, they used to come here to see him. There's his daybook, unless *she* has that, too."

"Daybook?" Saranna repeated.

"He kept account of his letters in it—who he wrote to and when." Damaris freed herself from the other girl's hold and went around the desk, this time opening another drawer. "Here it is!"

She took out a book not unlike a merchant's ledger, though not quite so large. "Why do you want to know about Grandfather's friends?" she asked, as she laid it flat on the desk top.

"I want to know if my brother is your only guardian, or if there is someone else in Baltimore who knows about you and Tiensin."

Damaris shrugged. "It wouldn't matter much, would it really? They'd only talk to *her,* and then they would believe what *she* told them. No—there's only one way—" She stopped abruptly as if her thoughts now outran her words in speed, or else they were such that she had no intention of sharing. Then, suddenly she smiled.

"I think I know—" she said. "If you will help me, Saranna. Then let her plan all she wants to! She won't find what she's after!"

"What do you mean?"

"We'll hide the treasure!" Damaris' eyes were alight. "If she comes back—and has some plan to take it—well, it just won't be here!"

"But how can we—" Saranna was again disturbed. She could understand Damaris' distress, her desire to put the collection beyond the reach of anyone who might sell all or part of it. But she had no intention of supporting the child in the belief that this could be done.

"We'll have to do it at night—" Damaris' voice quickened. "There are all those hampers stored in the cellar— the ones that most of the treasures came in. Grandfather never got rid of those. Perhaps he thought someday the collection might have to be moved. We can get those and pack, and then hide it. Yes, in the *one* place *she* would never dare to look! Oh, Saranna, it will work—it will!"

"But we can't—" Saranna's protest was silenced as Damaris leaned forward across the desk and caught her arm. The fingers of the younger girl's other hand were raised to her lips; her attention was centered beyond Saranna at the hall door.

Saranna took the hint. She picked up the ledger, being sure she would keep a hand on that. Damaris might be correct in believing that Honora's word would be taken over any complaints from them, yet there was a chance that someone would listen to them. Her own idea—to hide the treasure, Saranna took as a wild fancy.

Damaris spoke again, more calmly, and a little loudly, as if she wished her words to be overheard.

"That is what Grandfather always said, you know—" She might have been ending some speech, and the words had no connection, or little, with what they had been discussing.

Saranna was quick-witted enough to play her game. "Very wise, Damaris."

"Yes, 'Fishes see the worm, but not the hook.' He knew a lot of those. Like, 'To talk goodness is not good—only to do it is.' "

Her attitude was still one of listening. Then she nodded, and added in the faintest of whispers—pushing close to Saranna as she did so:

"If you stand straight, do not fear a crooked shadow. We can do what I want—you will see! Tonight! Promise you will help, Saranna!"

"But—it is impossible, Damaris—" Saranna, too, dropped to the lowest of voices.

The younger girl shook her head firmly. Her hand was tight now on Saranna's arm, drawing her to the far end of the room. Even there she continued to whisper. "No, I have been thinking. We *can* do it! You don't know, you see. It will not be easy, but we can do it. If you won't help, then I'll have to try by myself. There is a very safe place waiting. We have only to pack the pieces and put the hampers in a certain place—then there're others—"

"The servants? But they won't disobey Mrs. Parton—" Saranna protested.

"No—not John, or Rose, or Millie, or any like *them*. The other ones—from the garden. I—I should not tell you this, Saranna—'cause I promised. But Grandfather would say to now, if he knew. There are those in the garden—they'll help us." She gestured through the window in the direction of the hedge-walled, forbidden territory.

If this was only a fancy, Damaris was so deeply immured in it that it seemed real to her. And her voice carried conviction. There was only one small shred of proof that Saranna had—that jade pendant. Somehow the thought of that was bolstering her dawning belief that Damaris indeed knew much more than she told and that there might well be some source of aid in Tiensin itself. Though that did not quiet Saranna's uneasiness nor her decision to try to find some friend of Captain Whaley's who might be interested enough to stand as Damaris' advocate against any overt move of Honora's.

"I will do what I can," she promised.

Again in her own room, Saranna put the ledger down on the table and began to turn its pages. Apparently it had not been opened for some time, because some of those pages stuck together. And most of the entries were concerned with items of business which had no use or meaning for her. She found frequent references to the Judge, to Squire Barkley, and then to Mr. Sanders. Mr. Sanders! Why had she not thought of him before?

As a man of law, an attorney for her brother, one trusted enough to be asked to escort her to Baltimore, surely he knew something of the situation here at Tiensin. Had Saranna made impression enough on him of her own good sense that he might believe what she said if she spoke to him? She could not get to Baltimore, of course. But suppose she wrote him a letter, asked him to come to Tiensin? Would he heed such a request from her? Or would he speak of it to Honora and so immediately defeat any chance she had?

There were so many "ifs," yet if she found no other reference in this book, then Mr. Sanders must be her resource. Saranna sat with her chin propped on her hand, her elbow planted on the ledger to keep it open. She could write guardedly to Mr. Sanders. After all, she had a small excuse. The funds which Pastor Willis had promised to forward to her after the sale of the contents of their cottage in Sussex—Mr. Sanders was to collect those for her. She had every right now to enquire if he had received any such, or heard from Sussex. She would write such a letter tomorrow and it could be taken down to Baltimore with the weekly supply boat which was to sail the next day.

Cheered by the thought of this definite action, Saranna descended the stairs in a better frame of mind than she had had since Damaris had come to her with the report of the loss of the book. It would seem that the younger girl in turn had also decided to set that behind her. She spoke cheerfully at the table of their visit to Queen's Pleasure.

That Damaris had at all forgotten her own plans for that night, Saranna was sure was not so. She was even more convinced when the younger girl went quite willingly to bed at an early hour. So she sat up herself, uneasily writing, still unsure what she must do if and when Damaris came to demand her participation in the wild scheme.

Fair as the day had been, the night brought clouds and distant flashes of lightning, though as yet no storm hit Tiensin. Saranna had turned out her lamp, lit the cat lantern, and partially undressed, laying aside her weight of petticoats for a wrapper which was far less cumbersome.

She was not disappointed. There was the faintest of creaks from the door, then a small figure came into the very dim light. Damaris stood there, not wearing the skirts of a young lady, but trousers and a tight jacket not unlike those Saranna had seen in her dream on the old woman who served the Fox Lady.

"Come—"

"Damaris—this can't be done!" Saranna protested.

"It can—you'll see! I've asked for help. It'll be here. Come—now! We'll have to hurry or we'll never get it all put away!"

Saranna had no way, short of locking the child in her room, to prevent her attempting this. It was best that she did go and prove that this certainly could not be accomplished. Help? What help? What servant within these walls would dare to brave the Partons and help a mistress who was without any power?

Girding her wrapper tightly about her, Saranna crept along behind Damaris. The child seemed to have cat's eyes in the dark. Or else she had flitted on other similar expeditions enough times so that such adventures in the dark were familiar.

They descended the stairs and Damaris sped straight for the front door. She slid back the latch and opened it, her small figure hardly distinguishable in the heavy gloom. There was movement in that slit which gave on the outer world; two figures slipped through.

Who—?

Maybe if Damaris had no allies within the house, she did have among the field hands. But that was even more surprising—

"Come!" Damaris caught at Saranna's hand, drew her to the parlor. The other figures padded on down the hall, apparently on some errand of their own.

Damaris left her just inside the door, went to the table. A moment later, there was a flare of light from the lamp. The child turned quickly from that, hurried to open display cases. There was no doubt that she meant exactly what she said; she intended to see that none of the collection remained within Honora's reach.

There was a faint scratching from the door. Damaris, already lifting pieces of jade from their accustomed settings to stand them on table tops, pointed with her chin. Her voice was the lowest of whispers, barely reaching Saranna's ears—

"Open!"

Saranna, completely bewildered, obeyed.

Two men entered noiselessly, carrying between them two hampers of wickerwork, one placed upon the other. They set those down without a word and turned to go out again. Saranna caught sight of their faces—

Chinese! They were as alien as the elderly maid of the moon-doored house had been.

Neither glanced at Saranna, but were swiftly gone once more into the hall.

"Come on!" Damaris whispered impatiently. "You've got to help me pack." She flung back the lid of one of the wicker hampers and lifted out two inner trays, to clear the bottom portion of the container. Saranna, completely fascinated, saw that the inner part of the hamper was heavily padded, as was each tray in turn. And in that padding, were depressions of various sizes and shapes, each plainly intended to contain safely a certain one of the precious objects.

She found herself on her knees, carefully fitting into its proper place the pieces Damaris passed to her. They had not quite finished the bottom section when the Chinese returned—this time with three more hampers.

Back and forth trotted Damaris, pointing out to Saranna just where each piece must go. They filled the first hamper and Damaris knotted its cords. Saranna found that she fell into the rhythm of the work as if her whole life had been concerned with such packing. They finished with all in the parlor save the tall screen, moved on to the library, where another pile of hampers appeared as soundlessly, and with the same efficiency.

There were no more hampers, and Saranna caught sight of the two men who had never spoken, now carrying the loaded filled ones one at a time out of the front door, to return in what seemed a very short time and select another. Saranna's back ached from kneeling to pack, but Damaris had finished taking all the pieces from their display shelves and now squatted, as intent on fitting them away as Saranna was.

The older girl was so tense she feared her very touch might splinter some of the delicate porcelain. She kept listening for any sound which might herald a descent upon them by some member of the household. But what she did hear instead was the approach of the storm. The last two hampers had to be transported out into the rain. Transported where? And who *were* the two silent helpers upon whom they had depended this night?

Damaris shut and latched the front door. They were once more in the deep dark, since the lamps were now out. There was a crack of thunder which made Saranna cringe at its sudden noise. Then she almost cried out as Damaris' arm went around her waist.

"We did it, we really did!" The child's voice was full of triumph.

"But who were those men? And where did they take everything?" Saranna wanted to know. She felt as if she had been under some spell from which that clap of thunder had awakened her. Why had she obeyed Damaris so meekly without any questions? This almost had the same force as that dream.

"Don't worry." Damaris sounded far too blithe. Saranna's irritation first with herself and then with the child, grew. "They are safe—and the treasure is safe now. It is where nobody dares try to get it. I put it where Grandfather would have wanted it if he had known about Honora."

"Damaris—you've got to tell me where!" Saranna flinched from another terrific crackle of thunder.

"It's in the garden—safe in the Princess' garden. I can't tell you any more. I said that only because you have the fox head. So she must trust you a little."

That "she" did not refer to Honora, of course. But— did Damaris mean the Fox Lady? What was a dream and what was not? If she only *knew*!

"Come on—we've got to get to bed. Sometimes when it storms like this the Poker goes around looking for open windows—"

Damaris pulled her toward the stairs, and Saranna felt her way up. She must know—she *must make* some sense of this. But Damaris had slipped on ahead, and the older girl felt that even if she cornered the child in her room she might not get any more out of her tonight. But there was always tomorrow, and Saranna could wait that long in spite of her impatience and uneasiness.

XII

Hsü *Waiting*

But there was something Saranna could do besides demand explanations from Damaris; she could finish her letter to Mr. Sanders. She took out her small lap desk, brought out paper, made sure her pen was properly trimmed. Only when all her preparations were complete, she chewed at the tip of her quill, trying to think reasonably and coherently. She had a reason for writing, to ask whether he had heard from Pastor Willis concerning any small sum of money left after the sale. However, to that the lawyer could curtly reply yes or no, and she would have no immediate contact to ask him concerning Damaris' protection. At last Saranna believed that she had chanced on the proper formula. She was a young female, deprived of her natural guardian by Jethro's absence. Could she not play upon that note, suggesting that she needed mature, masculine advice concerning some problem which she did not wish to entrust to a letter?

A debt! That was it—some debt she had not formally known about. And with that excuse, she was only stretching the truth a little. For she did feel a debt of responsibility toward Damaris, though they were no blood kin. But she might word her letter in such a way that Mr. Sanders could believe her dilemma now arose out of the past.

Saranna wrote slowly word by word, weighing each sentence as she set it down:

136

Honored Sir:

Since my worthy brother is now at sea and will not return to us for many months, I am turning to you as his legal adviser and good friend, to ask a very great favor.

There has lately come to me knowledge that I have an obligation, to which I was heretofore blind. It is of the greatest necessity that I give an answer very soon to this problem. However, my ignorance of such matters is great. I feel that I need well-informed advice as to how I must now proceed in this affair which is too detailed and private a one to set out in any letter.

I am begging your indulgence when I ask if you can arrange a meeting wherein I may explain this difficulty and gain from you guidance as to my future conduct.

I am, sir, with respect—

Stiff and formal. However, such an approach Saranna judged would be to the taste of Mr. Sanders, perhaps impress him more than anything which was in the least effusive or struck a more friendly tone. She checked the page for both penmanship and any errors of grammar or spelling, gave a sigh as she folded and sealed it. The letters going out of Tiensin, though those were very few save during the days when Honora was in residence, were placed in a post bag which in turn was taken down to the wharf to be collected by any sloop inward bound to Baltimore. Saranna hated to entrust this missive to such an arrangement, but she knew no other way to send it.

Now she shivered as she turned down the lamp, undressed, and crept into a bed where the sheets seemed chill. She should be tired after their frenzied activities of packing below, yet she was never more wide awake. The tension of that work still held. And what would be the reaction in the morning?

In the absence of Honora or any guests the great parlor and library were kept closed. Yet surely before the

end of the day, Mrs. Parton, on some necessary household errand, would discover the loss. What would happen
then? Such a large-scale disappearance of the whole collection, with the exception of a few too large pieces (such
as the blue and white parlor screen), could not be the
work of an ordinary thief. No—it would be speedily
guessed who was responsible.

Then what—?

Saranna sought and discarded explanation after explanation which might be advanced for the stripping of
the room. That the action would be traced back to Damaris, she was entirely certain. And where *had* those
hampers been taken?

There was only one logical place that Damaris had
given—the hidden garden. The Chinese men were clearly
from that. Then was also the Fox Lady a truth? Were
they her servants? But who or what was she? And how
had she come to Tiensin?

What of Gerrad Fowke's story of how Captain Whaley
had imported Chinese servants to labor on the house and
the garden? However, Mr. Fowke had stated they had all
been returned to their native land when their work here
was done. Who had counted them—then? The Fox Lady
—Saranna now summoned to mind all her memories of
her meeting with that strange dancer in the moonlight.

The woman's grace, the jewel box of a house in which
she lived—if it was not all part of a dream (and Saranna,
against her will, was beginning to think that it was not)—
then the dancer was plainly no servant but a personage of
standing and authority.

The Captain's—wife?

Saranna wondered. Had Captain Whaley indeed married some lady of birth and breeding in China and then
hesitated to bring her openly to the attention of the
neighborhood here, fearing that some narrowness of
prejudice might well preclude her being received honora-
bly as she should be? All that was plausible, except for the
fox visage. No woman born could wear a fox's mask for a
face!

Some deformity of birth—to blight her life?

Saranna's hand sought the fox pendant which still lay on her breast. Against her skin it was not as chill as the sheets; it rather seemed to generate a warmth of its own. In the dark she traced the carving with a fingertip. A white fox—she had seen at least two among that silent company who had watched the dancer. Did it have some meaning?

Damaris' Princess—the Fox Lady? And Damaris said the pendant was a mark of favor. Perhaps, now that Saranna herself had aided Damaris in this late act to hide the collection, the younger girl would be moved to more and complete explanations.

The storm which had raged was now spent. There were no more fierce cracks of lightning, roars of thunder, though the rain fell steadily outside. Saranna's hand turned on the pillow. She found herself watching the two rounds of light which marked the eyes of the Emperor's cat.

Somehow as she lay there, her hand upon the pendant, her tension began to ease until at last she slept.

Millie, in a flurry, aroused her once more. So that Saranna was still half-bemused with slumber she had not completely shaken off, when she descended to the breakfast room. Damaris stood by a window looking out on a dripping world. She smiled back over her shoulder at Saranna. "It is still raining," she commented. "What if it rains forty days and forty nights again? We might be washed right away—"

The prospect of that did not seem to dampen her spirits any. She had an almost festive air about her as she came to the table. To Saranna the younger girl had the appearance of one relieved from some burden, now at peace with herself and the world. Did Damaris believe that their looting of Tiensin would simply go unnoticed?

"This is a good day to sew," Damaris observed, helping herself liberally to hot biscuits and then to comb honey. "I took my basket to the sewing room before I came downstairs—"

Such unconcern Saranna could not share. But perhaps she could and must counterfeit an appearance of it. She agreed that it seemed an excellent day for some indoors employment, and then was caught up answering a round of questions Damaris showered upon her. Apparently the younger girl had collected some of the *Godey Ladies' Books* which Honora had left behind and had been studying the various fashion plates, now professing a desire to learn how to make this or that elegant trifle until Saranna warned her that such skills might well be beyond both of them.

Every time the door opened to admit John or one of the maids with fresh coffee, hot breads, or the like, Saranna braced herself to hear the alarm raised. When that did not come she found, to her surprise, that she was growing impatient, that she wanted to face the worst and get it safely behind her. Did Mrs. Parton (of whom they had seen nothing this morning so far) not inspect the rooms under her care? Even though Damaris insisted that the maids not be allowed to dust the collection, still the carpets must be brushed, and other housekeeping chores waited within the closed rooms.

Mrs. Parton's continued absence added to Saranna's sense of all not being well. At length, as they finished the meal, and Damaris paused in her flow of comment on what might or might not be fashionable, Saranna dared to ask the first question of her own:

"Where is Mrs. Parton?"

"Down at the quarters," Damaris returned promptly. "Old Jane is ill." For a moment her smile faded. "I wanted to go, but the Poker wouldn't let me. Old Jane, she was my mother's own nurse when she was just a little baby. But the Poker says she has a fever and it could be catching. Always afraid of something catching—the Poker is."

"But she went herself—" Saranna pointed out.

"Yes, but you ought to see her. She has an herb bag around her neck and she smelled—" Damaris inelegantly pinched her nose between thumb and finger. "Saranna," she drew closer to the older girl as they went out into the hall, "what's the matter? You kept looking at the door all the time as if you were afraid something horrible was going to come in—"

"But, Damaris," Saranna was taken aback, "surely you know that Mrs. Parton, that everyone will want to know where your grandfather's collection is! The minute they discover the pieces gone they will—"

Her words grew slower because Damaris was slowly shaking her head. The young girl flipped up her apron and showed under the string which had held the key to the room upstairs with the four camphor wood storage boxes. There were two more keys jangling against it now, both large and heavy.

"Locked," she explained. "Oh, I suppose the Poker will be upset when she finds them locked. But if she looks in her key basket she is not going to find her keys. That will give us the time—"

"Time for what?"

"Time for someone else to make sure that the treasure is never going out of Tiensin." Damaris seemed entirely confident, though Saranna had no equal belief that any amount of time right now would solve the problem. It would only defer the reckoning which they both must face sooner or later.

But perhaps her letter would reach Mr. Sanders if Damaris could continue to cover up the disappearance of the collection, even by so crude a method as merely locking doors and hiding keys. A little heartened by that thought, she hailed John who was just turning into the breakfast room and held out the sealed envelope she had taken from her apron pocket.

"For the mailbag, John, please—"

It seemed to Damaris that he took the letter reluctantly, just as he would not look directly at either girl, but rather kept his gaze mainly at their feet.

"Yes'm. Bad on the water today. Maybe no one goin' in. But we puts the bag down anyhow—"

"Who were you writing to?" Damaris had none of the

tact demanded to make social contacts easier. And Saranna gave her the answer she had ready. If there were listening ears, they would have a plausible explanation.

"Mr. Sanders. He undertook to collect some money for me—money from the sale back in Sussex. I am asking if he received it."

"You need some money?" Damaris appeared surprised. "But what about that Mr. Stowell left you?"

It was Saranna's turn to be astonished. "Money Jethro left me? But he didn't leave me any money. I did not even see him again before I came here."

Damaris nodded. "Then *she* took it! I thought so. *She* wants money, quite a lot. You see, she wants bride clothes. I think she buys so much all the time that she doesn't have enough pocket money to suit her. She doesn't get any from Tiensin. My grandfather made sure of that. All *she* has is a little money my father left her, not nearly enough, or so *she* says."

"But this money you say Jethro left me—how did you—"

Damaris smiled. "She left those *Lady Books* here and I had Rose get them out of her room. I wanted to see all about the new dresses and bonnets. And this was in one of them— See?"

From some hiding place under her apron, she brought out a sheet of paper which had been much creased and which now smelled of Honora's favorite violet scent.

Saranna:

This is in haste. I am sorry that events have moved so that we have not had a chance to become better acquainted. But that is a matter which shall be remedied upon my return. Honora tells me that you are deeply effected by your mother's passing and have begged her to allow you to retire to quiet at Tiensin. This I can understand and I hope that you will discover its air to be beneficial to both your health and your nerves.

In the meantime, however, I wish you to have
funds that you may prepare to take your proper
place in the best circles in Baltimore, such a position as a Stowell may claim by right of name.
Please use the enclosed to any advantage which
seems to you necessary to accomplish that.

Your affectionate brother—

"But I never saw this!" Saranna smoothed the paper between her fingers. What *had* Jethro enclosed with the letter which she had not received? She could only believe
that Damaris was right and there had been a sum of
money which was now missing.

"How could Honora dare?" There was wonder as well
as anger in her voice. Such an act would certainly be un-
covered as soon as Jethro returned. Did Honora have her
father so bemused that he would believe any lie she might
utter to cover her own interception of his message and
the appropriation of a sum which had accompanied it?

"She doesn't expect you ever to see her father again."

"What!" Saranna halted on the bottom step of the
stairs, stared at Damaris enough ahead of her so that the
girl's face, as she half-turned around to deliver that statement was nearly on a level with her own.

"I told you—" Damaris had the ghost of that sly look
about her, "I listen. She's afraid of you, not that she told
the Poker so. The Poker guessed, and I'm sure she's
right. *She*'s afraid that your brother is going to give you
things. And *she* wants it all for herself. The Poker knows
that. *She* didn't just go back to town to shop, though she'll
do that, all right. *She* went to see Mr. Sanders—"

Saranna caught her breath audibly. Mr. Sanders—her
own letter—

"*She* wants to make sure that Mr. Stowell didn't leave
you anything in his will. They say Brazil's awfully unhealthy, such a lot of fever down there—"

Saranna gripped Damaris' arm hard. "You don't
know what you're saying!"

"Oh, don't I?" The old sly maliciousness was to the

fore now, more than Saranna had seen it for days. "I heard the Poker and Mr. Poker talking about it. They think Rufus is going to marry you, take you away. *She* wants that done before her father comes back. Then he'll be mad at you, good and mad. Because he'd think Rufus isn't good enough for his sister. So *she*'s promised Rufus some money to do it, and maybe some more later if it all turns out like *she* plans. So she wouldn't care now if you learned about that—" Damaris pointed to the letter Saranna still held.

The older girl wanted to say she did not believe a word of what Damaris had just said, that the child was spinning some fantasy. Unfortunately, her story fitted all too well. Saranna gave a harried glance around her, feeling much like a fox who hears the cry of the hounds behind on his trail. Then she steadied herself with the thought that Honora might scheme all this but she, Saranna, was warned and she could make her own plans. That she was like a gaming piece to be moved around on some board at Honora's pleasure and to Honora's profit was not and never would be true!

Swiftly, she refolded the letter and tucked it into the folds of her chemisette beneath the edge of her outer bodice. She wanted nothing less than to sit quietly sewing, but she felt that such an occupation this morning might steady her nerves and give her a chance to think clearly about what she could do to escape the web Honora seemed to be spinning.

Millie awaited them in the sewing room. And the maid hastened to lay out the unpicked lengths of dresses which Saranna had been reducing to their basic materials in order to create something passably wearable out of Honora's castoffs. She had discovered that the satin top of one dress could be agreeably combined with a cashmere skirt, using lengths of the unstained portion of the satin skirt to make two discreet flounces which would not be too indecorous for mourning. And the poplin could be turned and restitched to a very good advantage.

Both Damaris and Millie appeared fascinated by her

explanations. And Damaris agreed that even dull seaming could be an acceptable morning's task as long as the sewing machine which Saranna operated with authority took care of the longer lengths. They went down to lunch well satisfied with their accomplishments. For the satin dress was near finished and the poplin one well advanced. Damaris was excited and pleased, because several of the suggestions she had made from knowledge gained by her dipping into the fashion magazine had been useful. And Saranna could not help but know that her wardrobe was soon to be in a better state than she had dared to hope for years.

But their satisfaction with the morning's labors and each other was rudely broken in upon by the sudden appearance of Mrs. Parton who advanced upon Damaris swiftly.

"Where are they, Miss, where are my keys!"

Damaris made no pretense of not understanding her. "I put them away," she returned.

"You—you wicked child! Give them to me instantly!" For the first time Saranna saw Mrs. Parton give vent to strong emotion. Her round face wore an expression of anger which matched the flush on her overfull cheeks.

"Mrs. Parton!" Saranna had foreseen this moment. Whether she was properly armed against it, she could not be sure until she tried.

The housekeeper glanced at her. "This is no matter of yours, Miss!"

"But it is," Saranna was frightened, though she knew she dare not allow this woman to see any such break in her defenses. The housekeeper's present naked rage was so apart from the front she had always presented that Saranna knew the woman was moved beyond all bounds. "Miss Damaris was alarmed over the disappearance of her grandfather's catalogue. Rather than have anything of perhaps greater value disappear, she has locked the rooms in which the collection is displayed, and prefers to retain the keys until such a time as we learn exactly what did happen to the catalogue." She was inwardly proud that she had been able to speak quietly and with an air of assurance which she certainly did not at this moment feel.

Mrs. Parton had regained control. Even the smolder of anger disappeared and the flush was gone from her face.

"You meddle in matters, Miss," she spoke to Saranna, "of which you have no understanding. But it is not my place to reason with you. However," now she spoke once more to the younger girl, "if you know what is good for you, Miss Damaris, you will prepare to show better manners to those in a natural state of authority over you—" She tolled the words as unctuously as might a pastor from his pulpit. "There will be a report of this made as soon as possible to Mrs. Whaley—"

Damaris tossed her head and did not even look at the housekeeper. Perhaps she was overconfident. Saranna thought so. She hoped she could talk the child into a better and more biddable state of manners before the younger girl faced up to Honora. Though now she hoped she had several days to do that.

"It's clearing," Damaris announced as the housekeeper left the room. "I'm going to see Old Jane. The Poker's done her duty for the day and I won't have to worry about running into her down there a second time." She spoke decisively and Saranna guessed that she was not going to be turned from this purpose.

"May I go with you?" she asked quickly. The more she kept Damaris under her eye right now, the safer she felt somehow.

"Part way," Damaris answered. "But then you stay in the garden, because I'm going to slip in the back way. The Poker may have told Wiley to spy. I don't like Wiley. He always does what Rufe wants—"

Though the rain had stopped it was still damp outside and Saranna put on her stoutest shoes, took up her shawl. When she joined Damaris outside, the younger girl had a bundle of thick blanket under her arm.

"Jane always says her bones ache when it rains. I'm

taking her an extra blanket," she explained. "We go this way."

They did not take what Saranna thought must be the straightest path—among the buildings around the back courtyard—but rather a garden way. When they reached a section bordering on the peach orchard, Damaris paused.

"You'll have to wait here. I can squeeze through the back fence, you can't."

"Don't be long—" But Damaris had not waited for that admonition, she had already disappeared to the other side of the hedge. There was a bench nearby, but that was too wet with rain to offer a resting place. So Saranna paced up and down impatiently.

She had a feeling, which grew more intense every moment, that she was being spied upon. By one of the roaming foxes? Though she peered along the hedges at ground level, she could not see any hint of red-brown fur nor sharp eyes.

The foxes— Those made her think of the pendant and she drew the jade out of hiding, held it in her hand, marveling anew at the beautiful workmanship of the carving. As she turned it a little this way and then that, the gem eyes had their same appearance of life, as if knowingly they studied her in return even as she gazed upon them.

"Well, now, that there's a pretty trinket, ain't it?"

Saranna froze. In an instant, her hand closed about the pendant trying to slip it back out of sight. But somehow Rufus crept up on her. Now this hand moved around her upper arm, his fingers closed painfully around her wrist.

"Give us a look at your pretty," he drawled. "Seems like it's something maybe Missie gave you. Was that it? Better not take it for yours then. Missie ain't the right to give none of the Old Captain's stuff away. Let's have a look, I say!"

His painful hold tightened yet farther. Saranna bit

her lip lest she cry out. She tried to jerk free, but his strength was far more than hers. Then came a growl, echoed by a second.

From out of the shadows two foxes advanced, stiff legged, their lips lifted in snarls to show their teeth. They were larger than their fellows, and they were white!

Rufus dropped his hold of Saranna and she was able to pull free. The foxes did not even notice her. They were too intent upon the young man. He backed away one step and then two, his hearty high color fading.

"Get off, you vermin, get off!" He swung out with his riding crop. But this time, his prey was not netted, held fast for punishment. The nearer of the foxes sprang, caught the crop with ease between its jaws. Rufus aimed a kick which did not land.

Saranna waited to see no more. She began to run. Since Rufus was between her and the house, she went through the orchard, holding her skirts as tightly to her as she could to keep from catching on any low growing thing. The fear of Rufus so possessed her that she clung despairingly to the rail fence she came to, hardly seeing the road beyond, striving feebly to pull herself up over those rails.

"Miss Stowell!"

She had neither heard nor seen the rider who was bending down toward her from his saddle, concern in his face.

"Please—oh, please—"

"What is it?" Gerrad Fowke's voice was sharp as he swung off his mount and was at her side on the other side of the fence. His hands, warm and soothing closed over hers where they grasped the rough wood of the top rail.

XIII

Sung   Conflict

At that moment all her sensible prudence deserted her. She had difficulty controlling her voice but she was able to get out a strangled:

"Please—"

"What is it? Who has frightened you!" The sharp demand in his voice pierced through her wall of fear, brought her out of that terrible panic.

"I am sorry—" Her breath caught raggedly as she tried to regain control of herself as quickly as possible.

The weight of his gloved hands on hers continued to hold her palms imprisoned against the weatherworn wood of the rail.

"Tell me!" he commanded.

"I—" But how could she tell him? Only she could not get away from him either, though she was becoming more and more disturbed at the strange confusion which swallowed up her panic.

"Someone has frightened you," Mr. Fowke's face was stern and closed looking now. Saranna realized that he would be satisfied by nothing but the truth.

"I—" she tried to begin again. If she could only trust Gerrad Fowke, if she could only be sure that he was not so in sympathy with Honora that any appeal to him would be worse than useless.

"So there you are, Miss!"

Saranna could not suppress her start. Her hands

jerked in Mr. Fowke's grasp as Rufus spoke from behind her. And her eyes sought Mr. Fowke's with a plea she was hardly aware she expressed.

His lips tightened a fraction as he looked down at her. Then he loosed his grip and, deliberately setting hand on the rail, he vaulted easily over the fence, coming then to stand beside her. She had not yet turned to face Rufus, but somehow she could *feel* him. And her shoulders hunched as if he were physically threatening her with a blow.

"What are you doing, Parton?"

Saranna had heard that ring in a man's voice before, when her father had had some reason to bring a malingering seaman to attention. With one hand on the rail to support her, for she felt oddly faint and a little dizzy, Saranna edged around.

Rufus Parton, his face flushed, that same look in his eyes, that twist of the lips he had shown when he had been beating the trapped fox, faced them both. His eyes shifted under Mr. Fowke's deliberate measurement.

"Nothing out of the way—sir—" He added that term of respect as if it were wrung from him against his will. "We was just walkin' when this here mad fox, foamin' mad he was, sprang out. Miss Saranna—she ran—"

"No!" Saranna's denial had been forced out of her, but she wished the minute it had left her lips that she had not said that.

"No?" repeated Mr. Fowke. "There was no mad fox, Miss Stowell?"

She was caught. Having gone so far she must now go all the way.

"There were two foxes—white ones. Mr.—Mr. Parton was holding my arm. They—they came out of nowhere and flew at him—"

Rufus Parton's flush deepened. "And why was I a-holdin' you, Miss Saranna?" he demanded. "Because you had somethin' what belongs to Mrs. Whaley. I was asking where you got it, connin' it out of a poor, little weak-minded Miss like Miss Damaris. I was telling you she had no right to give it to you. That I was doin' for your own good, Miss Saranna. If you know what's the best for you—"

"I know what's the best for you, Parton!" Again the quarterdeck voice of Captain Fowke cut clearly across his babble of words. "You will be on you way, man, and that speedily."

Saranna saw Rufus' hand ball into a fist, half-raised. His face was near scarlet with wrath. But, after a long meeting of stares with Mr. Fowke, he turned and slouched off.

"Can you tell me now what this is all about?" Mr. Fowke's tone was quite changed. He spoke, Saranna thought, as he might to someone who had been hurt and needed his aid.

She drew a long breath. Honora's betrothed—but still he seemed ready to aid her. Maybe she could trust him in a little.

"I fear," she began shakily, "that this may be a foolish and perhaps foundationless dislike, Mr. Fowke. But I do not care to be alone with Rufus Parton. He surprised me while I was waiting for Damaris who had gone on an errand—to see her mother's old nurse who is ill in the quarters. I was examining this—" Reluctantly, only because Rufus had mentioned it, she brought out the jade pendant. "I found it on the dressing table in my bedchamber several mornings ago. But Damaris assured me she did not put it there."

He did not offer to touch the fox head, only surveyed it.

"I am no authority on such pieces. But I would say that it is old and perhaps quite valuable. But Damaris disowned it?"

"Yes. And I cannot be sure because the catalogue of her grandfather's collection has disappeared. Otherwise, I might be able to find it listed. But also, I cannot see any reason why Damaris would lie about such a matter. She quite openly urged upon me a yellow ceramic cat which she is sure was once a night lamp in the Imperial Palace."

"No," he agreed readily, "Damaris would not lie. When she is generous, she gives her gifts openly and makes no secret of the act. But if it is not from the Whaley collection, then from whence did it come?"

Saranna twisted her hands together. "I wish I knew!" she burst out. "I was afraid to leave it in my room before I learned. If it was seen by one of the maids, by Mrs. Parton—well, I have no explanation. And now when Damaris has—"

She stopped short. In spite of his sympathy at this moment, she could not share Damaris' secret with him. That the collection had gone into hiding might be discovered soon enough, but she was too uncertain of friend or foe to take him any farther into her confidence.

There was a lengthening moment of silence between them. She looked straight ahead into the orchard where Rufus had disappeared, waiting for Mr. Fowke's questions. But those did not come. Instead, he said at last, slowly and deliberately:

"Am I to take it, Miss Stowell, that you do not indeed welcome the attentions of young Parton?"

That was a subject now so removed from her mind that she answered again without taking any thought, blurting out the truth:

"Yes!"

"I see. You did not know him before you came to Tiensin?"

Now she did swing her head, indignation rising warmly in her.

"Certainly not! I never saw him before in my life."

Then she realized what she had done. If Damaris' eavesdropping had not been at fault, Saranna had given the lie direct to all Honora had told this man. And she had no reason to believe that he would accept an assertion which ran so counter to the confidences of his betrothed.

But to her surprise, he was not frowning, had not withdrawn again behind that front of command he had shown to Rufus. Instead he nodded as if he had no more questions.

"It seems that you have had some annoyances to face. But that can be easily remedied. Now, if I did not have this confounded beast to hand—" He glanced at the horse standing with dropped reins in the road.

Then he laughed. "But that need not matter. Hurricane is lazy; loop his reins on the nearest bush and he'll stand patient enough. There was never an animal who so belied his name."

Once more Gerrad Fowke nimbly vaulted the rails, brought his mount close enough to the fence to drop the reins over one of the jutting stake ends. Then he quickly returned to Saranna.

"Miss Stowell," he bowed a little, the smile lighting his face and suddenly chiseling years away from his rugged features. "You perceive in me," he continued extending his arm a little in invitation, "a most devoted escort to see you safely to your door, reports of rabid foxes or no."

"The foxes—" She felt herself unable to maintain the proper distance with this masterful man. Perhaps he now considered himself as one of the family, and she did not want to offend by not accepting his company. Though she thought that there would be eyes to watch their arrival at the house.

"The foxes," she began again. "I do not believe they were rabid. They might have a good reason to attack Rufus Parton—"

"So?" he encouraged. "And what would that be?"

She told him of the captured fox whose ill-treatment she had interrupted.

"I do not know whether animals are able to resent what happens to their fellows and avenge it," she ended. "But if such a sympathy exists among them, this might be the reason for their attack. And they were strange foxes—"

"White you said?"

"Yes. I have not seen their like—" Again Saranna hesitated, for she had. Among those of her "dream" were the white-coated ones standing out in vivid lack of color under the moon. Luckily Gerrad Fowke did not appear bent on following up her hesitancy.

"Albinos occur among many animal species. Though to find two together may indeed be a very unusual event. But I shall have a word with Collis Parton and with Mrs. Whaley. There have always been rules about any mistreatment of foxes here at Tiensin. The Captain had some which were quite tame. I remember, during my momentous visit here, that we chanced upon a quite large one sitting on a chair in the library, eyeing us as gravely as any judge from the bench. The Captain even nodded to the beast as he might nod to a good acquaintance he chanced upon in an inn parlor. He left strict orders in his will, you know, that the foxes were not in any way to be disturbed. I believe that Collis Parton and his wife were given a legacy with that condition attached. And I do not think that Parton would take kindly to his son's endangering that. I shall have a word with him before I leave."

They had passed through the orchard back to where Damaris had left Saranna. As they approached that small roomlike expanse between the hedges, the younger girl herself appeared. She surveyed them both questioningly, then smiled eagerly at Mr. Fowke.

"Did Saranna tell you?" she demanded.

"Tell me what?" he asked.

Saranna had quickly slipped her hand from his arm, wanted to warn Damaris, more than a little concerned that the child might blurt out something of what had happened. Though his kindness to her in the past few minutes had been very reassuring, and she knew he meant his promise of trying to curb Rufus' cruelty, yet there was no reason to tell him anything which might be repeated to Honora.

Damaris put her head a little to one side, watching him mischievously.

"Perhaps," she appeared to weigh the question carefully, "we had better not say—"

"Now you tease me, Miss Damaris, perhaps to the point where I must discover your secret in order to satisfy my own honor," he laughed. "Does that sound pompous enough?"

Damaris giggled. "You are trying to be Mr. Swain, aren't you? He is a silly, I think."

"Lady, you wound me deeply!" Mr. Fowke now struck such a pose that Damaris' giggles became laughter.

"I did hear him say that once, you know," she nodded. "He likes *her,* quite a lot. You don't have to worry though, he's not important."

"But you know something which may be." Now he swooped upon her. Though his words were lightly spoken, there was determination enough behind them. Damaris' face sobered. She stood tugging at her apron. Suddenly blank of expression, as if her attention were turned inward to study some problem.

"I know something," she agreed. "But it's not my secret; it's Grandfather's. And I promised—"

"You keep promises, Damaris—" That was not a question but a statement.

Her chin came up a little proudly. "I always have."

"Sometimes, Damaris, things happen which cannot be kept secret, no matter how many promises have been given. If that time comes and you need help"—now his gaze swept from the child to Saranna and back again, as if he included them both in what he would say— "let me know. Will you promise that?"

Damaris did not answer at once. She peered intently up into his face.

" 'A good neighbor,' " he added, " 'is a found treasure.' "

Damaris' face expressed a flash of surprise. Apparently she was not the only one able to quote the wisdom of another people. Then, quick as a stinging bee she retorted:

" 'It is your own lantern. Do not poke holes in the paper which covers it.' "

"And what is that supposed to mean?" he asked.

She shrugged. "You must certainly know. Saranna, we'd better get back." She was no longer a teasing, amused child. It was as if Mr. Fowke's quotation had slammed shut a door between them. Now she took Saranna's hand, plainly dismissing Gerrad Fowke with rude abruptness. But he only regarded her very thoughtfully and stepped aside, nodding to Saranna's flurry of thanks before Damaris' impatient and demanding jerks pulled her on.

"Why were you so rude?" Saranna wanted to know when she judged they were far enough down the walk to be out of hearing. "You owe Mr. Fowke an apology—"

"He had no right!" Damaris interrupted fiercely. "He had no right to say that. He's no good friend really, using Grandfather's words when he's going to marry *her*! I was—I was going to ask him about the collection book—if he knew *she* took it. But now I won't! *She* will tell him anything and he's going to believe it. Grandfather was the only one who knew *her*, knew all her tricks.

"What were you doing with him anyway?" she added a moment later. "What was *he* doing out in the garden? *She* isn't here!"

The child was getting so wrought up Saranna thought the best way to handle her was to explain. When she mentioned that Rufus had seen the pendant, then tried to take it from her, and the coming of the white foxes, Damaris stopped on the path.

She did not look at Saranna, rather stared at the ground as if searching for something which she must find there. So shut off did she look in that moment that Saranna's voice trailed into silence, a silence which seemed to grow like a shadowy cloud around them. Then Damaris spoke:

"I've got to believe now—believe that you are a part of it. But I promised Grandfather—I've got to think a while, Saranna, truly I have to."

It was as if she were begging some favor from the older girl. But then she added in a tone which held a trace of her old fierceness: "Where did you meet Mr. Fowke? Was he in the garden—hunting—?"

"Hunting what?" Saranna was bewildered by these abrupt changes of manner. "You mean foxes?"

"No! Of course not!" Damaris made a brushing gesture of one hand as if sweeping aside such a suggestion as absurd. "Looking for the hidden part. Maybe *she* put him up to that. *She* might think that because he knew Grandfather, he knows a lot more about everything. But he doesn't! Not ever!" She shook her head vehemently.

"He wasn't in the garden," Saranna hastened to assure her, fearing a return of Damaris' agitation. "I ran away from Rufus, down to the fence along the road. He was riding there and saw me." Quickly she added how Gerrad Fowke had faced down Rufus and added Rufus' accusation as a warning. Then she asked on her own account:

"Damaris, you have said this," she raised her hand to the pendant, "was not a part of your grandfather's collection. But can you prove that? It is plainly a piece of fine Eastern work and might well be taken by others, just as Rufus believed, to be a gift from you of something you had no right to give. If it is entered in the book and you are right that Honora has that—then we must give it back at once."

"I told you, no!" denied the younger girl. "That never belonged to Grandfather. It came from Kuei-Fu Yüeh. And I'm not going to tell you what that means either. But you'd better take good care of it—'cause that's why the foxes came, you know," she ended composedly. "It will protect you if you let it. Come on—I'm not going to talk about it any more. But you needn't think that *I* gave it to you. I wouldn't have the power!" With that parting word she darted away from Saranna, running lightly down the alley of the hedges so that Saranna had to gather up her full skirts in order to hurry and keep her in sight. Though first she tucked the jade fox back into hiding.

She heard voices raised before she was quite through

the door and there was no mistaking the disputants. Honora, in traveling dress, only the veil of her bonnet tossed back to reveal her angry face, had confronted the child who stood defiantly on the lowest step of the stairway. Behind Honora was Mrs. Parton, her hands folded at waist, over her apron, a very conscious air of virtue about her as she watched with her usual impassive countenance the struggle of wills in progress.

"Give me those keys instantly!" Honora advanced on Damaris. "I know that you have them hidden on you. Mrs. Parton has already searched your room. That is another thing; you are not to have those heathenish things about you constantly. They are a bad influence upon you, which can no longer be allowed. You will move into the west chamber. Rose has already transferred all you will need—"

"You can't!" Damaris' heightened color, the feverish look about her eyes, were danger signs to Saranna. Honora was provoking the child now into the kind of tantrum which would be to her own advantage when she declared Damaris unmanageable.

Swiftly she crossed the hall to reach Damaris, and so came into Honora's range of vision.

"You—you hussy!" The would-be mistress of Tiensin appeared to find in Saranna's sudden appearance another reason for anger. "Tripping out like a light young madam to make eyes at the nearest man. Yes, I have heard it, how you used this child for bait to get to Gerrad! Little good that will do you. It is plain that your country manners, or lack of those, are not conducive to any good conduct on Damaris' part. You will keep away from her, do you understand, until we have you safely married and out of here. I marvel that Rufus still wants a light miss such as you—"

Honora had worked herself up to such a rage that she, not Damaris, might well be the one thought to be of unstable mind. Saranna, unaccustomed to such an assault, was at first so unbelieving that she had no word of defense. But as Honora paused, perhaps to gather breath for a second berating, Saranna found her voice:

"I have not the least idea," she tried to make her tone even and cool, in contrast to the other's outburst, "of what you are talking about. Neither do I intend to marry anyone, least of all Rufus Parton!"

"You'll do as you're bid!" Honora flashed back. "I stand in place of my father as your guardian. If I want to set you outside these walls, leave you as a beggar—I can. Do you understand that, Miss? I can! And I will deal with you as I see fit. You are a common thief—oh," she laughed with rage, "I have my informants. You are wearing right now jewelry which is a part of the Whaley inheritance. If this silly child gave it to you, such a gift would never stand in the law. I can say, and will be believed, that you influenced her—not only to give you gifts, but to be defiant to her natural guardians—that you are an unwholesome influence upon her in every way. Then I shall have you out of this house!"

Now she swung back to Damaris. "As for you, Miss—Parton—take those keys. She has them under her apron I am sure."

As the housekeeper advanced, Damaris whirled and darted up the stairs. She paused for an instant just before she ran into the shadowy upper hall.

"You'll never, never find it!" she screamed down. "You'd better not even try."

"Parton, she has clearly lost whatever wits she ever had," said Honora. "Lock her in her room. I shall send for the help we need to deal with her. As for you," she rounded on Saranna. "You I shall also deal with—"

John came into the hall, in his hand was a hoop ring on which there were several keys. Honora snatched the hoop from his hand, went to fit them one after another into the lock of the parlor. But Damaris was now Saranna's first concern, and she hurriedly climbed the stairs after the housekeeper who had gone to obey Honora's orders.

Perhaps Honora had anticipated flight on the part of her stepdaughter. For Damaris had halted before the door of her own room, and was tugging frantically at the knob.

"It is locked!"

"Naturally, Miss Damaris. As Mrs. Whaley said, that is no longer your room. Come along now and none of your tricks!"

Saranna was still too far away to interfere. Nor could she have withstood the housekeeper armed as she was with the orders of the one Mrs. Parton at least considered to be her mistress. Though the knowledge of her helplessness did nothing to calm her conscience as she watched Damaris pushed within a room on the opposite side of the hall, the door slamming behind the child at once. By the time Saranna reached her side, Mrs. Parton was turning the key in that lock.

"You can't—" Saranna began.

"I take Mrs. Whaley's orders, Miss," the woman returned with that cruel spark showing in her small eyes. "Miss Damaris will stay safe until Dr. Meade comes. She is plainly too much of a handful to be allowed to run wild any longer. Just as Mrs. Whaley has so often said. And, Miss, if you will take any advice, you'll look to your own future a little. Mrs. Whaley has a strong will and in this house nobody questions her decisions."

Before Saranna could reply, the housekeeper brushed past, reached the head of the back stairs, and was on her way down. Saranna looked helplessly at the locked door behind which Damaris had been imprisoned. What would happen when Honora found the collection gone? It was plain in this house she was fully mistress.

Mr. Fowke—his offer of help. But even were he willing to try to curb Honora, how could Saranna let him know what was happening.

This Dr. Meade Mrs. Parton had mentioned, who was he? Someone well primed by Honora who would declare that Damaris was a danger to herself and must be carefully guarded? And where had the collection really gone?

If Saranna wanted to ransom the child by telling Honora that, she was powerless to help because she had only suspicions, no truths. She believed it was behind the wall of the hidden garden. But would Honora accept that suggestion? And could she betray Damaris—

Torn by so many thoughts which had no answers, she dragged back to her own room. Honora knew about the pendant. Therefore, Rufus must have told her. And her strange hints, Saranna's face grew hot; she raised her hands to her cheeks—

Their visit to Queen's Pleasure, Mrs. Parton must have reported as a fancy of Saranna's own; that she had deliberately arranged it so that she might be with Mr. Fowke! If Honora was jealous, then that jealousy (however causeless it was) might be fed anew by any well-colored story Rufus could give her of the scene in the orchard when Mr. Fowke had sent him about his business.

There was her letter—if Mr. Sanders did come (even if he believed her story against Honora's more plausible tale), was there anything he could—

Saranna stood staring. There had been a fire in the fireplace—and on the hearth lay a scrap of paper. Her own unmistakable handwriting was on that. She stooped and picked up the scorched fragment.

"Honored Sir—" she read. Her letter had been burned here, in this very room, and this scrap deliberately left to warn her.

Cold seeped through her though the room was warm. The iron threat of what she had found fostered that chill.

"Honored Sir," she whispered again. At that moment a click echoed behind her. Though she flung herself at the door, she was too late. As Damaris, she was now a prisoner in her bedchamber.

XIV

≡≡ ≡≡
≡≡≡≡≡
≡≡≡≡≡
≡≡≡≡≡

Kuai *Resolution*

Saranna fought a battle for self-control. If she beat upon the door, screamed for her freedom, as every nerve within her urged, she suspected all such efforts would be useless. Also, her pride and dignity would suffer, and Honora would have good cause to believe she had reduced Saranna to a state in which she would be biddable and her own puppet. Therefore—

The girl made herself consider the door carefully. Since she had come to Tiensin she had never had reason to use the key, to lock herself in. Such bolting and barring to achieve privacy was foreign to all her training. But with old keys sometimes there was a similarity of locks. As when little Jimmy Bains back in Sussex had locked his small sister in the parlor and then thrown the key down the well. Then the key to their back door had proved most efficacious in releasing the prisoner.

Keys— Damaris appeared to have her own private store of those. But Saranna had certainly never expected such a situation as this to arise. There was— Memory suddenly freshened. She went to the tall wardrobe, pushed back the few dresses hung within. Yes, she had remembered correctly! Hanging from a hook at the very back, secured by a bit of tape, was a key. Probably for the wardrobe itself, but it looked large enough to fill the keyhole of the chamber door.

She took it quickly to the door. The shaft slid in easily

enough, but would it now turn? Slowly, for fear that it might somehow break, or jam the lock, Saranna worked the key around. There followed another soft click.

Feeling weak with relief (for only at this moment did she realize the full strength of the dismay which had gripped her at being a prisoner), she turned the knob. The door responded.

But she would not go out yet. No, let them believe her safely confined. Their assumption would give her a chance to think, to plan. Her self-confidence grew. She had won the battle of the lock, but that might be only the smallest of trials now facing her.

That Honora would have her own answer for the vanished collection Saranna had no doubt at all. Sooner or later, Mrs. Whaley would descend upon Saranna—or Damaris—for an accounting. And, if Damaris was entirely defiant, the child would only bring more trouble upon herself.

Saranna returned to sit down in the chair by the small table where her workbox rested. She had been doing the last stitching on the poplin dress; its folds were now draped carefully across the bed. Now her eyes caught that unfinished task.

Busy her hands while she thought. Mother had always said that one's mind was clearer when one was at work. The girl pulled the waist to her, began to set small even stitches, making herself concentrate with one part of her mind on exactly what she was doing.

There was no chance of her reaching Mr. Sanders. Unless she could devise some surer method of smuggling out another letter. To entrust such to Millie, as friendly as the young maid seemed to be, was folly. None of the servants would venture to disobey any order from either the housekeeper or Honora. There remained now only Mr. Fowke.

Yet the few miles between Tiensin and Queen's Pleasure might now be equal to the distance between the river wharf and Baltimore, as far as Saranna was concerned. Unless— She carefully withdrew her needle, having made tight the last hook— Unless Gerrad Fowke came visiting.

Her old distrust of Honora's chosen husband-to-be stirred. Yet there was his promise given to Damaris, and to her, that he would be their friend in any emergency. Somehow that stayed in her mind, as if he again swore solemnly and irrevocably.

Saranna tensed at a knock at the door. But why would anyone knock when they knew, or thought that they knew, she was locked in? Could this be a trap?

Quietly she arose and moved forward, to stand at the door itself, her hand on the knob, her lips close to the crack.

"Who is it?" she asked softly.

"Millie, Miss Saranna."

"You are alone?"

"Yes'm."

Saranna opened the door. The young maid held a tray on which was a covered dish, a small pot, and a cup and saucer.

"I bringed you somethin' to eat." She sidled around the door. "Miss Saranna, Miss Honora, she's mighty mad. She is a-yellin' out that she's been robbed. She sent Albert ridin' over to Mr. Fowke's with a letter—"

Millie put the tray down on the table from which Saranna hurriedly cleared her sewing. Then she stood, big-eyed, watching Saranna as if she expected to see some alarming change in her person.

"Did she ask Mr. Fowke to come here?" Saranna asked eagerly.

"Don't know." Millie shook her head to emphasize her lack of knowledge. "Just see Albert ridin' off in a big hurry. And Mrs. Parton, she's fit to be tied. She's afraid of somethin'." At that, Millie looked almost cheerful. "Somethin' about Mr. Fowke. When she heard about Albert goin', she sent Zorbus, down to the fields to call Mr. Collis to come— There's a big somethin' what bothers her—"

Were the Partons afraid of Mr. Fowke? Had they al-

ready heard that Saranna had told him of the treatment
the foxes had received from Rufus? But how could anyone have overheard that exchange down by the orchard
fence? However—

"Stay here, Millie," Saranna made her decision. "I
have something for you to do."

"Yes'm."

"You can eat that if you wish." Saranna pointed to the
tray where Millie had revealed sandwiches lay under the
dish cover.

"But—what you goin' to eat then, Miss Saranna?"

"My usual lunch," Saranna returned firmly. It took a
great deal of inner stiffening of her will to carry out her
plan. But if she allowed Honora to control her life in any
way, then she feared she was lost.

"Miss Honora, she say you eat in your room—"

"I do not think it is going to matter," Saranna returned, hoping that she was speaking the truth, "what
Mrs. Whaley has said. She is very much upset, Millie.
When she has had time to consider the matter, she will be
of a different mind."

As she spoke, she unhooked the bodice of the ugly
calico, unfastened the skirt below, and let the clothing
slide to the floor in a discarded heap. The new skirt she
had so carefully put together went on over her head, and
then the chemisette of fine black mull; over that, the bodice was contrived from the worn poplin one, its deficien-
cies either eliminated by careful cutting and turning, or
hidden by the ruffling Saranna had devised from the
satin skirt.

She stood before the mirror surveying the results of
her handicraft carefully and felt a throb of excitement.
Not for a long time had she worn so well cut a dress, or
one of such fine material. During their poverty-lean years
in Sussex, her mother had never been able to produce for
herself and her daughter more than the plainest and
most utilitarian of clothing, never in style.

The black of the mourning made her skin fairer, her

lengths of ruddy hair even brighter. Too bright, Saranna decided quickly. Some of that must be extinguished with the new cap.

Memory of a new style of hairdressing which she had seen in one of the fashion pages Damaris had brought to the sewing room decided her to try something different. She had always worn her hair, not in any profusion of ringlets after the most popular fashion, but parted in the middle and drawn severely back, to be coiled up and securely pinned. Now she went to the dressing table and sat down before the smaller mirror.

"Millie, if you would be a lady's maid, you have to learn to dress hair—"

"Know that, Miss Saranna. Polly, she do Miss Honora—an' what a lot she got to do—curl papers an' curler iron in a candle flame an' all the rest. Polly—Miss Honora sent her to be learnt just how to make all them curls an' things—"

"Well, I don't want any curls, Millie. But you can make braids, can't you?"

Millie had come to stand behind her, looking down at Saranna's heavy, straight hair.

"That I sure enough do, Miss Saranna."

"Then this is what I want you to try for me, Millie. Part all the way, front to back, in the middle. Then make braids on each side coiled around over my ears—"

"But that ain't no fashion—" Millie began.

"It is in France, Millie. It was in one of those pictures we looked at while we were sewing."

"This ain't no France—" However, in spite of the last protest, Millie reached for the brush.

"No, but I wouldn't look right with a lot of curls, so let's try it," Saranna kept to her plan.

Millie was deft and she indeed could braid, tightly and evenly. The two braids were pinned up with Saranna's pins just as she had ordered, though she had to draw on a further supply of those dark shell holders before they were through.

She surveyed the results in the mirror, not with any

touch of vanity, but to hope that she had achieved her goal. The severe style was certainly in complete contrast to Honora's curls and floating ribbons, but Saranna decided it suited her well, and it certainly made her look older, more responsible.

"The cap now, Millie—"

That she took from the maid's hands and adjusted herself. It was a small puff of mull and lace with streamers cut from the black satin. And, once in place between the braids, she was herself astounded at the effect. She did not look like Saranna Stowell, penniless orphan. No, she had dignity, a kind of presence which she had never dreamed she could ever achieve. She was not pretty as prettiness was judged by the world, but she believed that she would not be overlooked in company either.

It was not for any need of compliments she had tried for this effect, but rather that in her person she could produce some sense of credibility for any countermeasure she might have to take against Honora. That clothes which suited a woman were her armor of defense was something men liked to deny, but women knew was the truth.

Then, on impulse, she picked up the jade pendant which lay upon the dressing table, even as it had when she had first discovered it. She slipped its silken cord over her head. But this time she made no attempt to hide it from sight under her bodice.

Against the dead black of her mourning, the white gem appeared to glow. She wore it for no reason of ornament, but because she had an odd feeling that it, too, would add strength to her determination to face the world in her own defense, and in Damaris' behalf.

Saranna gathered up her small silken reticule, her black bordered handkerchief, made a last careful survey of her person as a soldier might check his arms and equipment just before going into battle. The door key she slid into the purse.

"Miss Saranna," Millie stood round-eyed by the door, "you—you look like you be a Queen! That there little old

cap, it could be like a crown, it do look one, it sure do!"
She seemed astounded by the change.

Saranna held her shoulders straight. That Millie's
tribute was unrehearsed, she knew. And along with the
verdict of the mirror, the maid's words added a further
steeling of her purpose. Millie fumbled with the door
knob, and opened that portal for her mistress to sail
through.

Out in the hall, Saranna did not hesitate, going directly to the top of the stairs. She might well have tested
the key on the lock of Damaris' prison. But for the moment, she did not wish to try fate too high. Now it must
depend largely on the results of her confrontation with
Honora what further steps she would take to aid the
younger girl.

Below she heard a murmur of voices in the breakfast
room. And one was deeper—Mr. Fowke! Then he *had*
come to Honora's summons. She must not allow that to
make any difference in her attitude. Saranna must
present the picture of serene outward normality.

With her head high, she entered the room. Honora's
back was toward her, and her flow of rippling speech was
in full force. But Mr. Fowke glanced up at Saranna's
quiet but determined entrance.

She saw his eyes widen. An odd expression she could
not identify flitted across his weathered features. Then he
arose from his chair and, napkin in hand, awaited beside
the seat on his right. Honora swung halfway around, her
astonishment was plain only for a moment. Then she recovered with that rapidity which was part of her own ar-
mament.

"Saranna, dear! But I thought that you said your
headache was far too bad for you to join us—"

"I have sufficiently recovered, thank you, Honora,"
Saranna replied, holding fast to her courage. For what
Honora's narrowed, angry eyes told her was far different
from the tinkle of her words.

Composedly the girl seated herself in the chair Mr.

Fowke had drawn out for her, thanking him with a murmur. John appeared in the doorway, took in the situation, and a moment or so later Rose hurried in with an extra setting for the table.

"Do not let me interrupt you." Saranna somehow was able to preserve her outward calm, so that her words sounded reasonably prosaic in her own ears. "I know you have affairs of moment to discuss—"

She did not glance directly at Honora as she said that. But she felt the atmosphere about Jethro's daughter, as if the other's very rage gave off a fire's heat. Yet Honora's reception of Saranna suggested that Mr. Fowke was not to know of the situation at Tiensin. Which told the girl that she was a measure right in her trust. If Honora did not wish him to learn of the outburst which had greeted Damaris and Saranna on their return to the house, the reason must be that she herself feared some opposition to her handling of her stepdaughter.

It was the first time Saranna had ever eaten in a room so full of hostility aimed at her. But she did so with deliberation, as if nothing mattered but the food on her plate, chewing and swallowing bites of what might be dry and stale bread for all the real flavor the dishes held for her.

"It is a beautiful day," Mr. Fowke remarked into the silence which ensued upon Saranna's being served. "Perhaps I can persuade you ladies, and Miss Damaris, to ride to Queen's Pleasure."

Now Saranna dared raise her eyes and stare directly at Honora. How was Honora going to answer that? Two headaches might be a little difficult for Mr. Fowke to believe.

She saw that Honora's face was grave, her eyes avoided meeting Saranna's.

"Gerrad, I am so worried about Damaris. Her grandfather's preoccupation with those Eastern things has filled her mind to the point it has become an obsession. In fact, I have asked Dr. Meade to come for a consultation. It might be far better for the child to be out of these surroundings until she puts less store in this 'treasure' of hers. Dr. Meade has spoken of an excellent school for such children—very well managed and with the latest methods of handling hysterical cases. My father does not really understand what a problem Damaris has become. She has not been well supervised, instead given freedoms which have done her great harm. Dr. Meade will see her and then we can decide what is best for her—"

"Are you sure all has been going well here, Honora?" Mr. Fowke asked. "I know you have had trouble with governesses in the past. But from my observation, Miss Stowell has an excellent effect on Miss Damaris, and the child seems to be much happier and more cheerful."

"Damaris," Saranna spoke for the first time, "is very intelligent for her age. Her knowledge has quite amazed me—"

"What do you know?" Honora flashed out as if she could no longer restrain the temper boiling in her. "My late father-in-law filled her young mind with all kinds of heathen notions. And because she parrots what he taught her, everyone gets the false impression that Damaris is very learned. There is no truth in that, as you can judge when you have known her longer. She is highly excitable and can be easily influenced into rash acts. But this time she has gone too far—"

"Too far?" repeated Mr. Fowke.

"Yes!" Honora tossed her napkin onto the table. "If you do not believe me—come and see!"

Her skirts rustled as she arose so hurriedly from her chair that it rocked and nearly overbalanced. Saranna stood up in turn as Mr. Fowke pushed past her to where Honora was already going out the door.

Honora led the way to the library which was the nearest of the two rooms Saranna and Damaris had plundered in the night. She flung open that door with an extravagant gesture. "Look! Everything has gone!"

Mr. Fowke did indeed look, and his face expressed his amazement.

"But, Honora—where are—?" he did not try to finish

that question. Instead, he stared intently at first one and then another bare shelf, table edge—all the places which had been so filled the day before.

"Where has she put them?" Honora cried out.

Mr. Fowke turned to her, his face grave. "Honora, what you have just implied is impossible! No child could have looted this place. This is the work of men. Have you sent for the constable?"

"She did not do it alone." Honora pointed at Saranna who had followed her into the room. "This—this young—" Then she actually choked upon her anger. A phenomenon of which Saranna had heard but which she had never seen before.

"Nonsense!" Mr. Fowke was now a little aroused in turn. "You know very well such an act by two young girls is utterly physically impossible! Unless they had help."

"Perhaps they did!" Honora had lost more than a little of her fine coloring, her face looked near to haggard. "Perhaps they had help from—" She stopped short then.

"From the servants?" Mr. Fowke prompted when she did not continue.

"There is not one of the slaves who would dare," Honora replied impatiently. "But they did it—the two of them. Damaris as good as admitted it—"

"In jest perhaps, or because she was angry," Mr. Fowke said quietly. "Remember, I have seen the collection many times and—"

"It is all gone!" Honora interrupted him. "All but the screen, a carved table or such, and, of course, those pieces in Damaris' old room. Search if you will. We have, the Partons and I, and there is not so much as the smallest carving left. Except—" she turned quickly once more to Saranna "—that bribe she wears like the brazen little hussy that she is. Damaris gave her that for her help. There was no place else she could have gotten it—"

"I—" Saranna began indignantly, when Mr. Fowke raised his hand in a signal for silence.

"Honora, Saranna has already assured me that is no part of the Captain's treasure—"

For a moment Saranna did not catch her name, but Honora was quicker.

"So you call her 'Saranna,' not 'Miss Stowell' any longer? She has been busier even than I have believed. And, of course, it *is* part of the collection no matter how much she has tried to convince you otherwise."

There was very little expression on Mr. Fowke's face now and what there was Saranna could not read. But when he answered Honora he again used the "Captain" voice which had reduced Rufus in the garden.

"I believe there is in existence a catalogue of the collection. Maybe Damaris can give it to us. Then we shall know the truth about this pendant."

Perhaps Honora might have refused, her mouth was set enough to utter some mutinous word. Then she beckoned imperiously toward the door of the library where John now hovered.

"In my room," she spoke tersely. "I want the book bound in gold brocade—at once!"

John disappeared. So Damaris had been right. Honora had taken the book. Honora walked over to the desk, leaned one hand on its polished surface.

"Mr. Walsworth, and his friend, John Sheers—they will be here next week. They could not believe, even when they saw the pieces described. We have to find them—"

"You would have done better, Honora," Gerrad Fowke remarked in a level tone, "to have sent for me, and for the sheriff, the minute you discovered the robbery. Two young females have not the strength to carry any of the collection had it been carefully packed—"

"It was," Honora broke in. "Oh, at least Damaris can be trusted on that point. Parton went into the storage room in the cellar. Those boxes my father-in-law had made to his order in China to transport his pieces— they're all missing!"

"Those huge hampers!" Mr. Fowke raised his eyebrows. "That strains your story even more. The girls could not have moved them. And if they did not, what help had they? Field hands? You know well they would have buzzed such a story over the Manor long ago."

"I know who took them," Honora answered flatly. "In time, I shall get them back." The glance at Saranna was cold and deadly indeed. "But we have a way to settle you, *Miss Stowell.* Let me find reference to that pendant in the catalogue and I shall swear out a warrant for you as a common thief. You cannot brazen this out, my girl!"

John slid through the doorway as if he hated to enter a whirlwind of some storm. Honora held out her hand, but it was Mr. Fowke who stepped swiftly before her and grasped the book the houseman carried.

"I imagine this must be indexed—" he observed.

Honora's fingers crooked as if she would snatch the golden volume from him. Then she said with a sullen note in her voice:

"The jewelry is entered first. There is not too much of that. The pieces were kept in that single case over there." She indicated the empty one between the tall windows.

"Well enough." With deliberation, Mr. Fowke began to turn the pages. Saranna caught a glimpse of small paintings on them, and heavy block printing. Mr. Fowke turned that page, the second, and then he looked up.

"There is no mention here, Honora, of a white jade pendant in the form of a fox—"

Again she paled a little. Her hand caught the edge of the desk and Saranna thought she swayed, as if Gerrad Fowke's words were like a blow in the face.

"Then where?" she said in a half-whisper. Honora's eyes narrowed, she stared straight at Saranna. "Then—it is true! Every bit of it is true!"

For the second or two during which they locked stares, Saranna read Honora's fury. And, behind that, something else, fear. Honora certainly knew something which Saranna did not; perhaps a portion anyway of Damaris' carefully guarded "secret." And she herself must learn more in order to protect herself.

"I told you," for the first time Saranna spoke, "it was a gift." She put up her hand to finger the smooth jade.

Now that she was entirely sure that it was not of Damaris' reckless giving, her own need for the truth grew even stronger. "Since I am not a thief, and," she gazed around the room, using Gerrad Fowke's disbelief as a weapon, "it is so apparent neither Damaris nor I could have cleared away your treasure, I am going to Damaris—now."

If Honora did make any move to stop her, Saranna was unaware of it as she swept past John and into the hall, climbing the stairs with ahope that the key in her reticule could indeed free the second prisoner.

XV

Yî *Move with Fortune*

Saranna half-expected that Honora might have sent one of the servants to mount guard at Damaris' door. But there was no one within the upper hall. Firm of purpose she went to the door which Mrs. Parton had locked behind the younger prisoner. And, as firmly, she slipped the key from the wardrobe into the lock.

It went easily enough, but the turning was more difficult. At first she thought it would not do so at all. But, reluctantly, the lock gave, and Saranna threw open the door. She did not know what to expect—Damaris defiant, Damaris afraid, Damaris in tears— But what she discovered was an empty room and an open window, the lace curtain covering it billowing into the chamber as a rising wind drove against the house.

She ran to look out. A porch—a—?

There was a tree whose outermost limbs needed pruning, for the tips scraped against the house wall at this point. Had Damaris somehow made her way down it? Even to consider such a climb made Saranna slightly giddy.

However, the empty room was evidence enough that Damaris had made her escape. Where had the child gone? Was she hiding in the garden, elsewhere in the house? Or had she sought refuge in that hidden section behind the hedge? Was it Saranna's real duty to raise the alarm?

Even as she considered that, she closed the window, pulled straight the wind-ruffled curtains. Quickly she crossed the room, and, again in the hall, she locked the door. Let Honora and Mrs. Parton believe as long as they might that they had the real mistress of Tiensin in their custody. For somehow Saranna believed that Damaris was now safer than she had been behind that lock.

As she was restoring the key to safekeeping, Saranna lifted her head and sniffed. There was a scent growing heavier every moment, more clearly defined—a strange not unpleasant odor. The odor must come from around or beneath the opposite door, that of Damaris' Chinese room.

Saranna tried the knob. It was locked, as she had expected. And, though she lifted her hand to tap softly on the panel before her, she hesitated. If Damaris had somehow returned to her own private place, should she disturb her? Such a knocking might well come to the attention of a servant, be reported to Mrs. Parton.

Once more she groped in her reticule, brought out the wardrobe key, inserted it. This time in vain. She feared she might break the shaft off in the keyhole if she persisted in forcing it. Though she pulled the pins out of one carefully rolled braid so she could set her ear tight against the wood, she could not hear any sound for several breaths. Then came a distant murmur which rose and fell—not quite a song, and she could not distinguish any words. What *was* Damaris doing?

There was something about that cadence which suggested the younger girl was not indulging in any conversation, rather that she might be repeating some formal wordage—a prayer? Saranna had a sudden feeling that she had no right to pry into this secret. She backed from the door, and returned to her own room.

The tray was gone, and so was Millie. Saranna took the precaution of locking her door again. Though they knew she had gotten out, any tampering now with that lock would give her some warning—

Warning of what? She paced back and forth trying to

think coherently and logically. Mr. Fowke's attitude—in that she had found support. His denial that the collection had disappeared through Damaris' efforts and her own, while false, was so reasonable perhaps he could impress it on Honora. At least enough to make her reconsider her immediate plans.

Saranna was almost convinced that she could go to him with the truth. But from whence had those Chinese come, the ones who had carried away the hampers? Did they live in the hidden section of the garden, with the Fox Lady? Her head began to ache. She rubbed her fingers back and forth just above her eyes where the worst pain centered. If she went downstairs now, she would have little chance of speaking to Gerrad Fowke alone. Honora would make sure of that.

And what was Damaris doing? Throwing those painted wands again, trying to read the future by some superstitious trick? The heritage Captain Whaley had left his granddaughter might lead now more to her ruin than her happiness.

Slowly Saranna loosed the hooks of the dress which had given her so much confidence. As she folded bodice and skirt across the chair, pulled her faded and much-washed wrapper about her, plucked the pins from her braids so they swung free across her shoulders, she feverishly attempted to make some logical plan.

Suppose she were to write another letter to Mr. Sanders, and this time entrust the missive to Mr. Fowke? She could give the reason that she— No, tell him the truth! She still had that half-burnt scrap of paper. With that to show him, she did not think that she need worry about him accepting her story. Quickly she went to the table where the lap desk stood. But when she lifted the lid—no paper, no pens—it had been emptied! She was still staring down at that emptiness when there came a tap at her door.

"Who is there?"

"Me, Miss Saranna—"

Millie. How far she dared trust the maid now she had

no knowledge. Would Millie dare to take a message to Mr. Fowke for her? Or was the girl too cowed by Mrs. Parton to be relied upon?

When Saranna did open the door, Millie sidled in. Her arms were piled high with recently-ironed underclothing which gave off the very faint scent of lavender water used in the last rinsing.

Saranna settled in the rocking chair watching Millie sort, fold, and deftly lay her burden in drawers. The maid did not seem to want to even look in her direction, but kept her attention fixed on what she was doing.

She had patted the last petticoat into place and then arose from where she had been kneeling by the bottom drawer of the chest. For a moment she simply stood, her back half-turned to Saranna. Then she glanced warily over her shoulder.

"Miss Saranna—" she began, and then gulped as if she were choking on some word she feared to utter but did not know how to suppress—

"Yes—?" Saranna tried to show no agitation in return, keeping her voice calm and even.

"Miss Honora—she be very mad with you, with Miss Damaris. She say she goin' to fix that place, get rid of it—" Millie pointed to the window and Saranna guessed her meaning.

"The hidden garden?"

Millie nodded emphatically. "She sent Joseph downriver. He have a letter for a man in Baltimore. They come here with guns—kill the foxes, all of them—and kill people maybe—too—"

"What people?" Saranna demanded.

Millie shivered. Her hands twisted the edge of her apron, wringing the cloth as if she had it before her straight from the washboard.

"They say—say there is strange peoples back in that place. Sometimes the foxes they be people, sometimes foxes. If they catches 'em as foxes they shoot them all for sure; if they catches them as people—they does that, too.

Miss Honora, she says they is all gonna be done away with."

"When?"

"When the mens comes from the city—maybe two–three days."

"Millie, does Mr. Fowke know about this?"

"Maybe not. I ain't sure. Miss Honora, she waits 'til he leaves before she gives Joe the letter and sends him."

"Could you get a message to Mr. Fowke?"

Millie appeared to think for a second or two. "I dunno. That there Nemos—he's Mr. Fowke's groom—he's sweet on Rose an' comes over a-courtin' after dark. He ain't afraid of the Partons none. Maybe so he would take such—were you to give him somethin' for his trouble."

"How much?" Saranna thought of her pitifully thin purse. If she only had the funds which Mr. Sanders might even now be holding for her!

"Rose, she ain't sure she wants to settle down none. She's got an eye for pretties. Were Nemos to get him somethin' pretty, he could make bigger talk with her."

"Pretties—what kind?" Saranna followed that hint quickly.

"Somethin' to wear like. Rose, she does like to go to church dressed so all the men from the quarters roll eyes wide at her."

But Saranna was almost as destitute of such "pretties" as she was of money. Her small store of treasures were in the bottom drawer of the lacquered sewing cabinet. She pulled that open now.

Her mother's miniature painted before her marriage, a small locket of gold set with a pearl which contained her father's hair in a tiny braided coil; two rings much too large for Saranna's own fingers and unsuitable for her state of mourning. And, she drew out the last: the sandle-wood fan, its scented sticks carved into lacy open work. As she spread it wide, the heavy perfume of the wood was easily detected.

"Would this be a pretty?" Softly she waved it back and forth. Her mother had cherished it because of its oddity, the wood from the Sandwich Islands wrought by some workmen in Macao into this trifle. Meant to be used in summer when its strong odor was reputed to be able to keep mosquitoes at a distance, her mother had never carried it after they had gone to Sussex.

Millie drew nearer and touched a fingertip to the fan's smooth outer surface.

"Miss Saranna, that sure do be such a pretty as Rose never saw before in her live-long days! I think Nemos, he would swim hisself all the way to Baltimore were he able to lay that in her hand come next Sunday!"

"Good enough." Saranna tried not to regret her proposed bargain. She had such a strong sense of impending danger that surely a fan, even one so long cherished, was nothing in the way of a price to pay for help.

"I have to have some paper, and a pen—" She had already handed Millie the fan and the girl was holding the wood close to her nose, inhaling its scent in delighted sniffs. "Someone has emptied my desk while I was gone."

Millie's interest in the fan quickly dissipated. "Miss Saranna, I don't know how you can get those. Do I try to get them for you—they is kept in the part of the house where I ain't never supposed to show myself. And do Mrs. Parton or that John see me—"

But Saranna was already trying to improvise writing materials. On the hearth! There was charred wood—dark ashes. She quickly knelt and scraped the blackest of these onto the dish-bottomed holder of the bedside candlestick.

Paper? The book she had brought to her room. Ruthlessly she tore out the flyleaf. Then she drew out from her store a knitting needle.

"Millie, can you get me some vinegar—very little—perhaps a couple of tablespoonfuls?"

The maid nodded vigorously. "I can and no one will ask none about that. 'Cause ladies rinse their hair in vinegar. I can wash your hair and no one will say it be somethin' as we ain't ever do."

"Good enough!" Saranna was already unbraiding her hair. "Get it right away. Oh, leave the fan here until later."

Millie laid that on the table and was gone. How well her plan might work, Saranna did not know. But she did believe that were Gerrad Fowke to know of what Honora planned, he would put an end to it.

Millie was back shortly with an armload of towels, a jug which she announced contained rainwater, the only proper rinse for any lady's hair, and a much smaller jug of vinegar.

"Miss Honora," she announced, "is a-lyin' in her room with a headache. She got that triflin' Polly, who think she's so mighty big 'cause she's Miss Honora's maid, a-sittin' there a-puttin' cloths on her head and a-gettin' her things. I heard tell as how Mr. Fowke, he talked sharplike to her before he rode off. And she didn't take kindly to that nohow—"

While Millie got ready the towels and washbasin, Saranna experimented with the vinegar and the charcoal from the fireplace. She mixed a black enough liquid, but whether it would last after drying was a question. In the meantime, she thought of what she must say.

"I go an' get the hotted water now," Millie announced. Saranna nodded absently in reply.

She dipped the point of the needle into her mixture and began to print out letters. Since she had neither the time nor the space on her torn-out page to be formal, this must be terse and to the point.

Mr. Fowke:
    They plan to attack the hidden garden. Men from the city. Kill the foxes and whoever may be within. I must ask help for Damaris—and for Tiensin.

She made her signature a single S. Saranna was sure he would not have any difficulty in knowing who had sent this. She laid her message out to dry. Though she had gone over each letter in those words twice, she could not be sure of the staying power of her improvised ink.

When Millie returned, she went through the lengthy ritual of washing her hair, applying towels from the mammoth pile the maid had provided, as well as brushing and sitting in the full sunlight of the afternoon in order to dry it. But the strands were still faintly damp as she had Millie rebraid it for her appearance at dinner.

Honora and Damaris might not attend that meal; if so, Saranna determined to dine in solitary state, so asserting her independence before the household. She had Millie once more hook her into her dress, deciding not to vary that with the more formal satin waist, and descended the stairs with a firm step.

As she entered into the breakfast room she found it in semitwilight, no candles lighted, no place set. They had not expected her then. But with a determined will, she pulled at the bell cord. It was Rose, not John who came in answer to that perhaps overforceful ring.

"Where is dinner?" Saranna said. "Surely this is the hour—"

"We—Mrs. Parton—she say you take a tray in your room, Miss Saranna."

"Nonsense. I am perfectly well and able to be here. You will bring my dinner now." Saranna had never been so authoritative in her life. But she sensed that she must prove that she was not a nonentity in this house. The spirit and pride which had carried her and her mother through the dark days in Sussex had come back to her full force. She was young, that was true. And were Jethro here, her duty would be to obey the wishes of the master of the household. But that did not mean that she had to let Honora stand in authority over her.

She waited, watching the appearance of John, who eyed her first as if he were going to protest, but then turned to set out silver and fine china before the chair which had been hers since she had come to Tiensin. Saranna fully expected Mrs. Parton to confront her with some prohibition from Honora. But the housekeeper did not show herself, and Saranna ate slowly and methodically as if this was the only possible arrangement she could countenance.

There was no reason to sit alone in the parlor. Having achieved her purpose so far, she returned to her own room, lighted the lamp, and took up her book. Though she found that even when she had read several pages, she had no idea of the story. Finally, she laid it aside.

The storm last night had seemed to clear the air. There was a moon rising. She looked down from her window to the hedge which walled in the hidden garden. How very tall that growth was, cutting off the view from even this second-story window. And it was thick, too. If Honora ordered that cleared away, the hands who did it would have a very difficult job before them.

Suddenly, Saranna was tired. There had been so much happening this day and she had been up well half the night before helping Damaris repack the treasure collection. Slowly she undressed, aware of the aches of fatigue in her body. She put on her muslin gown, tied her nightcap firmly in place, and settled herself among her pillows. But, once she lay prone, her desire for sleep seemed to have fled. There was something else, a sensation she had not experienced before—a little nagging feeling that she had left something important undone. Yet as she went over all her memories of the day, she could not locate that omission.

Done—or undone?

Had she made a bad error in judgment in her appeal to Mr. Fowke? Or was it that she must make sure before she slept of Damaris' whereabouts? With a sigh, Saranna sat up.

Then she heard it!

Out of the night came that strange off-tone music again. She scrambled over the edge of the bed. Her wrapper— Where had she left her wrapper? This time she had forgotten to light the Emperor's night lamp and she bumped forceably in the dark against the chair where she had hung the wrapper. With that about her shoulders, her feet forced stockingless into her slippers, she crept to the door and unlocked it. She then threaded the key onto the tie of her wrapper.

Damaris! She was sure Damaris might be bound for the hidden garden. And this time she herself had not awakened from any sleep, she was very certain that what she heard was no part of any strangely vivid dream.

She went first to Damaris' door. That was tight shut and did not yield as she turned the knob. She dared not knock or call without perhaps arousing Honora's maid in the chamber near the fore of the hall where a crack of light showed strongly at floor level.

Damaris—could she have already gone on into the hidden garden? If that were where the treasure had been taken, then there was good reason for the child to check upon it. Saranna moved cautiously down the dark hall. Now her hand was on the pendant she wore, both night and day. The gem seemed not to be chill and cold, rather warm—though that was certainly only a fancy.

Step by step she descended the back stairs. There was a light glow from the direction of the kitchen, the sound of voices, but all safely muted. She was at the outer door now and had lifted the latch.

The night wind was almost too fresh for the gown and wrapper she wore. She wished she had taken more time and dressed. But again that urgency gripped her. It was here and now she must move!

Around the house she went, to front the hedge. The eerie trilling of a flute had risen slightly above the other sounds which combined to make a harmony which, to her Western ears, did not sound like music at all.

Saranna felt her way along the edge of the hedge and then she stopped, pulled aside brush limbs with both hands, and found the concealed doorway. Once more, she fought her way on into the garden, down the twisting path, beyond the small house of the flower-grated windows until she could see the terrace.

But tonight, in spite of the music, there was no fox-faced dancer swaying gracefully under a waning moon, no company of foxes transfixed by her movements. The musicians sat back in the shadows under the overhang of the eaves as they had done before. But in the moon door of the house stood a woman who could only have been the dancer save that tonight it was a human face she wore.

Her robe was not the loose-flowing, high-belted one which had swirled about her in the moon dance, rather it was richly heavy, stiff with embroidery, high-collared and clasped upon the shoulder. Her hair was stretched over a frame in a formal fashion, decorated with pins which glittered, as did the long earrings hanging from her exposed ears. She was as majestic as a Queen in her own courtyard, and if this was Damaris' "Princess," the title was very fit.

Her eyes were upon the path and, as Saranna emerged from the growth behind her, one hand arose as her very long sleeve folded back upon the wrist to show the fingers with their gemmed nail guards. She beckoned, and Saranna, again feeling neither awe nor fear, rather that this was an ordained act, came forward upon the terrace, approaching she who stood in the moon door.

"*Mei*—" The lady stepped back into the room where the lamps were lit, and once again Saranna followed.

"You are welcome, younger sister." Though the lady spoke English, her words had a slightly sing-song quality. Now she pointed to that wide bed which was also a place to sit. Once more the table divided them as they settled themselves upon its padded surface. But this time no tea service was waiting.

Rather the Fox Lady put her hand upon a box of lacquer work whereon were many foxes patterned in red and gold on the black surface. From that she took a bundle of small ivory sticks like those of a dismembered fan, yet of the same width throughout. Then Saranna saw that some were divided by an inset bar of dull red, while others were untouched.

"Younger sister, you have come and the hour is a propitious one. At such a time, the Great Ones make known what may lie ahead for those of us who have not yet ascended. For my own life, I know all readings well, but this is the moment when I must also find what influences lie before you, and whether the path which is yours is also, for this space of time, mine.

"Therefore, take these into your hand, let them fall upon this surface. And while you still hold them, do think about that which troubles you and clouds your way—"

She held out the bundle of ivory sticks and Saranna found herself taking them. In this time and place, it seemed entirely natural that she should obey this regal woman who had about her the air of one who had never had any order she had given put to question.

Saranna held the wands. But her mind was a chaotic whirl of bits and pieces. She could not think of anything else *but* troubles, yet those were difficult to place in any order.

Then she dropped the ivory sticks. The music on the terrace had ceased. In the silence of the room, the clatter of the ivory pieces as they struck the lacquered surface of the table seemed almost as loud as a drum.

"It is *Yî*," the Princess inclined her head a fraction to better read the pattern. "Which denotes advantage in every movement."

The tip of one of the nail casings tapped by the rod farthest from Saranna. A solid one:

"The first nine undivided—for you to make some great movement. The second nine—oracles which cannot be opposed if you stand firm—good fortune. The third six, divided—increase through that which means you evil—with no blame to you. The fourth six, you can be relied upon in the aid you will give others. The fifth nine, undivided—you are of sincere heart and this will lead you to such fortune as you have not dreamed. The sixth nine—undivided—ah, here stands one to whom no one shall join, while the evil in that heart will deliver judgment."

For a moment she was silent, her attention given entirely to the wands in their supposedly random pattern before her. That she utterly believed in what she said was manifest. And that belief began to influence Saranna. The confidence of this dweller in the hidden garden was so assertive that she could not deny this as mere superstition and folly.

"It is well. The Old Ones have spoken." The Fox Lady gathered the ivory sticks together, fitted them once more into the fox-patterned box. "Now, younger sister, attend to what I say to you. We have seen what may be, and the reading of the wands was in all ways auspicious. But a faint heart may put to naught the brightest of foretellings. I say this—be strong of heart, trample down your fears even as a Bannerman spurs his horse to trample down the barbarians of the outer Hordes. She who you must strive against is strong of will; therefore, your will must be as steel to the iron of hers.

"There advances soon upon us an hour of judgment. At that time, do you come to me. For scattered forces defeat a general before he does battle. Do you understand?"

"Yes," for the first time Saranna spoke. And then she added in a rush of words. "They—Mrs. Whaley has sent for men to come from the city. They want to shoot the foxes, destroy this garden, all that is in it."

There was no change of expression in the lady's face, which might have been carved from the same flawless and aged ivory as fashioned the wands she had cast to foretell the fortune.

"Rumors of such madness have already been reported, younger sister. Remember, fear you must hold from you as you would avert a sword pointed to your throat when you have a shield in your hand to raise between. When the time comes you shall know it; then you and the younger one must come hither. I have certain powers which are the heritage of the women of my mother's ancient clan. But in times of great danger one standing alone may be as a too-lightly rooted tree facing a storm of wind. I would not be uprooted before my time, and thus you can help in another way—

"Now," she clapped her hands together and out of the shadows beyond the bed the old serving woman came bearing a tray on which were two handleless cups, covered.

The Fox Lady took up one, motioned for Saranna to lift the other. As the girl set aside the saucer lid, she sniffed again that flowerlike odor of the tea.

"Let us sip to fortune and an hour when all debts shall be settled," the Fox Lady said.

Saranna sipped, then drank more deeply. The red and gold, green, blue, all the color of that magnificent room beyond the moon door began to swirl around her. Did that ivory-skinned face before her suddenly sharpen, nose and jaw become another shape, russet fur covering that muzzle, or was that only some fantastic flight of imagination?

XVI

Chen _Shock_

Saranna had a confused dream. She was in her own chamber at Tiensin but there were two people there with her and the room was poorly lighted. They pulled and tugged at her, and, against her will (which seemed dulled so that she could not summon any resistance) they were clothing her in that same drab and shabby dress in which she had traveled from Sussex. Then, when she was fully clothed, one of them supported her while the other pushed a cup so tightly to her lips, that, in sheer discomfort, she opened her mouth, to be choked by a bitter tasting liquid swiftly poured therein.

Between them they then led her, or rather half-dragged her toward the doorway. There was another dusky figure waiting in the hallway. Dimly she heard a buzz of whispering amongst the three now surrounding her. Then that dream ended abruptly after the manner of dreams.

Saranna was first aware of a slight rocking of her bed. The sway reminded her of something else from long ago. But it was so hard to think, to remember. Above her closed eyes was an area of pulsating pain and she felt wretchedly sick. She turned her head on her pillow. The wave of pain answering that movement, slight as it was, made her gasp and then moan. She was so ill—

Mother—where was Mother? She could help—

Now that her head remained still, the pain was not

189

quite so acute. Slowly, Saranna opened her eyes. The bed on which she lay— Where *was* she? This was not her small chamber in the Sussex cottage. No, the area was even more cramped. And Sussex—she had left Sussex, hadn't she?

Mother— Mother was dead!

Memory was returning in bits and pieces and with it stalked fear. She could already guess that this was no normal awakening. She had gone from Sussex to a ship—

A ship! The foul odors she could smell now, the swing of the narrow bed on which she lay—she was on a ship!

But how could that be? Because there had been houses after the ship—one in—in a city. And then one— Saranna's dulled wits strained to piece together those bits of memory.

Tiensin!

The recalling of that name might have turned a key. Because now flooded back the days—and nights—at Tiensin—with all their perplexities and threats of danger.

This was not Tiensin, and it was certainly not the room behind the moon gate which was her last clear recollection. She had drunk tea with the Fox Lady. After that had followed that queer dream. And now she awoke here. Where was she?

The throbbing pain in her head, those waves of queasiness which rolled over her with every movement were so weakening it was hard to think clearly. But she could use her eyes.

They told her that she lay on a very narrow bunk in what must be a small ship's cabin. There were the smells of an unclean place to further upset her uneasy stomach. Such light as there was came from a hooded lantern pegged to a low beam overhead.

There—there was her sea chest! Draped over it her shawl, her bonnet, the creased ribbons dangling. In spite of her sickness and the pain in her head, Saranna began to believe in the reality of what she saw.

Then that queer dream of hers. Someone or ones had half-roused her from a very deep sleep and dressed her.

Who were *they*? Not the Fox Lady and her people, of that Saranna was certain. And why was she on a ship? Where were *they* taking her—and why?

There was a mug standing on a shelf at the other side of the cabin. Her mouth was so dry—if she only had a drink! Could she reach that? And if so, did it hold something which would alleviate her thirst? She ran her tongue tip over her lips as she stared at the mug.

Thirsty—so thirsty— On board a ship— Though she must have gone to sleep somehow in the house behind the moon door. She began to listen intently, trying to pick up the sound of wind and wave as she had heard it when she had come south.

There were instead small creakings, the slosh of water. And Saranna thought that, though she was clearly afloat, the ship in which she now lay was making no headway. Were they docked? The small spark of hope that thought brought made her move.

As she struggled upward, pain in her head intensified, to bring a moan from her lips. But she had swung her body half off the bunk, clawed at the edge to steady her, that she might not fall to the floor. Nausea surged to wrack her.

Only that fear which bolstered her determination got her somehow to her feet. So low was the cabin that she had to bend her head a little. She lurched to the shelf, reached out one hand for the tantalizing mug as she kept the other in a tight hold to balance her on her feet.

Liquid did cover the bottom of the mug, but as she raised it to her mouth the sourish fumes of the stuff made her stomach twist once more, and she dropped it to the floor.

Air—if she could only get into the fresh clean air, that might do her good. Holding on as best she could to the cabin wall, Saranna took four or five small steps which brought her to what was plainly the door. Against that she put her flattened palm, pushed with what little strength she had. To no purpose. She must be locked in!

Why?

Her head hurt so that she could not keep her feet. Now she half-stumbled, half-fell, aiming for the bunk, and landed on her knees, her arms across the stained and rumpled covering upon which she had lain earlier. She was a prisoner here—but why? And who had done this?

It would be very easy to claw her way back up on this noisome shelf, lapse back into unknowing, uncaring unconsciousness. But that she must not do. She rested her head on the surface of the bunk and tried to think in a clear and logical way.

Now she could most vividly recall all which happened in the hidden garden, every word and gesture of the Fox Lady, how she had thrown the wands in that strange manner of foretelling Damaris had called *I Ching*. And what had been then her urging? Stand firm, hold fear from her—come with Damaris when danger arose.

"But I can't," Saranna whispered. "I can't."

Stand firm, hold fear from her—

She straightened her shoulders, levered herself up and away from the bunk. Now she looked down at her crumpled dress. She forced one shaking hand into the front of her chemisette. It was still there! Whoever had dragged her hither had not taken the fox pendant.

Dragging that out of hiding, Saranna centered her gaze upon it. She was moving by instinct alone, yet there was that which suggested that this was what she must do. Cupping the pendant in her hand, she raised it to her forehead, the seat of that sickening pain. And there she held the piece of jade between her sweating palm and her head.

She began to breathe slowly and evenly. What she was attempting she could not have explained, it was as if her body rather than her mind, obeyed some unconscious order. Now Saranna closed her eyes, tried to picture the Fox Lady as she had seen her first, dancing before her followers, her furred and pointed face turned up to the moon.

Clearer and clearer came that vision. Now the head of the dancer was turned directly to face Saranna. The eyes

of the Fox Lady met hers and held, grew larger, larger—
filled the whole of the world—

Did the girl make some plea during that meeting of
eyes—perhaps even of minds? She was not consciously
aware of doing so. Nor was she now still plagued by the
miseries of her body. It was as if what she, Saranna Stowell, really was, the element of her true identity, assumed
command and the body was fully subject to her.

She arose from her knees. But she still held the pendant in one hand, her left. Now she looked around the
room with purpose, knowing just what must be done, and
seeking for the tool with which to do it.

Nothing—nothing of what she needed. She turned to
her sea chest, threw its contents out upon the floor. Her
hand closed upon her second pair of stays. She dropped
the pendant, letting it swing from its cord. Her workbox
was not there she noted, nor either of the dresses she had
worked upon the past few days. She had only her teeth
and her fingers.

Working with haste but carefully, she ripped and
chewed at the tough cloth. At last that gave in a tear large
enough for her purpose and she drew out the wide front
busk, the thickest and strongest of those whalebone ribs.

She paid no more heed to the tangle of clothing lying
on the dirty floor but gained again the cabin door. With
infinite care and all the skill she could bring to bear on
the task, she began to force the narrow, but strong strip
of whalebone between the jamb and the edge of the door
itself.

Time and dampness were on her side. The wood was
warped enough to let the busk slip through the narrow
crack. With that much of her purpose achieved, she
crouched to listen. There was nothing to be heard but the
murmur of water. She was sure she was on a river sloop,
and one now docked. Was there some guard on board, or
had she, in her drugged state, been deemed so safely captive she was left alone?

She could not continue to wait; time might be of the
utmost importance. Now she began to wriggle the busk

upward, seeking contact with the bar which bolted her in here. From her journey on Mr. Fowke's sloop she knew such fastenings were simple. She could only hope that this would prove to be of the same nature.

There! The busk had encountered opposition. She had touched the bar. Slow, steadily, using all the pressure she could obtain from the pliant length of whalebone, Saranna began to lever that sealing bar up out of its holders.

This action seemed to take all the time in the world. The girl was wet with perspiration, weak with the effort she was forcing from her body. Then—suddenly, the bar rattled loose!

There was a clatter from without as it fell, sounding to Saranna nearly as loud as the thunderclaps on the night of the storm. She tensed; if there were any guards on board, that would bring them running. However, when she heard no thud of boots or feet along the planking of the deck, she gave a quick shove and had her door to freedom.

After the gloom of the cabin, the bright light of day half-blinded her. But the air—the good air! Saranna staggered forward, out into the sun. For a moment, she was so glad to be free that she was unaware of anything else save that fact.

And she had been right in her guess. The sloop was tied up at a wharf. As she tottered around to face land-ward, she saw the hedge-walled alley which led from the water to Tiensin. At least she was still in familiar territory. But she was not safe.

No, those who had taken her from her bedchamber were of Tiensin, or at least they had been given full run of that house. They need only sight her again and—

Saranna crept forward along the deck, watching feverishly for any sign of life ashore. She edged down the plank walk to the wharf. Could she hide out in the garden? She must—! Perhaps she could even reach the hidden garden where the Fox Lady might grant her some refuge. But there were gardeners ever at work around the estate. If she were sighted—

She made the best speed she could to the shadow of the hedge, then edged along that, trying to be alert to any sound, any glimpse of someone at work here. Should she try to reach the road beyond the orchard, and, with that as a guide, head to Queen's Pleasure?

But with Honora here—

That odd strength which had come to her during that moment in the cabin when she had envisioned the Fox Lady seemed to be now fast ebbing. Her head was once more aching cruelly, and her body was so weak she could barely keep on her feet and moving. No, she must discover some hiding place until she was stronger. She could not hope to round the house in the open to reach the hidden garden, not in the full light of day.

In the end she fell and so found a hollow beneath the low spreading limbs of a clipped shrub. There she lay, crouching as small as she might in a dark huddle. Perhaps she fainted; perhaps she slept. But she did not remember much of what followed.

There was something pulling at her shoulder, a voice whispering in her ear:

"Please, Saranna—please! Wake up—wake up!"

Saranna tried to twitch away from that hold, close her ears to that voice. But, both were insistent, and would not let her rest.

"Saranna!"

She choked, coughed. Her nose was full of a pungent scent. She opened her eyes. In the dark, someone crouched beside her. She tried to brush away the scent, and her hand struck against that of another. Saranna seized upon a small wrist.

"What—what are you doing?" She sniffed and coughed again. But the irritating scent was waking her, clearing her head. "Damaris?"

"Yes. Oh, Saranna, where were you? They said—I heard them—you went away with Rufus. Mr. Fowke came and they told him that. He—he was very angry, I think. He would not talk to *her* after she had Mrs. Parton and Millie out to tell him it was so. And when I went to your room—everything was gone. Except your new dresses. Millie said you gave them to her. But I didn't believe her at all. Millie was awfully afraid. *She* says she's going to sell Millie, sell her deep South! Then—the Princess—she sent one of her people, told me to hunt in the garden. Saranna, what happened to you?"

"I'm not sure." At least that headache did not wrack her, as it had at her first waking. Rather the pain had subsided into a low throb which was bearable. But she had to gather her wits with firm purpose to understand Damaris' fast gabble of recent events.

"I was on a boat—" Saranna tried to make sense of what had happened. "First—I went to the garden and the Fox Lady. She threw wands and read something about the future." Through the dark, she heard a small gasp from Damaris. "Then we drank tea. And after—there is a queer dream about people dressing me—leading me to a door after they made me drink something nasty. I woke up in the boat and I was sick—"

"How did you get here?"

"I—I don't really know. The pendant—there was something about the pendant made me think in spite of my being so sick. So I got out of the cabin—and then I hid—" At that moment her adventures had once more begun to take on the aura of a dream—rather a nightmare. Yet she *was* out in the garden in the dark with Damaris crouching beside her.

"*She*'s awfully angry," Damaris whispered. "*She* put off the company that was coming. I think she wants to tear down the garden before she has anyone here. Rufus is gone. Maybe downriver to meet those men she sent for. I've been listening all I can. She thinks I'm locked up." Damaris gave a soft laugh. "I—I called the Princess and told her about your being gone. It was she who had her people look for you. She said you are part of what must come."

"Who is the Princess?" Saranna had loosed Damaris and crawled out of the hollow which had hidden her. She was very hungry, even more thirsty. "Do we go to her now?"

"Not yet," Damaris returned promptly. "She is drawing her forces, I think. When she does that she can only have her own people, the ones who know her, around her."

"I have to have something to eat, drink." Saranna was not sure she dared trust her cramped legs as yet. Where would she find shelter if she could not reach the hidden garden which now took on the semblance of an island of safety in a world where she could not trust anyone save Damaris? Mr. Fowke—for the first time in her life Saranna found herself crying without being aware of her tears until their salt-flow down her cheeks dripped upon her lips.

Mr. Fowke believed she had gone with Rufus Parton. Their lies must have seemed overwhelming evidence or he would not have left. Her painfully composed message had been worth nothing.

"I can't get into the kitchen," Damaris stood to her full height. "They would see me. Listen, Saranna, you can get a drink at the fountain. They cleaned that out and started it running, 'cause they thought company was coming. If you stay there I can go to the quarters. Old Jane, they don't watch by her at nights now, she sleeps so much. I can get some corn bread, something there—"

At the thought of water, of any kind of food, Saranna was ready to move. But she found that she staggered when she tried to walk, and Damaris had to half-support as well as lead her. There was no moon tonight, even a waning one. And Saranna did not know how the younger girl found so direct a path through the hedges, until they emerged in a round open space, in which a fountain did play, and there were benches placed here and there among the greenery.

The water brought her stumbling forward to fall to her knees while she scooped it up with both hands, sucking avidly at a portion cupped to reach her lips. Then she splashed droplets over her face and down the front of her already ill-treated dress. When they had clothed her in that dream time, they had made no attempt to fasten up her hair. And her braids, half-undone, fell down her back, leaves and twigs caught in them.

Altogether, she decided, she must look like some road-tramping beggar.

"Damaris—" Drinking left her voice less of a croak. But, as she looked over her shoulder, she could see no other beside her. The younger girl must have already slipped away on her try at getting some rations from the old nurse's cabin. Saranna drank again.

When she wiped her face with the hem of her bedraggled skirt, she suddenly sighted the creature which had come noiselessly out of the darkness to face her from the other side of the fountain basin. In spite of the darkness this ghostly form had lines she could distinguish, one of those large white foxes, the like of which had attacked Rufus.

However, Saranna felt no fear. Doglike, the fox sat on its haunches. The longer she surveyed it, the clearer she could make out its form, as if the white fur had some glow of its own. Its head might have provided the artist who had carved the jade piece she wore as a model. Was it a sentry, a guard, dispatched through another's will to make certain that she remained safe? Saranna no longer questioned whether such things could be. The Fox Lady, somehow she was above and beyond the limitations of Saranna's reality.

She remembered now that Damaris had not answered her first question as to the identity of the Princess. How had the Fox Lady found her way to this land? With the Old Captain who had loved the beautiful things of China so completely that he also had collected her in some fashion as his crowning treasure?

Yet Saranna, having had even so small a contact with the dweller in the garden, was certain that the Fox Lady obeyed only her own will, and that if she lived in the shadow of Tiensin, behind her own moon door, it was because she would have it so.

The white fox arose, faced a little away from Saranna, pointing its muzzle to the left. However, the beast did not growl or show any signs of uneasiness. So warned, Saranna lost no time in crawling on her hands and knees, not even taking a moment to rise to her feet, back to the nearest bench. There was a rustling in the shrubbery.

Saranna, breathless, tried to watch the fox and also the space from whence that noise came. Still the fox showed no sign of more than just interest. She could only depend upon the animal's warning—

"Saranna?"

"Damaris!"

"Here!" Thankfully she answered whisper with whisper. The small figure slipped out of a narrow space between two of the high-growing shrubs and came to her.

"Corn bread and it's all cold. But I dabbed some honey on it." She thrust a crumbling mass into Saranna's hands. "It's the best I could do."

Saranna, lost to all thought of manners, crammed the sticky, dry stuff into her mouth in as large bites as she could manage. She chewed and swallowed, and then had to seek the fountain side again for a drink to help that mess down. But when she had eaten the cold slab to the last crumb she could lick from her fingers, she felt much better.

"I saw the Poker. She was going down to the wharf. She had a basket." Damaris had seated herself beside Saranna. "Maybe she was going to take you some food—"

Saranna started up. It would need only one glance at that open cabin door and the alarm would be out. They would realize very well that she could not have gone far. Which meant the garden would be searched. Where—?

Damaris' hand closed upon hers.

"You've got to hide," she stated the obvious. "I guess promises sometimes have to be broken. Grandfather would do this if he were here. You come with me."

Once more they made a circuitous way from one piece

of shelter, under tree, bush, or shrub to the next. Saranna saw that white shape slipping along in their wake, and then the first fox was joined by a second.

Damaris did not turn to the house but kept a course which led to the courtyard with its cluster of small buildings all designed for special uses. There were two lighted lanterns set up on posts, but luckily the circles of radiance about them were not great.

The younger girl, still hand clasped with Saranna, made her way to the spring house. She pushed upon the door and slipped inside.

"Now," she told Saranna. "I have to feel my way, and I have to use both hands. You hold on to my skirt, tight. And we have to go slow—it's all dark here."

They shuffled along against a damp, cold wall where Saranna's shoulder brushed the stone blocks of its building.

"Stop here," Damaris ordered.

That dark was so utter Saranna could not see anything of the younger girl, but she did hear a series of scratching noises. Then a faint grating sound.

"Stoop down—way down," Damaris said. "Then come up—slow."

Saranna did as she was ordered. Now both shoulders brushed against walls as she moved forward half-crouched.

"Wait here. I have to close the door."

Damaris squeezed back by her in a space so narrow that Saranna's breath came faster, her fear of being shut in some kind of box was awakening. Once more Damaris pushed past her.

Holding tightly to the girl's skirt, Saranna crept forward step by reluctant step.

"You can straighten up now," Damaris' voice echoed hollowly. "And I'll tell you when the stairs start—"

Stairs? A secret way into Tiensin?

"Right here," Damaris spoke with the confidence of one who had made this trip before. "We have to go down—twelve steps—"

Saranna felt cautiously with the toe of her shoe. She began to count in her head as she went down. Twelve— then another flat surface.

"Straight ahead now—until we go up again—" Damaris said.

"What is this—a passage?"

"A secret," Damaris replied. "It's a secret I promised not to tell. But we have to use it. Anyway, *she* don't know about it. Nobody in Tiensin did after the workmen went back to China, nobody but Grandfather and me. He never even told my father. Straight ahead—and it won't be too far, I promise, Saranna."

XVII

Huan *Dispersion*

As Saranna climbed the second flight of stairs, she was completely confused. Why had this hidden way been fashioned to Captain Whaley's order? Had he feared some vengeance and so set up a way of secret escape? And where within Tiensin would they emerge?

"Wait!" Saranna had counted only five steps when Damaris' voice brought her to a halt. "Now I have to open the other door."

There were sounds probably magnified by the darkness in which they stood. Then light burst upon them. Those beams were faint enough but seemed dazzling to Saranna after her long (for it seemed very long) period in the total dark.

Against that light showed Damaris' silhouette. Then the younger girl climbed a step or two and vanished. Saranna followed as quickly as she could, so eager to be out of that black passage that she did not fear what might lie ahead.

However, this room she entered through a trapdoor was no part of Tiensin she had ever seen. And piled around its low walls were those wicker hampers she herself had helped to pack on the night of the storm. A single lantern hung from a hook in the ceiling right above the door. This was plainly a storeroom, but how near those ordinarily used by the household, Saranna wondered?

Damaris appeared fully at ease, showing no wariness. She lowered the trapdoor, which moved easily as if designed to be handled by one without great physical strength. Then she walked confidently to the door.

"You wait here—just a minute," the younger girl ordered, slipping through the narrowest crack she could manage.

As she stood there, Saranna's nose twitched. There were strange odors in this place. Not the damp of underground, nor the familiar mustiness of most storerooms. The scent she picked up was spicy, a little like perfume. She knew it of old, this was that same smell she had caught in Damaris' bedchamber. Also in its concentration was a mingling of those pleasant perfumes from the chamber behind the moon door. Had the secret way brought them so into the domain of the Fox Lady?

Saranna was given little time to speculate. The door opened as softly as Damaris had closed it. Now the child had returned followed by that old woman who so noiselessly and deftly served the tea and played the lute in the moon house. The ancient one studied Saranna and gave a tongue-clicking sound which could only express dismay.

"It is all right," Damaris said. "You must go with A-Han. The Princess cannot be disturbed while she summons the forces. But afterward, she will need us."

A-Han came to Saranna. Gently she took the girl's scratched and grimed hand, patted it reassuringly. Smiling she drew the older girl with her, out of the door into a courtyard around which stood the four walls of a building. Gleams of lanterns shown through latticed windows, diffused by those blinds to dim radiance.

With A-Han, Saranna stepped up on a narrow terrace and entered a shadowy room. The servant pushed her down on a chair, hurried to light another lantern, this covered with pale golden silk so that its light was golden, too. She scurried about at a pace which belied her age-marked face, bringing first a large but low tub, then an array of pots and jars, and lastly an armload of what could only be towels.

There was a scratching at the door, a low word. A-Han opened a sliding panel, brought in a huge pitcher from which steam curled, after that two buckets, the contents of which she splashed into the tub, adding the heated water more slowly with much testing by her fingers.

Saranna lay resting, half drowsing, on a low divan sometime later. She had been bathed as if she were a child, then her body rubbed with a fragrant oil to ease her aches. Tea had been brought her and small cakes which were not sweet, but crisp and filled with a paste of meat and vegetables. She wore not her torn and shabby clothing, but rather a long robe styled much as that she had seen last on the Princess. This thick brocade was a rust-brown red in color, and it was overpatterned with fine embroidery in a design of pine branches and cones— the cones being picked out with threads of gold, so her every move awakened a spark or two of glitter.

Her hair had been smoothed with a comb dipped in scented liquid between each stroke and then formed into a soft coil at the nape of her neck into which pins with flower heads had been skillfully placed to hold safely. In all her life, even during the good days in Boston, Saranna had never known such care, or been surrounded by such luxury and beauty.

A-Han's hands had somehow driven even the ache from her head, as the old woman had kneaded and worked upon the girl's neck and shoulders. She drifted now on a sea of drowsy contentment. Those dangers and fears which had driven her for hours seemed very far away and of little matter. She did not even ask for Damaris who had vanished again. No, it was enough to lie here in the golden light of the lantern, to feel clean and safe—

Saranna's eyes drooped shut, and she must have slept. Then into that sleep came a summons which she knew she must obey.

"Younger sister, it is now the hour!"

Saranna stirred. She tried to cling to slumber; there was something waiting her when she waked—something she dared not—

"Younger sister, wake!"

That command she could not withstand.

She opened her eyes. The golden lantern no longer glowed. Instead, sunlight struck across the floor. Full in the path of that natural light stood one she knew.

A robe of blue-green, so stiff with silver embroidery that it was like armor rather than any conventional dress, covered this woman from throat to floor. Above the high collar the fox face turned toward her, and above that an awesome headdress of what must be royal rank.

The Fox Lady raised her hand, beckoned. Saranna struggled free of the last dregs of her sleep and arose. Then she saw that a little behind the impressive figure of this ruler of the hidden garden was Damaris.

Even as Saranna, she wore an embroidered robe, her hair nearly all hidden under a small crown of filigree and flowers. She held her hands stiffly before her, carrying, as if it were a small shield for her breast, a round piece of polished metal. Nor did Damaris give any greeting as Saranna moved to join them. Her expression was one of concentration, as if she were intent upon some serious act for which she alone was responsible.

The Fox Lady passed into the courtyard beyond the room where Saranna had lain, and the girls followed behind her. They crossed a pavement between tubs in which small flowering trees and shrubs were rooted, and entered yet another door. Here was the room Saranna had seen twice before, that which was the chamber of the Fox Lady.

Incense curled before a statue in the corner, the statue of a woman who held within her arms, as she might a nursing child, a fox cub. While from the folds of her carven robe, where the long skirt trailed a little on to the base supporting her hidden feet, were the heads of other cubs, their sharp muzzles a little elevated as if they sniffed the air, something very alert and waiting about them.

Before the statue, the Fox Lady bowed her head. Her voice arose in a sing-song chant. From beneath the concealing length of sleeve, her hand advanced to pick up a small carven stick lying at the feet of the statue. With this the Fox Lady struck a jade ring hanging suspended to her right. The chime of the sound seemed to fill the room, roll out across the garden with all the power of a thunderclap, musical as the note was.

That must have been a signal, for, beyond the moon door, from the terrace without, there now began the slow beat of a drum, low, almost muffled. Saranna felt the rhythm through her body as if the soft beat kept time to the beating of her own heart. The Fox Lady bowed once more to the statue and then paced, as one heading a formal procession, through the moon door onto the terrace.

This time they walked into the full light of day; no moon helped to make the world a mystery. Yet here were also the foxes gathered in a line which extended from one end of the terrace to the other. Motionless they sat so. They might well have been carved from red stone. Save for the larger two just before where the Fox Lady came to a halt. That pair was silver-white, larger than their fellows.

There were men stationed behind that gathering of foxes—four, two on either side. They, too, had the appearance of strange dream creatures, for their bodies were entirely encased in armor. And those helms which completely covered their faces were giant fox heads wrought in burnished and lifelike painted lacquer. Their hands were closed upon the staffs of banners at the folds of which the wind tugged fitfully.

Saranna could now see the drummer, a man with a face as aged as that of A-Han, a man with a whisper of white beard on his chin. He tapped out that monotonous beat with the fingers of his right hand, holding the drum before him as he sat cross-legged on the terrace. There were two others beside him, older women, one A-Han, the other even more aged and bent. Together they tended a brazier. Incense smoke arose in great gray curls from its pierced top.

Beat—beat—the drum rhythm was the only sound. The rise and fall of those fingers which induced it the only movement now among the party on the terrace. They all faced in quiet watchfulness the direction of the path down which Saranna had twice found her way.

There was a distant shout, a crashing. Saranna started, then noted that those with her betrayed no such sign of surprise. They seemed fully ready to confront what came in their own fashion. Not even one of the foxes showed any uneasiness.

A second crash, then the sound of trampling through bushes which the low beat of the drum could neither disguise nor cover. Saranna's heart beat faster than the drum now. She guessed what was happening; the men Honora had planned to bring from the city must be here, already beginning their destruction of the hidden garden. Yet those on the terrace did not move—they waited.

There followed sounds of crashing stone, of splintering and chopping, which made Saranna sick. Still the Fox Lady faced unmoved, as far as the girl could perceive, the source of those sounds. However, now her hands reached forth—pushing free of those long sleeves—one to Damaris, one to Saranna. And the older girl knew instinctively what was expected of her at this moment. She clasped the left hand of the lady with her right, those nail coverings cold and hard in her grasp. While Damaris, now holding the round piece of metal with her right hand, took the lady's with her left. So linked, they stood, still impassive.

A bush was shaken furiously, dragged free of the soil, and tossed aside. Into the open crowded a crew so ugly that Saranna wanted to shrink away, only to understand that at this moment she could and dare not. But, having broken into the open before the terrace, the men stopped, amazed at the party waiting to receive them. Saranna saw uncertainty cross the faces of the foremost. Then their party parted to give Honora passage.

She stared in turn at the Fox Lady. Then her mouth twisted as she screamed:

"Shoot! Kill those foxes—!"

Saranna saw guns swing in on their targets. Not one of the waiting animals moved from its place in line. Nor did any of the armored men make a gesture of defense. They would all be killed! Her fear was like a sudden ice-cold knife thrust through her. Still she could not now have broken the hold which linked her with the Fox Lady, even if panic fully possessed her.

And she must not let that happen, she must not! There was a reason for this gathering of the garden inhabitants and in this moment Saranna bowed her will, stifled her alarm, tried to become in turn part of whatever they would do.

In the same instant she made that decision, she experienced something else. It was as if some inner strength which was hers, but which she had never known before she possessed, was being drawn out of her. She could actually feel that energy draining from her body, through that hand linkage. This force was what the Fox Lady must have.

For the first time the Fox Lady herself spoke. Her words were strange, they seemed to echo eerily in one's head in the way the gong sound had echoed earlier. Three times she repeated that series of sounds.

"Shoot!" Honora's face contorted. "Shoot, I tell you!"

Then Saranna witnessed the unbelievable. Those guns did come up, center on the terrace, and—

The weapons dissolved! There were no guns in the hands of the invaders. There were only sticks. Then the sticks twisted, turned, became living ropes of scaled flesh. The men cried out, threw the living horrors from them. Those behind edged away, their faces expressing their panic and horror.

"No," Honora caught at the sleeve of the nearest.

"Don't believe what you see. She can make you think anything is true. Look there—it's a gun—a gun!" She pointed
wildly to the weapon he had thrown away in terror.

She spoke the truth. Now a shotgun did lie upon the
path. But the man eyed it as if it were still a snake. He
jerked free of Honora's grasp with an oath, continued to
back away.

"Out—" he called to the others. "Let's get out of
here!"

They stampeded back through the broken brush.
Honora stood there alone. But she did not retreat. All
color left from her face. She wore a mask of ugly fury, as
alien, and far more dreadful, than the furred visage the
Fox Lady turned upon the intruders.

"You—witch!" Honora no longer screamed, her voice
was low, ragged, with the intensity of her rage. "You heathen witch! I know your tricks. Just as you played them
with that old fool, the Captain. You cannot play them
with me—ever! And they—" she gestured behind her to
where the men had disappeared, "when they have a
chance to think, they will realize the truth. Then no trick
of yours will save you—any of you!" Her gaze swept
along the line of Bannerman and foxes, Damaris, the
lady, and Saranna.

She began to smile, and that smile was as dreadful as
her grimace had earlier been.

"All here—all of you! Which is my good fortune, not
yours. You—" she pointed at Damaris "—with you out of
my way I shall have Tiensin. You—" she came next to the
Fox Lady "—you and your tricks have had their day.
Now, you heathen witch, you shall have an accident—a
fatal one! You—" she had reached Saranna, and her lips
curved venomously "—you who would dip into my father's pockets, and, most of all, want to—" Her mouth
tightened as if even in this hour she could not bring herself to say plainly what was the core of the hate which
blazed in her eyes.

"I am not tricked, nor shall I be by any of your mind
witchery." She spoke again to the Fox Lady. "I know that I

hold this, and I shall use it." She held out the hand which had been hidden in the folds of her skirt.

Saranna saw the sun glint on the barrel of the small gun—a round, fat barrel. Honora held a derringer. She was raising her hand—about to aim at one of them. Which one?

The white foxes moved. They leaped forward together, as if they had been trained for just such an attack. The fangs of one fastened on Honora's wide upper sleeve, the other dashed, growling, to her left.

She screamed. But the fox on her right had achieved its purpose. The beast had loosened her grip on the derringer, and it spun away, to land beside the discarded shotgun on the path. Honora shrunk back. Now the foxes circled her, growling and snapping. They were herding her on toward the terrace as sheep dogs would handle a straying member of the flock they were set to guard.

Beating with her hands against the air, her breath coming in whistling gasps, Honora stumbled forward.

"No, no, no!" Fear and rage fought together on her face. She had no beauty now as she was forced by the leaping, snapping foxes onto the edge of the terrace. Yet, in spite of all, her anger was greater than her fear. And she fixed her gaze in a defiant stare on the Fox Lady.

As Honora came to a halt directly before her enemy, the foxes settled a little behind her, sitting up motionless again. Even the beat of the drum had stopped.

It was Honora who broke the silence, her voice hoarse:

"You have not won! They will regain their wits, and they will not be the easier on you because you tricked them."

"That is so," the Fox Lady answered her with majestic calm.

"Then—you had better listen to me." Honora made brushing motions along the outward swell of her skirt, as if ridding herself of the effects of her momentary panic. "I want you gone! I will even make you the same offer

Captain Whaley made to the rest—passage back to your own country."

"You are generous—" the Fox Lady returned, a remote tone in her voice. "Before you expend your breath in promises, remember that the swiftest of horses cannot overtake a word once spoken."

"I want you gone, you and your tricks!" Honora's tone lost some of its control.

"That we have always known," conceded the Fox Lady. "This I say to you now: Before you beat a dog, learn his master—or his mistress's name."

"You know I can do as I wish—" Honora's hand shook a little. As if she were aware of this betrayal, she whipped her fingers hiding once again in the folds of her skirt. "I shall send the men again—better armed—"

"So it is written—"

"You cannot escape a second time—"

"Perhaps not. Yet there is something which still must be done."

The Fox Lady's hand turned in Saranna's, seeking freedom. And the girl relinquished her grip upon those slender fingers with their gemmed nail guards. Damaris must have broken linkage at the same time, for, Saranna, glancing sidewise, saw the lady reach out and take from the younger girl the round of metal which she had so carefully held.

With this in her two hands, the Fox Lady lifted it to the level of her sharp pointed muzzle, stared straight into the polished surface as if it were a proper mirror and she would make sure of the correctness of her toilet. Then she stepped forward until she was within touching distance of Honora.

Reversing the mirror, she held it out and a little down, so it was now directly before Honora's own face.

"Look upon yourself, woman," the Fox Lady ordered. "Look and see what is to be seen in you!"

Honora's eyes centered upon the strange mirror. Slowly her face changed, anger receded, fear grew—such an agony of fear as Saranna would have believed no human countenance could ever frame. Then Honora screamed, a cry of both terror and despair. Her hands flew up to hide her face. She swayed back and forth, as if she no longer had strength or will enough to keep on her feet.

"Go!" ordered the Fox Lady. "Go, rally those barbarians you would turn upon us. Go, seek in every mirror you can find for what you once thought you were, what others saw in you, those who knew you not as your heart has made you. Go!"

Honora tottered as she turned, then she staggered away, her hands still half-covering her face. She blundered against bushes, gave another scream, broke through the opening between the battered shrubs once again where her crew of raiders had entered.

They could hear her rough passage, and the two white foxes ran a little ways after her, came trotting back, whining like dogs who scented danger, and waited for orders to be on guard.

"They will come again; she was speaking the truth," said the Fox Lady. "Because of their fear, these evil ones will be doubly angry this time."

"But you can—" began Damaris.

Slowly the Fox Lady shook her head. "Not so, younger sister. Once can I call upon the eye-magic and hold the minds of barbarians so. But my strength of purpose is now exhausted. Even if you lend to me again your wills, even then I cannot summon such as give us safety. I have attacked with all I have—" She looked from Damaris to Saranna. "Younger sister, the wands of *I Ching* speak ever the truth. If we would come to fortune out of this trouble, then yours must be the effort. What help can you summon?"

"Help?" repeated Saranna. "But—there is no one. The servants—they will do nothing except what Honora orders and—"

"Mr. Fowke!" Damaris interrupted. "He would come—he would!"

"Even if we could get a message to him—would we have time?" Saranna rubbed her fingertips over the heavy gold embroidery of her borrowed robe. Gerrad Fowke believed that she had gone with Rufus. But her very presence, if she might be able to reach him, would be proof enough of the falsehood of that. Somehow, at that moment, she was sure of his help—though how to summon it—

"We must go!" Damaris ran to her, caught her hand. "We have to, Saranna!"

The older girl glanced from the determination written on Damaris' face to the alien features of the Fox Lady. She could read there no expression in the beast's sharp muzzle and eyes. Yet there was a sense of approval somehow carried to her.

Saranna laughed shakily, twitching the rich robe. "This is not made for running along the highway—"

The Fox Lady clapped her hands and A-Han was at her side. She spoke, giving some order and the old woman nodded eagerly, beckoning to Saranna.

Back in the chamber behind the moon door both Saranna and Damaris struggled out of the robes. A-Han produced a bundle of dull-blue cloth which shook out into trousers and high-collared jackets. Damaris pulled on hers with the ease of one who had done this before. But Saranna, though seeing the advantage of such garments for one in haste, hated to wear them.

"Hurry—!"

"But—these—" Though Saranna fastened the cord of the trousers about her waist, she felt very strange—almost undressed.

"You can run better in them," Damaris pointed out tartly. "Come on!"

The old man who had drummed waited for them beyond the edge of the terrace. The Fox Lady had dismissed them with a nod, retreating to the inner chamber where once more she bowed her head before the statue. Their guide did not take them back along the path which would or should lead them straight into trouble. Instead, he struck on into that portion of the garden lying directly before the other end of the terrace, weaving in and out among the shrubs.

Saranna caught hasty glimpses of a stream, a hump-backed bridge, of flowers and shrubs, but there was no time to really note the wonders through which they hurried. Then they fronted the wall again, but at a different point.

Their guide placed his dark, wrinkled hands on two of the bricks and pushed with all the might left in his shrunken body. Slowly, a whole block of the closely fitted masonry pivoted leaving a narrow space through which they could squeeze. Saranna would never have made it in skirts, she admitted to herself as she struggled through. And it was true that her legs were freer in these queer heathenish garments.

Then her feet found no solid ground and she pitched forward, out and down, landing beside Damaris in a roadside ditch. Behind them there was a crack of sound and Saranna guessed that the wall had again closed, sealing the hidden door.

XVIII

Chi Chi *Completion*

"Well now, ain't this a bit o' luck!"

At first, Saranna cringed closer to the ground like a small animal cornered by death. Rufus!

"Yes, siree—here's a pretty catch. Two of them pesky heathens right in my hands, as the saying goes."

"Damaris—run!" Saranna scrambled up somehow, to face Rufus Parton. He held a shotgun in the crook of his arm as he stood grinning down at her. If she could divert him only for a few seconds, Damaris might get free.

"Let little Missie run," he agreed. "She won't get far—Mrs. Whaley has her guards out. You're in a pretty pickle, ain't you, m'girl?"

His bold eyes roved over her figure. Saranna wanted to cringe again. But before Rufus—no, she would never do that!

"Now, you just come up out of that there dirty hole, m'girl—"

She heard Damaris scuttle away to her right, but she did not even turn her head to watch the younger girl run. Perhaps Rufus was right. Damaris might be caught before she reached the edge of Tiensin land. On the other hand, there was always a chance that she could elude Honora's guards and reach Gerrad Fowke. Though Saranna could not believe in any rescue for herself now.

Rufus made no attempt to help her climb the steep bank of the ditch. She would not have accepted his assistance anyway. But as she stood at last on the narrow road, he laughed.

"You wearing them heathen clothes, girl, that sure can give a man ideas."

"Now," he added briskly, "you jus' start walkin', m'girl. I'll get you outta my hands back on the sloop and go an' collect from Mrs. Whaley for takin' you away. Then we'll be off upriver to where a parson's waitin'—"

"You can't marry me against my will," Saranna found her tongue at last.

"Oh, you'll be willin', girl," he said. "My mam, now, she knows a bit about fixin' up doses. I'll see you get one of those and you'll be as meek as any lamb. Makes you think muzzy, them do. If I tell you 'yes' then, you'll say 'yes.' Don't you worry none about that. Get a-movin'—"

He caught her by the upper arm, pushed her around, and then applied a vicious shove which nearly sent her spinning to her knees.

"You jus' keep right on a-walkin'. Don't take it all so hard, girl. You an' me, we can do right well for ourselves. I won't never lift a hand to you 'less you try that lookin' down your nose like I was dirt. You'll be m'wife and that's somethin' to be proud of—"

Saranna stumbled on, prodded by his fist between her shoulder blades now and again. She recognized the road: this was the one over which they had come from Queen's Pleasure on Sunday. It would have guided them both back there. Damaris—could Damaris really reach Gerrad Fowke? And what if she did and he came too late, after Rufus Parton had gotten his promised fee from Honora and had taken the sloop upriver?

She tried to think clearly. But Rufus' sudden appearance to halt their escape was such a shock that as yet she had not adjusted to it. She was tired, so tired that it was impossible now to do more than just endure.

"See?" queried her captor. "You can be as nice and easy as the next girl, do a man handle you right. I tell you, girl, where we're goin' you can be big as Mrs.

Whaley. 'Cause I'm not goin' to be any hired man. No, siree. I got me land and the cash to buy more! Someday I'll have us a house as will make this here heathenish place look like a stable! Jus' you wait an' see!"

But Saranna was no longer listening to his boasting. She thought she heard something else—the drum of hooves coming toward them. Some of Honora's city ruffians now mounted to ride sentry duty?

She dared not let herself believe that this could herald the coming of some outsider who might be an aid to her.

"Wait up!" Rufus' voice held a harsher note. "Someone's comin'! Get down!"

The heavy slam of his palm against her shoulders tumbled her off the lane into the brush which masked the ditch, and once more she sprawled into that. But this time Rufus joined her, pulling her farther down into hiding.

Saranna thought by the vibration through the ground that there was more than one rider. And it was quite apparent Rufus did not expect the newcomers to be friendly. He had the shotgun ready, and was a little way up the side of the ditch intent on sighting at whoever came into view.

He was so intent that Saranna, her eyes fixed upon his back to catch any move he might make, began, inch by inch, to slip along the ditch. Not that she had any real chance of escape, but she would not stay meekly there and wait Rufus' future pleasure.

At first she could not see up on the road as did Rufus, as he was perched in a place where the brush was thinner. However, as she edged farther and farther from him, there came another opening. Through that, the riders came into sight.

There was a flash of blue—Damaris! Damaris mounted before Gerrad Fowke on the gray horse he favored. Behind him were men, armed with shotguns, pistols. Saranna recognized two of the riders as men she had seen working the sloop upriver. What would Rufus—?

Saranna glanced quickly from the road to her captor. He was grinning, that grin he had worn as he tormented the captured fox. Whether he would ever have dared shoot she would never know. But with a cry of warning, Saranna threw herself in his direction.

Rufus snarled as his head whipped around. Saranna opened her mouth to scream a second warning and he struck at her, his fist crashing against her cheekbone, the force of the blow sending her back and down into the very bottom of the ditch. She only half-consciously heard Damaris' high voice, the shouts of the men on the road.

Rufus crouched beside her, his hand on her throat, closing, cutting off her breath. She saw him only through a haze of pain as she tried to struggle free. Then, suddenly, he was gone as if some giant's hand had plucked him away. She drew deep gasps of air into her empty lungs, unable for the moment to care about anything but the fact that she could breathe again.

"Saranna! Saranna, did he hurt you?" Damaris was trying to raise her head, peering into her face anxiously. There were threshing sounds from the road above, grunting, a half-stifled cry.

"Mr. Fowke, I met him," Damaris poured into her ear. "He had already heard there was trouble here, he was coming. Oh, Saranna, did you *see* him? He just grabbed Rufe and jerked him up on the road. Now he's pounding him—really licking him!"

She had pushed up to her knees to watch the struggle beyond.

"There!" she added with great satisfaction. "Rufe is just laying still while Sam Knight is tying him up. Oh, Saranna, I never saw a real fight before—"

Apparently, that very unladylike exploit fascinated her.

"Rufe—I'm so glad that he caught Rufe. What was he going to do with you, Saranna?"

The older girl was gingerly rubbing her throat. When she spoke her voice came out as a croak. "He said," she returned in a half-whisper, "he was going to marry me—"

Suddenly she began to shake with broken laughter. It all seemed wildly insane, like part of a nightmare. Yet she could not wake up. Rufus' big plans which he had poured out with such self-importance and confidence enough to frighten her—all brought to nothing in a moment or two.

"He hurt you!" Damaris cried indignantly. "There's a big red place on your cheek, and marks on your throat. He was trying to choke you when Mr. Fowke caught him."

Saranna laughed until she found herself crying instead. Each gasp she drew hurt her bruised throat.

"Saranna!" Damaris' hand fell on her shoulders, shook her. "Please, Saranna, what is the matter? I know he tried to hurt you, but he's gone now and—"

"It's all right, Damaris," a deeper voice broke in upon hers. "Now you just move out of the way and let me lift her—"

Damaris disappeared. In her place was someone else whose firm grasp swung Saranna up and out of the ditch, but did not restore her to her feet; instead, held her as if her body had no weight at all.

"It's all over," Gerrad Fowke reassured her. "I'll get you to someplace quiet—"

"No!" She still could only half-whisper, but now she remembered the urgency which had brought her into this last near-fatal action. "The men Honora brought—they will overrun the moon garden. The Fox Lady says she cannot hold them off a second time—"

"I know. Damaris told me. We have an answer for that. Don't you worry. I'm going to send you back to Queen's Pleasure with Lorenzo, both of you. I want you safely out of this."

She heard Damaris protest and Gerrad Fowke's authoritative answer. Then she was on a horse, arms about her, trotting down the road. Her head had begun to ache again, the pain running from the place Rufus' fist had landed. She felt queasy and sick, and wanted nothing more than what Gerrad Fowke promised—to be safely out of all action.

There was a confused memory of a big black woman who oh'ed and ah'ed and chattered, but who made her comfortable in a strange bed. And then Saranna thankfully allowed herself to sink into a dark world where, mercifully, there were no dreams this time.

"Now, Mr. Gerrad, don' you go wakin' up this child. Just look at her face—that there big bruise a-turnin' green! I declare, you is got no feelin' 't all—not 't all!"

Saranna moved her head on the pillow. The room was light but this was not her chamber at Tiensin; it was smaller, paneled, gave the feeling of a greater age. She could now see the broad back of a woman whose head was tied up with a yellow turban scarf and who was vigorously protesting, even as she backed into the room, apparently unable to withstand the will of the one who confronted her.

"Now, Aunt Bet, you know I wouldn't be here unless it was of importance—"

Gerrad Fowke! It seemed to Saranna that she had always known his voice, would know it even if she never saw his face. She pulled herself high among the pillows, holding the quilt to her chin.

"Please," she called. "What is it?"

The big woman turned around. Her dark face was concerned.

"You see?" she snapped over her shoulder. "You done woke her up with your foolishment!"

But Gerrad Fowke pushed around her, came to stand at the foot of the four-poster.

"Saranna, I hate to ask it of you—but—" For the first time, she saw him without his customary air of authority. He ran one hand through his hair, reducing that to even more disorder. "Damaris is too young, and I've sent the Partons to their quarters. I have to have someone to get to Honora. She's—she seems entirely distraught."

"She hates me," Saranna spoke what she believed to

be the truth. "What makes you think I can help—"

"I don't know if you can. But there has to be *some-one*—"

His hand again went to his head. Saranna wanted to say "no." The last thing she desired was to set foot within Tiensin again. Surely by now, Gerrad knew what Honora had done. Was he upholding her? Saranna could not believe that was true even at this moment.

"All right," she said flatly. "I'll have to have some clothes—"

She was not going back to Tiensin in the strange apparel provided by the Fox Lady. Tongues would wag enough about this venture anyway.

She saw the relief in Gerrad Fowke's expression and knew a pinch of misery in answer. In spite of everything he did care about Honora. Saranna only hoped that he could control her once they were married.

"That's all right. I brought your things. And I would not ask you to go back except that I cannot get to her. She's locked herself in her room and she's screaming all kinds of nonsense. She's even threatened to destroy herself if I come near her—"

"Give me a chance to get dressed." Saranna could no longer watch his distress. She was so tired—tired of all the intrigue and troubles at Tiensin. Though that she would have any influence with Honora was impossible.

Aunt Bet grumbled but she did help her dress, shaking her head over the creases in the dress which Gerrad had apparently caught up without much care. There was, also, a hasty collection of underthings, even stockings and slippers. And when Saranna looked into the mirror as Aunt Bet braided her hair and wound it in a coronet fashion on top of her head, she saw the dark bruise discoloring near half of her face. A pretty sight and there was no bonnet nor veil to hide it either. Gerrad had forgotten those.

She was not to go without some food in her. Aunt Bet insisted on that. And produced such a wealth of eatables that Saranna felt it was better sustenance for an army than one thin female. Only, as she looked at the loaded plate, hunger did return and she did justice to as much as she could.

"Where is Damaris?" she asked when she joined Mr. Fowke outside. He had the Tiensin carriage waiting. But the driver of that was a stranger to Saranna.

"At Tiensin. Or rather with someone in the hidden garden. We ran off those toughs, took their leader prisoner. The sheriff is on his way to tidy up. I've given the Partons notice, though I feel sorry for Collis; I don't think he was a party to what has been going on. He's a slow thinker, but a good overseer."

"And Rufus?" Saranna asked as he took his place beside her and the coach rocked down the drive.

"Rufus," his quarterdeck voice was winter-cold, "has been given a choice. Though I would dearly like to break his neck," a certain warmth colored that, "he has too much to say which would hurt other people. He was told to light out here and now for the West, or face the sheriff. It did not take him long to make up his mind."

Hurt other people—Saranna's thoughts seized on that. Gerrad meant Honora, of course. He had to protect her from gossip, and Rufus need only tell the sheriff of her plot to ruin Saranna.

"You need not fear him again," Gerrad Fowke was continuing. "I have sent a couple of my men to make sure he makes it to the state border. But I think he is frightened enough of the consequences of what he had done not to try to double back. There is nothing for him here now anyway and he knows that very well."

Saranna's bruised face ached. She had a strong desire to put her head in her hands and cry. She was not sure why, but the tears pricked behind the eyes she tried to keep uncaring. Just as she hoped that her face did not betray her present state of that unhappiness, the cause of which she dared not explore.

So she stared straight ahead and asked no more questions. The sooner they reached Tiensin and she did whatever Gerrad Fowke asked of her, the sooner she would be free of all of them. Saranna did not believe he would try to keep her here after what had happened. There were the Sanderses; perhaps they would give her shelter for long enough to let her write Pastor Willis to see if Sussex could present any haven.

The carriage rocked, it was plain that the driver had been given instructions to make as good a pace as he dared. Saranna swayed, held the strap at her side, eluding the arm Mr. Fowke half-advanced as if to steady her.

Then they were in the driveway at Tiensin. There were scars from trampling on the lawn. She knew that the garden which had been breached must show even worse damage. But with Gerrad Fowke she went inside. There was a scared huddle of servants in the hall, John at their head. He turned to Mr. Fowke quickly with an expression of relief on his face.

"Mr. Fowke—Miss Honora, she do act like she ain't right in the head no more—"

"It's all right, John. We're going up—"

Mr. Fowke had taken Saranna's arm, was leading her purposefully to the stairs. As they mounted, he said in a lower voice:

"She will not let me in. But if she will open the door to you, I shall be with you. She has threatened to throw herself from the window if we tried to break in. I do not know what has brought on this terrible wild hysteria."

Saranna remembered that confrontation with the Fox Lady's mirror—could that have been the cause of this? Then what had Honora seen on that polished surface which had driven her to this state?

Honora's maid stood before the closed door. She looked at the two who joined her and, though she was crying, her eyes were also wide with fear. Mr. Fowke motioned her to one side, nodded imperatively to Saranna.

With some hesitation, she stepped forward and knocked at the closed panel.

"Honora—?" Her voice was no longer a hoarse whisper, but neither could she use it without being reminded of Rufus' brutal grip on her throat.

"Honora?" she called again.

"You—!" There was a sharp sound to that single word. Then—again— "You—!"

Through the silence which followed that, Saranna thought she could hear movement on the other side of the door. Mr. Fowke had flattened himself to the right against the wall.

Now Saranna did catch the click of a key in the lock. Mr. Fowke made a small signal with his hand and the girl guessed his purpose. She would be the only one in plain view when that door swung open, but Gerrad Fowke could move in from the side.

The door was opening now—jerked back as if Honora had a purpose which she must accomplish. And Honora did confront her. But this was not an Honora which Saranna had ever seen before. Her dress was wildly disordered, torn lace hanging from the bodice as if she had ripped madly at it with both hands.

Her hair hung down in witchlike, uneven lengths, lank and sweaty. While the face so framed was strange. She constantly worked her lips in grimaces, she might have been chewing on some exceedingly bitter mouthful.

Saranna was transfixed. So startled that for a second or two she did not glimpse the pistol in Honora's hand, the twin to the one she had attempted to use against the Fox Lady.

"YOU—!" Honora's voice shrilled up crazily. Left hand joined right to steady the small gun which wavered as she fought to point it straight at Saranna.

Gerrad sprang. Honora had had eyes for no one but Saranna and he caught her easily, twisting the derringer from her, hurling the weapon out into the hall. She fought him wildly, crying out with sounds like an aroused animal. But Fowke bore her backward, forced her to sit down on the chair before her dressing table, the nearest seat.

The mirror there was smashed. But as Honora faced

where it had been she uttered an inhuman howl.

"No—no—!" Her struggles grew the stronger. He looked to Saranna.

"Get me her robe—over there—!" He pointed with his chin. Saranna at last found the ability to move. She grabbed the garment and took it to him. Somehow he used it to bind Honora's arms to her sides, to keep her captive.

"You kill that she-devil—" Honora looked up at him, a vestige of sanity returning to her face. "See what she has done to me. Monster—I have a monster's face!"

Gerrad looked to Saranna for an explanation. Swiftly she told him of the meeting at which Honora had been shown the mirror.

"So that is it! Some of the Princess' work. Well," he shrugged. "When one is fighting for one's life any weapon will serve. But she," he looked down at Honora, who had her face averted stiffly lest she face the ruined mirror, "is not changed."

"The—the Fox Lady said Honora saw herself as she really is," Saranna repeated. "But when she made their guns, the guns of the men change, she said that was an illusion and she could not do it again."

"There seems to be a more lasting illusion here," he commented. "But for the sake of Honora's sanity, we had better see if matters can be remedied. Come on!"

Muffled as she was in the prisoning garment, he swung Honora up in his arms and headed toward the door, Saranna hurrying after him. Honora buried her face against his shoulder as if she dared not let anyone see her features.

Down the stairs they went, and not one of those in the household followed them. Then outside, to that wreckage of the wall and hedge which had protected the hidden garden. They had pushed on in sight of the terrace before they saw anyone. There Damaris stood in the open, one of the large white foxes on either side.

She viewed their coming first with surprise, and then with an expression which mingled fear and anger.

"Go away!" she shrilled. "Don't you dare bring *her* here!"

"Not so, younger sister." From the moon door came the Fox Lady. But this time her face was wholly human. In one hand was a thing wrought of fur, and Saranna recognized it for a mask, very realistically made.

"Why do you bring her here?" Now the mistress of the garden addressed Gerrad Fowke.

"Because of your woven illusion, Kung Chu Yüeh," he answered.

"You call me by a name forbidden, a rank no longer acknowledged. How do know you that name and rank?" she asked coldly.

"I have been in the Eastern lands, Kung Chu Yüeh. A story as strange as yours is not easily forgotten. No; rather passing years have already made it a legend oft-times repeated. The tale of the daughter of a Prince of Banners who was stolen by coast pirates, rescued by one of the Western barbarians (as your people name us) to become the First Lady of his inner courts—"

"I am a nameless one. No such woman as you speak of could have returned to her clan after that had happened to her. She would be dead to her house. That I found refuge with one who paid me honor, for that do I thank Kwan Yin. Had I been a worthy daughter of my blood I should have put an end to my own life, so was my face blackened by the act of the tiger ones from the sea. But my mother was of Ping-yang, of a very ancient House whereof the women had the Old Knowledge. And it was given to me in my hour of need that I was more of my mother's clan than of my father's—great lord though he was.

"So I lived, and I found contentment. For my Western lord paid me honor and gave me my wish, though I must come to dwell in a far land and learn an uncouth tongue that I might talk with him. In his way he was kind, and I was another of his treasures which he loved. But with A-Han who had been my mother's nurse, I learned more and more of the ancient wisdom. For it is legend that my mother's clan had many born among them who were blood-kin, heart-kin to the furred ones." She held up the mask.

"It amused my new lord that I could bring the furred ones to me, and he ruled that they should not be harmed." She was silent a moment.

" 'The messenger of death enters and all business stops—' " she quoted. " 'When the waters sink, the stones show.' My lord wove about this place such protection for the future as he could. But with his passing, who cared for rules made by one already Gone Above? This younger sister," she touched Damaris lightly on the shoulder, "was also under threat. The rule of a child means nothing in the eyes of those grown to full stature. So again I sought the Old Knowledge striving to protect her, for she is of the true blood of my lost lord.

"Then came this other—" She glanced at Saranna. "And in her spirit there rests that which is kin. Like knows like upon first meeting. Also, the reading of the wands said that she was the key to my lock. I set upon her the sign of my furred people, that in her hour of need, they would protect her.

"The Old Knowledge may warn, it can foresee, but it is hard to use. Though these younger sisters gave me of the strength in our hour of danger, yet there is only so much that I may do. But *she*—" now she indicated Honora, "had a blackness in her heart which opened the gates for my magic. She looked upon the Mirror of the Goddess and saw herself as she really is. Now she would hide from that sight, yet the memory of it sears her mind."

"It will drive her mad," Gerrad answered. "If you have any pity, let her go."

"Let her go? But I do not hold her. She has laid the curse upon herself."

"It is an illusion," he repeated stubbornly. "Having woven it, you can also destroy it."

Then the Fox Lady sighed. "Perhaps—perhaps—"

"No," Damaris caught at her sleeve. "If you do, *she'll* try to get rid of you again—"

"Not at all," Gerrad's voice was clear. "I will promise that!"

For a moment which seemed to spin on and on, the Fox Lady eyed him. Then she nodded, as if she had read something in his expression which answered an unvoiced question.

"Get the mirror, young sister. No, this shall be well. There are other forces at work here, a choice has been made and it is the right choice—one which will lead to the lifting of a cloud."

Reluctantly, Demaris went. When she returned through the moon door she carried the mirror and gave it into the Fox Lady's hands.

"Hold her head high," Kung Chu Yüeh ordered. "If Heaven allows, she shall see what is granted her to see."

Gerrad forced Honora's head up. She whimpered, fought against his hold. But at last, she was facing the mirror, her eyes squeezed tightly shut.

"Open your eyes! Look!"

As if that command had stitched threads to Honora's eyelids, and drew them apart, now she stared into the mirror. Her face contorted in horror and then slowly relaxed as she continued to gaze.

"It is gone—all gone," she said with a child's wonder.

"It is gone unless you summon it again, for it pictures the evil within you," answered Kung Chu Yüeh.

"Now listen well." Her sweep of gaze included them all. "It is not my desire to play your games longer. I and my people wish only to be left in peace, contained within our own small world as the meat is contained safely within the shell of an uncracked nut. My lord's treasures shall be returned to his house, those of his kin shall be left to follow their own path. Between my dwelling and theirs, the door shall be closed—"

"*No*, please, no!" Damaris cried out.

"But yes, younger sister. 'Teachers open the door, you

enter by yourself.' You have lingered nearly too long in the courts of childhood, it is time you walk into the future. I grow old and tired, and elder ones wish to sleep easily among the dreams of years past, not be called to confront problems of the future. For that belongs to you, my younger sisters," now she included Saranna, "not to one such as I. Such good fortune as the Old Knowledge has given me to summon, that do I leave unto you both."

She turned from them, and walked with her dancer's grace across the terrace. Damaris took a step as if to follow and then hesitated. Saranna could guess why. There was about that regal figure now such an air of withdrawal as they dared not intrude upon.

Within the moon door she vanished. And then, for the first time, Saranna saw a screen panel slide across that round opening, shutting them out. Damaris began to cry softly and Saranna went to her.

"Don't," she said. "How do you know—she may change her mind someday. And if you become the woman she thinks you will, then she will want to see you."

"Yes," Damaris smeared the back of her hand across her eyes. "Yes, at least I can hope—"

Gerrad Fowke, leading Honora, had already started back through the torn garden. Saranna and Damaris came behind. But Saranna, seeing how he led and supported Honora, felt desolate and empty. At that moment, she wished that she could also draw shut a moon gate, shut out the life as it was for a dream of illusion.

But when she picked her way across the broken wall, she found him waiting there alone. Honora was moving on around the house, her maid with her.

"I wonder," he was examining the stones which had been torn from their settings to make that opening, "if she expects us to rebuild."

"You believe her then," Damaris asked, "she won't want to see us again?"

"I should think," he returned, "after the activity of this day she would have no wish to see more of the Western barbarians. She has a legendary past, you know. Even in her own country, they speak of her carefully and with deference. One does when one discusses someone with her powers. I would take her at her word, Damaris. Suppose you get ready for the return of the collection; she ought to be sending that back forthwith—"

Damaris put her head on one side, glanced from him to Saranna, with a little of the malicious awareness which she had shown what now seemed weeks ago, though the real time could only be measured in days.

"Very well—" she replied with the ostentatious virtue of one being very good and obedient.

"Honora"—Saranna said as the younger girl hurried on ahead—"she will be all right now."

"Doubtless—for a while. But Honora being Honora will not turn overnight into any pattern of good will," he answered coolly. "She needs a husband to keep her busy, and someplace beside Tiensin where she can play the lady."

"She has that—Queen's Pleasure—" before she thought Saranna blurted out.

"Not Queen's Pleasure—never!" To her vast amazement Gerrad Fowke shook his head. "I am not the kind of man Honora can make and mold. And I am afraid if we were wed there might come sparks and then a roaring fire, or else a hurricane to drive our ship on the lee shore. No, I'll have none of Honora—"

"But she—" Saranna was amazed past prudence.

"Oh, Honora always believes what she wants to. Have you not learned that by now? We shall find her a husband after a while, if she has learned her lesson sufficiently well. No, the lady of Queen's Pleasure will abide there in due time—in due time—" he repeated as if he were Kung Chu Yüeh repeating some spell of noted potency.

Saranna's hands went to her bruised and scratched face. She felt very hot and was sure she was blushing. Could one ever be too happy? Maybe she would discover that—in Gerrad Fowke's "due time."